DAUGHTER
OF ISIS

So fun sharing,
this with you!

Reina

DAUGHTER OF
ISIS

REINA CRUZ

Boyle
— & —
Dalton

Book Design & Production
Boyle & Dalton
www.BoyleandDalton.com

Paperback ISBN: 978-1-63337-439-3
E-book ISBN: 978-1-63337-440-9

Printed in the United States of America

— To Mom —

For believing I am capable of anything I put my mind to.
I did it!

"Two possibilities exist: either we are alone in the Universe or we are not. Both are equally terrifying."

ARTHUR C. CLARKE

CHAPTER 1

Sunday Elm could smell it, a familiar sickeningly sweet scent. She looked up from her email to study the closed door, listening. The heavy thump outside of the room confirmed it: she was no longer home alone.

Normally this would frighten someone living on her own. Sure, Maurita, Arizona, wasn't considered overly dangerous, but that wouldn't stop a person's heart from pounding at the strange noise on the other side of the door.

Sunday wasn't bothered, though.

If she were frightened by every unexplained sound she heard, she wouldn't just be going to therapy, she'd be living in a loony bin.

Sunday kicked her long legs out from under her desk and tucked her unruly brown curls behind one ear.

Another thump.

Something heavier had fallen to the floor this time.

Why do they have to bug me at home?

It was the first visit since the accident. Sunday stepped into the hallway, her breath growing short. She'd done this before. Dozens of times. But this time, she didn't feel up to it.

Outside her office, the hallway looked as it should, art and photos hanging on the wall. A picture of Sunday wearing a black cap and gown was prominently displayed—a smile spread across her young face while her father wrapped his arms around her in a proud hug. Most people didn't notice the resemblance between them until they actually saw Sunday and her father standing side by side. It was easy to miss since her skin was several shades darker than his. She got her complexion from her mom, but the way her eyes wrinkled and her large teeth took over her face when she smiled—that was her father.

A tangle of joy and heart-wrenching sadness washed over Sunday. She rushed past the photo, distracting herself by calculating how many years it had been since she'd graduated high school. She could hardly believe she would be invited to a ten-year reunion next year.

Her bedroom on the right appeared normal, the bed unmade and a pair of flip-flops discarded in front of her closet. The living room still bore the evidence of her late-night binge-watching session, including an empty wine glass, candy wrappers, and her favorite blanket abandoned on the couch.

Sunday stood at the end of the hallway where the small kitchen opened up beside her. Two cans rolled across the floor, stopping at Sunday's bare feet where the hardwood met the kitchen tile. A can of tomato paste and one of refried beans. The woman on the beans label smiled up at her.

She picked up the cans and carried them back into the kitchen. The disturbance had obviously started there. The cabinet door above the oven hung open.

She took her time replacing the cans, examining the cylinders for any dents.

She knew it was best to let them come to you. The cans were a cry for attention, and so Sunday made herself appear busy so they could interrupt her when they were ready to talk.

Well, not talk in the traditional sense. The dead didn't really talk.

"Rosarita, you look all right," she said to the refried beans woman as she placed both cans back into the cupboard and shut the door with a soft clunk.

Her fingers were still wrapped around the cabinet handle when a cool breeze brushed past her. It wasn't the bone-chilling cold that Hollywood depicted. Only something really powerful could have that effect on her. Instead, it felt like the sort of breeze that blew across the beach; pleasant, especially in the Arizona desert.

Sunday followed the cool air to the living room.

The spirit sat on the couch beside Sunday's discarded blanket. Still playing coy, the dead woman didn't raise her gaze when Sunday sat in the chair next to her, but instead picked at the purple fuzz the blanket left behind.

There was always something off about them. The spirits from the Other World typically took a human form. Almost. They had some control over their appearance, and most preferred the comforting look of the living.

But there was always something off.

Sometimes a missing feature, like no feet or eyes.

Sometimes a body part replaced by a tentacle or a pig snout.

Sometimes their hair was on fire or their arms were made of water.

Sunday didn't understand the logic or reasoning behind these strange features. Maybe they related to how a person lost their life, or to their death life. She had a theory that the length of time a person spent in the Other World affected their manifestation. She believed that the longer a person had been dead and existing in the supernatural realm, the less control they had—as if they were losing the strength to keep their human appearance.

She waited for the spirit on the couch to acknowledge her.

The spirit used to be a woman. She wore a nightgown Sunday had only seen in old TV shows from the '70s. Her hair hung loose, limp and pale like a waterfall cascading around her face. She sat with her horse legs stretched out in front of her. The hooves were adorned with ballerina slippers.

Unless the woman was an equestrian ballerina who had died in a tragic bedtime accident, Sunday couldn't explain the state of the spirit. She did look a bit like Sunday's most recent ex, though.

Eventually the spirit faced her. Her colorless skin faded into the grey couch behind her. Her eyes, dark-rimmed like a raccoon's, were downcast; she peered up at Sunday like a forlorn child. Her lips were as blue as her eyes.

"Can I help you?" Sunday typically treated these visitors like door-to-door salespeople: unwelcome, but tolerated until she could get them to leave.

The spirit spoke to her.

"Coffee?" Sunday questioned. She wrinkled her nose, put off by the obscurity of the request. She could taste it and smell it, but she didn't understand why.

Spirits didn't talk. They communicated in other ways, like knocks or flickering lights. All that Hollywood stuff had to come from some grain of truth.

As for Sunday, she just *knew*.

It was part of her "gift."

She insisted on putting the word in air quotes. Her "gift" was usually anything but.

Spirits talked to her by dropping images and ideas into her head. Not only could she see them, she could hear, taste, and smell their memories and thoughts. Their ideas became her ideas.

Sunday saw a coffee shop.

The large storefront windows revealed a sidewalk dusted with snow. Customers came in shaking the white powder out of their hair and peeling off their coats to dry on the rack next to a space heater. The walls were decorated with colorful pieces of teacups, saucers, and mugs, a chaotic mosaic of china. The smell of roasting coffee permeated the fabric of the chairs, and the hum of chatter was only drowned out by the coffee bean grinder. Customers and employees alike were smiling and laughing.

Then the scene changed. Outside, snow still covered every surface, but inside, dust covered just as many surfaces. The colors of the decorative dishware on the walls had dulled. Even the lights appeared dimmer. One man wearing a faded baseball cap sat at a table in front of the window reading a newspaper. The man behind the counter had asked if he wanted a refill three times. He wasn't going to ask again.

The coffee shop was going under. Sunday understood. She knew that when the spirit was alive, she'd built the business from the ground up. She appreciated the hours that the woman had put into her tiny hole-in-the-wall coffee shop in Petoskey, Michigan. Tourism ran the town and now, forty years later, the shop floundered. The spirit feared it would close.

Sunday felt for the woman, and not just because she spilled her sorrow into Sunday's head. The spirit had come all the way from Michigan, but Sunday couldn't help.

The dead woman would have to stick with knocks and flickering lights to communicate with the new owners in Michigan.

"I can't help you," she told the horse-legged spirit. "I really wish there was something I could do, but I can't. I'm sorry."

The spirit frowned. Sunday prayed she wouldn't get angry. Angry spirits made a mess.

Despite her silent pleas, the spirit woman developed a red hue. Her dark eyes glowed as she pressed her blue lips tightly together. She lifted herself off the couch to hover over the rug.

"Shit!" Sunday jumped to her feet, but not quickly enough.

The horse hooves slammed into Sunday's stomach, sending her over the armchair and into the dining room set across the room.

The hooves had knocked the breath out of her. Her feet dangled above her and her arms were twisted up in the legs of a chair. The seconds dragged as her mouth gaped open and shut like a beached fish.

The air couldn't fill her lungs fast enough when she finally got a breath in. Coughing and gasping, she struggled to sit up. She raised her head high enough to see a DVD player sailing in her direction.

With a shriek, she ducked. The machine crashed into the wall behind her. The spirit screamed in her head, dead lungs never needing to stop to take a breath.

"Fuck!" Sunday shouted, curling into a ball behind the chair. Above her an onslaught of knick-knacks and books were flung across the room. They piled on top of the broken DVD player. She needed to get out from behind the chair, but the thrown objects were unending.

"I get it, lady, you're upset. Just leave!" she shouted over the sound of screeching in her head.

The half-woman, half-horse spirit floated to the front door, ravaging the apartment like a tornado. Sunday covered her head with her arms. The spirit threw a lamp and overturned the couch. The scream in Sunday's head packed a punch of rage and despair.

She'd worked so hard. She fought for everything she had in life. People like Sunday, young and surrounded by life-easing technology, had caused her business to crash. She's gone, and the people she trusted with her life's work failed.

What was the point? Why had she worked so hard for nothing?

The spirit finally hovered out the front door, slamming it behind her. A few picture frames and a mirror crashed to the floor.

The quiet that followed was deafening.

Sunday peeked around her chair shield.

Empty. No spirit.

Sunday sat alone in the two wrecked rooms.

She shuffled out of her hiding place and immediately grabbed a large bag of salt from behind her dining room curtains. She emptied half the bag along the bottom of the front door. After replacing the bag, she pulled paper curtains down over all the windows in the apartment, installed in front of the blinds. Red pentagrams enclosed in circles covered the cream-colored paper drapes. The pagan-marked windows cast a warm hue over the apartment. Sunday finished the ritual by lighting a bundle of sage that had been tucked under a pillow in her bedroom. She placed the burning herbs on an incense tray to allow the smoke to dissipate throughout the front room. Typically she avoided the salt-strewn, sage-smoked mess. The neighbors tended to complain when passing her pentagrammed windows, but sometimes these measures were necessary.

Suddenly her front door shook, the two horse legs of the spirit splintering the doorframe. She leapt back, reminding herself that the spirit couldn't make it past the line of salt. Another kick rattled the door. Sunday dove for the sack of salt and poured another layer across the entryway, just to be safe. The spirit was not welcome back.

CHAPTER 2

Insurance companies should sell a supernatural plan; that way, when an aggrieved horse spirit destroyed your living room you wouldn't have to pay for replacement furniture out of pocket. Sunday resented cleaning up after her visitors. She didn't think she would be the only one who would take advantage of that insurance plan.

What would be worse? Stepping on salt that had been tracked from their line across the entryway and throughout the whole apartment, or cleaning up after the occasional angry spirit? Sunday leaned on her upturned couch, counting the number of visits that had ended in property damage. Three? Four? And it had been six years since she'd moved into the apartment. Or was it seven?

She sighed.

Cleaning up was a lonely job. Sunday gathered the unsalvageable pieces of her dining room table in a pile by the front door. She had nobody to call for help or to vent to about the extra housework. She was used to being alone, though. It wasn't exactly practical to tell your childhood friend how you spent the weekends shepherding spirits into the Other World. Instead, she told half-truths or flat-out lies about her life.

Sunday left the pile of broken furniture to get ready for work. She had to leave for her appointment in an hour and then work right after—enough time to shower, but not enough time to clean her uniform like she'd planned. Marinara sauce was splattered across her white button-up blouse from her last shift, so she hunted through her drawers for an old one and hurried into the bathroom to shower. Wetting her curls would make them more manageable when she pulled back her hair.

Even after shaking out her shoulder-length brown tresses, they stubbornly stuck out in every direction but down.

Manageable, but not actually obedient.

As she pulled and tucked at her hair, her mind wandered to the mess in the living room. The chaos reminded her of how alone she actually was. There had been one person in her life who understood the aggravation of Other World creatures. Her dad. He called their Sight an endowment, their personal ability. Stephen Elm had been a Seer too, making him Sunday's supernatural companion from the moment she saw her first spirit at seven years old. Sunday grew up and helped her father with his antique dealing business. They'd been inseparable. The furniture from his online antique shop would've come in handy now that her table and chairs had been demolished. But it had all been sold off after the accident.

Sunday blinked quickly, focusing all her energy on taming her hair. It had been six months; she was sick of crying. Work helped distract her, but it didn't stop the grief. With no one to share the whole truth with, Sunday just treaded water day by day with no plan for when she would grow too tired to keep her head up.

•••

"You're a little early." Dr. Morris's receptionist greeted Sunday with a smile. Her name plate read Cheryl. "She'll be ready for you soon. Sit."

Cheryl motioned to the couches with her long manicured nails and returned to the computer in front of her. Sunday picked up a magazine and did as she was told. The ticking clock behind her interrupted every word she tried to read. Cheryl sneezed.

"Bless you," Sunday said.

"Thanks." The receptionist smiled again. Sunday wanted to let her know that some of her pink lipstick had smeared onto her tooth, but she couldn't push her voice past her nerves. "Do you want some water?"

Sunday shook her head and returned to the magazine. The incessant clock was still a distraction, so she closed her eyes and rotated her neck. The muscles had tightened after she'd been kicked by the spirit. She'd be lucky if those ghost hooves didn't cause internal bleeding. The home insurance for supernatural disasters should partner with medical that included acupuncture and massage therapy. The biggest downside to having an angry ghost attack your home had to be the sore body. Being kicked into her dining room table had made her twenty-seven years feel closer to fifty.

She hadn't seen Dr. Elle Morris since her father had taken her. He'd found the family therapist after her mother left, but that was fifteen years ago. Could she help Sunday now?

"She's ready for you." Cheryl grinned the lipstick-stained smile again. Did her cheeks hurt?

Sunday dropped the magazine back on the table and followed Cheryl's gesture through the door behind her desk. "You've got…" Sunday rubbed her own front teeth.

"Oh!" Cheryl used her phone to check her lipstick. "Thanks."

The room seemed to have grown smaller than how Sunday remembered it. Two bookshelves no longer towered over her, instead standing behind Dr. Morris like sentries. The doctor had aged. Her chestnut hair was now highlighted with gray and her eyes were framed in wrinkles.

She greeted Sunday and invited her to take the empty armchair next to her.

"I was taken down memory lane seeing your name on my schedule," she said. "How long has it been?"

"I think fifteen years." Sunday wiggled in the seat. She spotted a desk across the room, the same one she'd sat at as a child, coloring pictures.

Dr. Morris tucked her hair behind her ears. "Time flies. I saw the information you provided. I was so sorry to hear about your dad."

Sunday bit her tongue and nodded.

"Did you want to start there?"

Sunday shook her head.

"Okay," Dr. Morris said. "When you're ready, then. When you're alone and thoughts of your father come up, try taking a deep breath and exploring those thoughts and feelings. Don't be afraid; they won't hurt you."

Sunday tugged on a loose thread along her shirt hem. "Yeah, okay."

"Why don't you tell me how you two were doing after you stopped coming to see me?"

She shrugged. "We'd gotten into a routine. That's why we stopped coming. Dad didn't think we needed you anymore."

"That's great to hear." Dr. Morris jotted notes on the pad in her lap. "Tell me about the routine."

"Did Dad tell you about his beliefs?" Sunday asked, frowning. Her father had warned her all those years ago. There was a fine line between being honest with your therapist and providing symptoms of psychosis.

"Sure. I appreciated the wholesomeness. It was refreshing."

Sunday smiled and pictured the barista spirit. Wholesome? What had her father told this woman?

"Did you take over his store? The online one?" Dr. Morris asked.

"No. That helped pay for the funeral and some other bills. I'm a restaurant manager."

"Oh? Any place I would know?"

"Bokka's?"

"Sure." Dr. Morris nodded. "Went there for my anniversary last year. It's nice."

Sunday studied her fingernails, pressing her thumb against each one to watch the color fade back.

"So have you seen your father's spirit? Were his theories right?" Dr. Morris asked.

Sunday shook her head. "Well, yes, about his theories, but no, I haven't seen him."

"And how do you feel about that?"

She inhaled deeply. How did she feel about her father's spirit moving on to the Other World? He wasn't troubled in his death, which could have led him to stay here. Sunday knew she should take comfort in that, and she did, but she couldn't deny the small feeling of hope at the first hint of a spirit. Would it be her dad? Would she ever see him again?

"I don't know," she said. "Lots of conflicting feelings."

Dr. Morris nodded like she understood. "So you didn't join his business, but did you follow his faith?"

Sunday nodded.

"Are you still following after his death?"

Tears filled her eyes.

She didn't help the barista that morning. She told the poor woman she couldn't, convinced herself that it was geographically impossible. Could she afford to take the time off of work? How would she pay for a plane ticket? Her father had always managed it before. Were her circumstances all that different now?

"I don't know," she whispered.

Dr. Morris leaned closer with a tissue. Sunday accepted it.

"That's fine. Understandable, really," Dr. Morris said. "Your faith must have been completely wrapped up in him. Now that he's gone, it must be like Christianity without a Bible. You've lost your guide."

Sunday wiped her nose.

"Have you thought at all about helping someone else, about using his faith?"

Of course she had.

Every spirit and creature from the Other World reminded Sunday that she should be helping the dead move on. She should protect the living from the monsters in their closets or under their beds. At the very least, she should check her father's email, see who had reached out for his help, but she'd done nothing.

"Yeah," she replied.

"I remember a little girl telling me how proud she was to have helped her dad by using her gift to help others. She told me that it helped her when her mother left. Do you remember that?"

Sunday nodded. "I just don't know if I can do it alone."

She sunk back into the chair. Dr. Morris offered her another tissue, and Sunday wiped away the tears.

"I'm sorry." She forced a smile. "I've been crying so easily lately."

"Understandable." Dr. Morris cleared her throat. "Let's stop here for today."

Sunday glanced at the clock between the two bookshelves. Time had moved so fast.

"I can recommend all my typical suggestions," the doctor continued. "But I have another idea, if you're up for it."

"Sure."

"You should try journaling. I'm sure you remember the one I had you write all those years ago. But I'm thinking that instead of just letting your mind guide your pencil, you should try writing out your father's faith as well. Everything he taught you about spirits and the afterlife. Use that as your guide now that your father is gone."

The thought of putting pen to paper made Sunday nauseous. She couldn't help a spirit move on; how could she bring herself to write all about them and the Other World? It would hurt too much, a reminder that she was all alone.

"I'll try the journaling." She stood up.

"Good," Dr. Morris said. "Use the journal to probe a little into your memories of your father's faith. Explore it. Don't be afraid of it."

As Sunday left the building, she thought over Dr. Morris's advice. She'd write about her feelings, but she couldn't write about her father's faith. She'd leave the Other World behind, an old chapter in her life. Dr. Morris could help her start her new one.

PRAYERS OF JAX FRASER

God, I fear I am losing my mind. I see them in the church pews while I give my sermon, on the sidewalks when I leave the church. The dead. Twisted and mixed with animals by the Devil. What curse is this upon me, God? Please hear my prayer. Please guide me. I don't want to see them, Lord. I shouldn't be seeing them. I fear I'll be taken by the Devil and made just like them.

CHAPTER 3

The bus dropped Sunday at the nearest bus stop, a block away from the actual downtown strip. Downtown was only a three-block stretch of banks, restaurants, and overpriced boutiques. The buildings maintained an old-fashioned façade of brick storefronts and decorative awnings. The city kept the shrubbery and trees nicely trimmed. At night, with the twinkling lights shining above the sidewalks, it had a romantic date-spot vibe. Great news for Sunday.

Job security.

Even if she had owned a car, Sunday would prefer public transportation and walking. It took her longer to get to work, but she skipped metered parking and enjoyed a walk through the aromas coming from the bakery and taqueria. It cleared her mind and occasionally her sinuses.

She loved the quaint view, the smell of cinnamon and the sounds of laughter and chatter of tourists and families getting out to the shops or relaxing at the large park that took up one side of a block. She watched a couple walking hand-in-hand across the street. When was the last time she had walked side-by-side with someone? Not romantically, she didn't have the energy for that, but a companion, a friend. She didn't want to figure up how long it had been.

Sunday pulled a Bluetooth earpiece out of her purse for hands-free calling and slipped it into her right ear.

"Reap," she hissed. No response. "Reap!" She gave a quick shout, scanning the street for a reaction. No one paid attention.

"You rang?"

A breeze tousled Sunday's hair and a figure appeared beside her. He wore a black fedora and a black trench coat that brushed along the tops of his Oxford wing-tipped shoes. The dark ensemble stuck out on the warm fall afternoon.

"Hey, Reap." Sunday smiled. The skeletal creature beside her cheered her up, unlike the first time they'd met. She saw Reap beyond his surface now, but back then the rotten flesh and dark empty eyes had terrified her.

A few years ago when she had been hired at the restaurant, Sunday spotted Reap for the first time. His fedora had kept most of his face in shadow, but the visible bottom half revealed a grotesque jaw of peeling skin and exposed bone underneath. The rest of the Grim Reaper's skeletal body was hidden beneath dark gloves and the trench coat. Only that fraction of skin stubbornly stuck on. She'd spied him through a haze of panic. Her thoughts had whirled through her head as she held her cell phone to her ear, listening to the dispatcher and watching a man perform CPR on an elderly woman at her feet.

"She's not breathing," Sunday had gasped.

The skeletal man in the fedora had stood just beyond the small crowd that had gathered. The collapsing woman had drawn an audience who shuffled their feet, anticipating more drama. But Reap hadn't been interested in the scene. He just waited. It sent a chill down Sunday's spine.

She understood then who he was. She knew what would happen once the paramedics arrived. Her eyes fell to the woman on the ground, to her closed eyes and slightly parted lips. She had appeared peaceful, ready for what lay ahead.

Paramedics lifted the woman onto the gurney. No one rushed. The siren had long ago been silenced. The crowd had dispersed, but Sunday waited on a bench. The Grim Reaper still stood vigil, watching the woman be wheeled to the ambulance. The doors slammed shut. The vehicle rolled into traffic leaving no evidence of the afternoon commotion. The skeletal being turned to follow the ambulance. Sunday jumped to her feet and rushed to him.

Her father would disapprove. His voice sounded in the back of her mind: *It's not our world. We have no business meddling in it.*

But her curiosity had driven her to the Grim Reaper. Why shouldn't she know about the Other World? Why have the Sight and not understand the creatures she saw?

"Hey!" She jogged to close the gap between them, waving to catch the Reaper's attention.

He turned slowly, each movement gliding through molasses. Sunday halted before him. He gazed down at her, her eyes wide with panic.

"You're here for the woman, right? She's going to the Other World?" Sunday's heart pattered in her chest, more from the excitement of interacting with a being from the Other World than from her rush to catch up to him. Instead of fearing the rotting flesh of the Reaper's face, she'd smiled, exhilarated.

"Yes." Reap's eyes narrowed as he studied her.

The word dropped the smile from Sunday's face. Her mouth hung open. He could talk? She'd expected his life story to play in her head like the spirits she'd come across already. But he spoke to her.

"What?" Reap raised an eyebrow. "You need something? I really should be going. I don't have time to talk to the living."

"You talk," Sunday said.

"I do, and this was a good one, thanks." He turned, his trench coat blowing dramatically behind him.

His words, sarcastic and real, had floored Sunday. Her lips moved, but no words came out. She forced herself to say something. Anything to stop him from leaving.

"I can see things from the Other World!" she had shouted, no doubt drawing the attention of the few people around her, but she didn't care.

Reap turned around again. "I gathered as much. Do you have a question for me or something? This is getting weird."

"I've never talked to someone from the Other World before," she replied.

"Ah." Reap walked back to her. He removed his fedora to reveal a skull beneath, holding the hat against his chest. "I guess I'm honored, then. *Guten tag.*"

Sunday frowned. "You're German?"

"No," Reap sighed. "Haven't had such luck. Just a fan."

"Of Germans?"

"Of humans! 'Being human is a complicated gig,' but I envy you for it. That's Nietzsche, by the way. One of the good ones."

Sunday nodded, more out of politeness than understanding. "So, if you're not human, then what are you?"

Placing the fedora back on his head, he waved a hand down his body. "Isn't it obvious?"

"Grim Reaper?"

"That's the name some humans have given me. I'm just a glorified usher, really." He checked his empty wrist. "I have to go. I'm sure I'll see you around, though. This is my district."

His district? Did that mean there were more Grim Reapers? It made sense to Sunday. One creature couldn't usher the dead of the whole world, or even the entire state of Arizona, into the Other World, She didn't get the chance to ask him that day. He'd hurried after the ambulance, disappearing in a haze.

They had run into each other again. Despite her father's protests, Sunday maintained a friendship with this Other World being. Reap often hustled down the sidewalk with Sunday, each rushing to work. He quoted Nietzsche and she peppered him with questions about the Other World. Now, as Sunday fell into step with him, Reap looked at her. The skin above his eyes lifted, the eyebrows absent.

"Where're you off to?" Sunday asked.

The earpiece made it appear that she was talking on the phone. She'd learned that trick after getting strange looks for seemingly talking to herself. It was easy to forget that she was the only person around who could see the creatures from the Other World, especially since she used to share these experiences with her father.

"Not your restaurant, so you don't have to worry about it," Reap replied.

The Reaper could talk, unlike spirits. Sunday believed that this was the cosmos's way of making Reap's job easier. Most people could not telepathically understand the supernatural realm, so speech allowed him to explain the folklore: There really was a man dressed all in black who showed up to guide you to the Other World after death. Sunday had a strong suspicion that Reap wasn't good at charades.

"What are you laughing at?" he snapped at Sunday, who had giggled at the image in her head of Reap attempting to act out *Fiddler on the Roof.*

"Nothing!" Her arms flew up in surrender. "Why are you so on edge today?"

He sighed. "I'm sorry. You'd be surprised, but with summer winding down, the accidental death rate is shooting up. I feel like I can't collect them fast enough."

Reap had confided in Sunday before about his occupational woes. His job was the prime reason for his existence, but he never actually enjoyed his work. A Grim Reaper with an existential crisis.

"Most beings in my realm don't have the awareness to know there are other options out there!" Reap continued with exasperation. "I get to know all about Earth and humans just to help them in death. Why couldn't I have been a Grootslag or a Kappa and exist in ignorant bliss?"

Sunday patted Reap's bony back. Both had slowed their pace as they approached Sunday's building.

"That which does not kill us makes us stronger." She offered one of his favorite Nietzsche quotes.

Reap sighed and then flung his scythe out of his sleeve and over his shoulder.

She scanned the block again. People crowded the storefronts and sidewalk, typical of a sunny weekend.

"What colors do you see today?" She pointed at the couple in front of them.

Reap's shoulders lifted and then dropped.

"Come on!" Sunday urged. "At least do me. I need a pick-me-up today."

He sighed. "Fine." He gestured to the couple. "They're this aquamarine color, a mix of her green and his blue." He let out another sigh. "They're so in love, even their auras have meshed together."

Sunday nodded, enjoying the game with Reap. As a Grim Reaper, he perceived people in colors, auras. They changed just as people changed. More often than not, the auras were inconsequential, like fun facts about a person. "What about her?" She pointed to a mother pushing a toddler in a stroller across the street.

"She's a muddy grey." Reap cocked his head to the side. "A bit depressed, I'm afraid."

Sunday bit her bottom lip, bummed. "And me?"

Reap gave her a side glance. He tilted his chin down, examining her aura.

"I'm going to call it orchid today. You have more red in your aura. I still don't like how shaky it is, though."

Sunday shrugged.

Typically her aura was a light shade of blue, but Reap had been seeing her aura in more red tones and shaky ever since her father's accident.

"Thanks for letting me vent. I feel better, really." He looked behind him. "I was supposed to turn back there. Think blue today, okay?"

Without another word, Reap spun around on his heels and trudged away.

Sunday shook her head. Only she would be comforting the Grim Reaper on a Saturday afternoon. She checked her watch. A minute after one-thirty.

Bokka's had long been a staple of fine dining in town. Son graduated from high school? Celebrate at Bokka's. Grandma's eightieth birthday? The family came together at Bokka's. Thinking of proposing? Drop the question at Bokka's.

Sunday enjoyed the fast-paced work. She skipped through the back door, pulled her apron out of the top right locker, and tied it around her waist as she made her way through the kitchen.

"Hey, Maggie," Sunday greeted the head chef for the night. "I thought Ben was supposed to be in tonight."

"He called in sick." Maggie looked up from a simmering saucepan that smelled like garlic and oysters and rolled her eyes. "Again."

Sunday shrugged. "You're on overtime, though. Right?"

The head chef nodded. She grabbed her water bottle, took a swig, and went back to stirring her sauce.

"I'll talk to Carol or Rob. Explain why you're doing overtime," Sunday promised.

Maggie thanked her as Sunday walked on.

She almost made it out of the kitchen to check in with the host before being ushered aside.

"Behind you!" the sing-song voice of Shelly James warned her.

The bouncing blond ponytail continued on her quest with a platter of soup and salad. Sunday enjoyed her shifts with Shelly. She watched her weave her way through the maze of tables and chairs. The waitress didn't claim to be angelic; she was the type of girl used to getting her way by manipulating others around her. Sunday had nodded and smiled through many stories of how Shelly didn't have to pay for a single drink the night before, but the confidence the waitress exuded pulled Sunday in. It brightened Shelly's smile and shone through her eyes, a fresh presence compared to Sunday's doom and gloom.

The air cooled as Shelly rushed past her, drawing Sunday's gaze down. She sighed. Not again.

A creature the size of a child followed behind the waitress. Around its waist it wore a ragged towel that used to be white. A strap made of a few twisted shoelaces hung across its bare chest and tied around a black sock holding who-knows-what at its hip. It wore no shoes, and its overgrown, broken yellow toenails clicked against the tiled floor. Its repulsive feet matched the thin greasy hair patch growing out of the top of its head and trailing down over one shoulder.

The gremlin glanced at Sunday as it passed by, red eyes laughing at a twisted joke she wouldn't understand. It smiled, revealing yellow and brown fangs, before following Shelly into the dining room.

CHAPTER 4

It was a good thing restaurants didn't have regulations for Other World creatures. The Toko following Shelly around definitely didn't meet health codes with its grimy makeshift clothes and rancid oily hair. Tokos were trickster demons. Only someone with old knowledge of the Other World could curse a person with a Toko. Shelly must have pissed off someone powerful; Sunday didn't see the disgusting creatures often.

This ugly gremlin did a great job of scaring the hell out of the waitress. Shelly described herself as a jumpy person, but she didn't know about the curse. When she came to work talking about the noises she heard all night or the terrifying monster she thought she saw in the mirror, Sunday bit her lip. She knew. It was the Toko.

Tokos could actually hurt people. They caused illnesses and accidents, but this one was harmless. In fact, Sunday suspected that Shelly enjoyed the drama and relished the attention she received from her fright-filled stories. The Toko hadn't worked out as planned.

The workday shot by. Weekend nights tended to be busy, so Sunday always had something to do. The last customers left just after ten, a treat when working the late shift, and the cleanup went smoothly.

Just shy of eleven, the staff headed out the back door, eager antic-ipation over Saturday night buzzing between them. Kitchen and wait staff alike chatted about their plans. Sunday followed a bit behind them. She'd stayed behind to lock up the cash in the safe and double check that all stoves and ovens had been shut off. By the time she walked out, most of her coworkers had rounded the corner. All except Maggie and Shelly.

"What are you up to tonight, Sun?" Maggie's voice pulled Sun-day's gaze out of her purse.

"Not much." Sunday tucked the restaurant keys away and joined the chef and waitress. "My place is a mess, so I might work a bit on that, have a glass of wine."

Shelly scoffed. "You can't seriously be thinking about cleaning tonight."

Sunday shrugged.

"Join us," Maggie said. "Omar invited us all to McFlahrety's."

"I don't know," Sunday said. She didn't want to spend the night drinking.

"Come on." Shelly hooked her arm around Sunday's. The warmth of Shelly's skin radiated through the thin fabric of her shirt sleeve. "Just stay for an hour. Then we'll let you get back to your cleaning and wine."

Sunday sighed, weighing the options. Go home, alone, and face the mess the horse spirit had left behind, or have a drink with some coworkers. The comforting heat of Shelly next to her pulled her feet along. There was no convincing herself that the first option was better. The three of them walked half a block to the bar. Music and voices filled the air as soon as they turned onto the main street.

Sunday followed them through the pub entrance. A man dressed in all black checked their IDs at the door, barely glancing at the card between Sunday's fingers. Maggie pushed her way through the crowd milling around the bar. Close behind, Sunday squinted at the large board above them listing the beers on tap.

"Tequila!" Maggie leaned close to the bartender, holding three fingers up.

"Oh no." Sunday waved the glass away when Shelly held out the shot filled with gold-colored liquor perched between her fingers.

"Come on!" Shelly shoved the glass into Sunday's hand. Part of the contents spilled on the floor. "Loosen up a little."

Sunday hated that loosening up typically required pouring burning liquid down her throat. That tended to get her the opposite of loosened up. But Shelly's grin pulled Sunday's fingers to the shot. Her two coworkers tipped their heads back and poured the liquid into their mouths. Sunday stared at the liquor, ashamed to be caving under peer pressure. She leaned over a couple to drop her now half-filled shot glass behind an empty glass of beer on the bar while Maggie and Shelly grimaced with their eyes closed.

Shot glasses discarded and hands now filled with glasses of beer, they made their way to the porch. Gas fueled heaters warmed the outdoor seating space. Smaller tables with seats made from old barrels were scattered around the area, all filled by an adult softball team sporting jerseys with the pub's logo printed on the back. Booths lined the enclosing fence. Shelly led the way to a side booth filled with the rest of the Bokka's staff.

Two waiters moved over to allow them to sit together. Sunday squeezed between the two women, holding her beer on the table with both hands.

"Cheers." Shelly held up her glass, smiling. Her eyes jumped to each coworker around the table, landing on Sunday and motioning for her to lift her own drink.

After a few drinks, the voices at the table layered, each person talking over another, all following a different conversation. Between the chatter and the beer she had been sipping, Sunday's head spun.

"I should be heading out." Maggie stood up, empty glasses clinking against each other when she disturbed the table.

Sunday thought about following Maggie out and finding her way home. She checked her wrist for the time, but Shelly's hand guided her arm back in her lap.

"It's still early." She leaned close. Sunday caught a whiff of her floral perfume. "Stay for another round?"

Sunday didn't remember agreeing to stay, but another drink appeared in front of her. She took a sip and watched the conspirer of the whole event, Omar, wave his arms as he told a story. She couldn't figure out what tale, so she turned to Shelly for an explanation.

But Shelly wasn't sitting beside her. Instead of the young blond woman, she saw Shelly's Toko leaning against the table and resting its head in its grungy hands. Its feet stuck straight out in front of it, legs too short to hang over the edge of the booth. Sunday frowned, irritated that Shelly had left her. The gremlin smirked and gave her a wave before hopping off the edge of the booth and wandering into the crowd.

She watched the Toko as it found Shelly at the bar, leaning both elbows on the bar top, wedged against a tall man. Her head flew back, mouth hanging open with a squeaking laugh Sunday could hear from her seat at the table. Shelly playfully slapped the man's shoulder and took a drink of beer Sunday assumed he'd bought her. When Shelly walked away from the bar, he followed her, two more beers in his hands.

Shelly collapsed beside Sunday again. The man took a seat on her other side, his cheeks hiding his eyes with a large smile. From what Sunday knew, he seemed to be Shelly's type. Tall, dark hair, bearded.

He put Sunday on edge. She couldn't tell if it was the smug smirk or his insistent eye contact. She had never been uncomfortable with eye contact, but his eyes bored into her like he feared she'd disappear if he looked away for a second. Sunday squirmed in her seat, her gaze on an empty pint glass.

"Matty got this round," Shelly said, introducing the man.

"Thanks." Sunday took the drink he offered her.

She took a sip, no longer a part of the conversation. Each glance in the man's direction sent a shiver down her spine. She couldn't focus as Shelly shared yet another story of how the Toko scared her. Sunday's eyes kept sliding to Matty, who was listening, entranced.

What was wrong with her? Sunday couldn't make sense of her unease. She searched the man, hunting for red flags. He wasn't threatening. In fact, he joined the group seamlessly, charming and handsome, asking questions to make the others feel heard. He bought another round, earning more favor from her coworkers.

She wiped her sweating palms along the tops of her legs.

Maybe she was jealous. She searched inside herself. Her attraction to Shelly wasn't a new discovery. Her beautiful coworker had caught her eye the day the owner introduced Shelly as the new hire, but Shelly was into men, not women. Sunday had never been bothered by Shelly's dates before.

She gulped the rest of her beer, hoping to settle the nerves twisting her stomach.

Matty's eyes were dark and brooding, but when he smiled they lightened, growing friendlier. He wasn't just Shelly's type. Did Sunday have a crush? Was she jealous of Shelly meeting him at the bar and not her?

She snuck another glance in his direction. The knots in her stomach squeezed tighter. These were not the butterflies of a budding romance but the nausea of anxiety. It didn't feel like any crush Sunday had ever had before.

"Can I get some more?" Sunday pushed her empty glass toward the pitcher. Omar filled it.

Sunday forced her eyes away from the table. She'd go after this last beer, order a ride share. She watched as more tables emptied. The night wound down, and a group of what appeared to be underage high school students slumped against the table next to hers. Security, the man who had been checking IDs at the door, made his way to the passed-out teenagers. He shook the blond football player's shoulder. Slowly, bleary-eyed and pimple-faced, they got to their feet. The football player leaned against his friend, still half passed out. The security guard followed close behind them, arms held out as if he expected one of them to crash to the floor.

Sunday thought that one of them must have already fallen under the table. Eyes shone between the security guard's moving legs.

She blinked.

The group left, but the eyes were still there, staring. Sunday squinted, forcing her alcohol-influenced vision to focus. Definitely eyes. Large and yellow.

The ache of panic settled in the back of Sunday's throat. She took a gulp of beer to help it pass, but panic threatened to close her throat altogether. She knew those yellow eyes. The beast behind them resembled the big bad wolf on steroids. Hounds.

The first time she'd seen a Hound had been on her walk home from middle school. Not only was her body changing in uncomfortable and embarrassing ways, but twelve-year-old Sunday also had to navigate spirits visiting her in school bathrooms.

One afternoon, she walked past a neighbor's bush and froze. Something growled. She turned and found herself looking at a beast with spindly legs that reached to her chest; its shaggy dark fur stood on end. The beast's smooth, ratlike tail extended away from its body, pointing to the sky. It faced away from Sunday, hiding its face and teeth. It didn't notice her staring at first, but then she screamed and booked it the last two blocks home.

Her father had found Sunday in the fetal position in a corner of her parents' bedroom. He explained what the Hounds were.

"They're bad omens." His chest had vibrated against Sunday's cheek when he spoke. She'd nestled herself into her father's arms. "They feed off of negativity, so they like to hang around when tragedy is about to strike. Grief is a strong emotion. And fear. All of these feelings attract Hounds."

Her breath had caught in her throat. It occurred to her that the Hound was feeding off of *her*, which meant something bad must be about to happen. For the first time in her young life, Sunday realized that she wasn't invincible. She could get hurt. She could die. So could her parents. The thought had made her cry.

"What's going to happen to me?" Sunday croaked.

Stephen had chuckled, and Sunday pushed herself up, watching him with tears rolling down her cheeks.

"You're fine, Pumpkin. It wasn't following you. The only reason it chased you was because it knew you had the Sight." The smile fell from his face. "Their existence isn't known to our world, and the Hounds want to keep it that way. They don't want to become a warning and lose the shock of a tragedy. Sunday, they will kill you if you threaten their existence."

People said the unknown made everything scarier, but knowing that the Hounds were bad omens who could tear your throat out hadn't made Sunday feel any better about them. This, coupled with the fact that she knew they weren't the worst creatures from the Other World, made Sunday want to stay in her father's arms for the rest of time. The Hounds, creatures straight out of the bowels of Hell, were merely at bee-sting level on the scale of monsters that existed in the Other World (as long as you weren't allergic).

The first Hound hung around for a neighbor's death. A heart attack killed him before he could get out of bed in the morning. He was forty-five; the tragedy devastated the whole family. Sunday had to say goodbye to the man's son, her playmate and the first boy she ever had a crush on.

No one saw it coming.

Except for the Hound.

The second Hound appearance happened when Sunday was in college. She'd been visiting New Orleans over a school break when she'd seen a few Hounds sniffing around an alleyway. Loud tourists had stumbled by them, but the Hounds paid them no mind; they were waiting. Not long after flying home, a hurricane big enough to be named had hit the infamous city, killing hundreds.

The third experience she'd had with Hounds hit closer to home.

Back at the bar, Sunday sat up straighter and attempted to join in the conversation. She wouldn't allow herself to think about the third experience. Her eyes continued to flick to the Hound under the table.

The shadows hid the Hound's shape; only its eyes shone through the dark. It slunk out of its hiding place, glancing at Sunday. Her gaze snapped to the beer in her hand, pretending not to notice the large monster surveilling the downtown bar.

Another one. The bad omens seemed to be following Sunday around. She understood the others, but why this one? Whose pain were they there for?

Panic pushed bile into Sunday's throat. The same fear she'd felt when her father explained the presence of the Hounds came rushing back to her. At twelve, she'd no longer felt invincible. The realization scared her more than a reality where a Hound actually targeted her. Now, the reality felt all too real. Were the Hounds following her? Hadn't they already fed off of her grief? What other horror was in her future that would bring them to her now?

The monster slunk around the security guard's legs. Thick strands of saliva dripped off its wet lip as it locked its beady eyes with Sunday.

It saw her, knew she had the Sight. She'd die right there, mauled to death by an invisible beast. She prayed the pain would be invisible too but had little hope.

The next thing she was aware of was sitting on the ground with her head between her knees. The cement floor cooled the backs of her legs and a hand rubbed her back.

"That's it." The owner of the hand spoke softly above her. "Just breathe. You'll be okay."

Sunday wanted to roll her eyes.

You knew you'd hit a new low when you were getting kudos for inhaling and exhaling.

It all came back to her in chunks.

She took slow breaths in and out, but her chest felt heavy like a weight had been placed on top of her. She couldn't get a full breath in. Then her whole body broke out in a cold sweat. The Hound wasn't going to kill her; she'd suffocate to death instead.

As Sunday continued to regain her breath on the cold floor of the bar, she figured it out. Again, she wanted to roll her eyes. She could laugh at the absurdity.

She'd had a damn panic attack.

She wanted to shrink smaller and smaller until she disappeared. The badass monster fighter, sidekick to the bravest man she would ever know, had a panic attack over a Hound.

She was ashamed.

She felt weak. Cursed by her Sight.

She wanted *nothing* to do with the Other World. Ever.

CHAPTER 5

"Hey, Sun. Are you okay?" Shelly placed a hand on Sunday's shoulder. Sunday barely heard the question over the sound of her heart pounding in her ears. Her sweaty palms slipped down her arms. She squeezed tighter, holding onto herself to keep the shaking at bay.

Shelly brought a glass of water to her lips.

"She's so pale," the hostess said.

"Are you going to be sick?" Omar asked.

Sunday attempted to take a deep breath. It was shallow. The Hound sniffed around the bar, the patrons unaware of the menace at their feet.

"Come on." Shelly took Sunday's arm and pulled her to her feet. "Why don't I get you a cab."

Sunday allowed herself to be guided toward the exit. Even with her gaze fixed downward, she could still see the Hound in her peripheral vision. It took all her energy to keep herself standing on shaking legs. Before she made it out the door, her knee buckled and she staggered to the floor.

Omar jumped up to catch her, but Matty beat him to it. He had his arms around her waist before she collapsed completely.

"My car is parked out back," he said. "I can take you guys home."
Shelly agreed.

Sunday tried to keep an eye on the Hound without staring at it directly.

"Breathe," Shelly encouraged as she and Matty supported Sunday on both sides through the exit.

Leaving the bar put the Hound completely out of Sunday's sight. She took one large breath and stood a bit more steadily on her feet.

"There you go." Shelly's voice rang clearer as she rubbed Sunday's back.

They walked around the bar to the back parking lot and Matty placed her in the passenger seat of his car. Sunday stared at her shaking hands while attempting to take long, deep breaths. They still felt shallow; she forced her breath past her chest and into her stomach.

"How are you feeling?" Shelly's hand reached from the back seat to Sunday's shoulder again.

Sunday balled her sweaty hands in her lap, giving Shelly a curt shrug.

She wasn't going to die. Sunday took a deep breath and reminded herself of this. The Hounds were scary, yes, but they didn't typically cause full blown panic. At least, not until she'd seen her third Hound six months earlier.

"Explore it," Dr. Morris had told her this afternoon. "Don't be afraid."

Sunday had seen the third Hound right before her father's accident. The beast prowled around her dad's backyard all evening. She could hear it snarling and growling even with the house closed up. She should've known.

It had been a Thursday night, their weekly dinner date, but Sunday had been waiting at the house for a couple of hours. She thought her dad must've been caught in traffic. But why didn't he call?

She had checked her phone again and was surprised by a missed call. She hadn't heard it ring. Had the call not gone through or had she been distracted? She listened to the voicemail. Her father's message had left her trembling.

He never made it home that evening. Five-car pileup; the worst the area had seen in a long time.

Sunday saw the news of the accident on TV. The Hound's nails scraped on the concrete as it paced the back porch, feeding on her fear. Sitting in the dining room, Sunday watched the television hanging on the wall across from her and kept an eye on the backyard through the sliding glass door behind her. She glanced back at the Hound and unease swept over her. She called her dad's cell again. No answer.

She'd never felt hatred before, but she *hated* that Hound sniffing outside.

Lost in her memory, Sunday hadn't noticed where Matty was driving them. He stopped in front of Shelly's townhouse, pulling Sunday away from her thoughts. Shelly climbed out from the back seat and hung over the driver's side door, smiling at her bar pickup.

"Will you text me?" she said.

"Of course." He grinned back.

Shelly walked away slowly. Sunday watched her rotating hips, which turned out to be a great pace keeper for her breathing. Just as Shelly approached her front door, she turned and smiled one last time. Then she disappeared into the dark townhouse.

Matty cleared his throat and put the car in reverse.

"Can you guide me to your house from here?" he asked.

Sunday stopped him outside of the apartment complex. He parked on the street and walked around the car to open her door. She pulled herself out of the low sedan with shaky limbs.

"Feeling better?" he asked.

She shrugged. "I'm getting there."

He didn't ask what had happened. Sunday appreciated that.

"Well," she pulled her purse higher on her shoulder so she had something to do with her hands, "thanks for the ride. Really."

"Not a problem." He stuffed his hands in his back pockets. "Good night."

She began walking into the complex, but his voice stopped her. "Do Hounds always scare you like that?"

PRAYERS OF JAX FRASER

Heavenly Father, I'm grateful for your guidance and your wisdom. Faith has been my life's work, but I never felt the power of your love until you gave me this gift.

CHAPTER 6

Sunday frowned. She must have misheard him; the anxiety screwed with her mind. Did he mention the Hounds?

"Did you hear me?"

"Yes."

"I'm just curious," he said. "I saw the Hound in the bar and then you just freaked out. Is that normal?"

Sunday turned around on the ball of one foot. Matty leaned against his car. She couldn't read his face. Unlike her wide eyes and open mouth, his face appeared blank. He watched her, waiting patiently for an answer as if his question hadn't just upturned the small world she lived in.

With the exception of her father, she had never met anyone with the Sight. Sure, her dad had mentioned others with their gift, but Sunday always pictured them in some far away world like Brazil or Alaska. There couldn't possibly be someone else with Sight in Maurita, Arizona. Her dad would have known, and he would've told her.

"No." Her voice scratched her throat.

"You don't normally scare like that?"

She shook her head and walked back to his car.

"No, I don't." She crossed her arms across her chest. "That's new."

Matty nodded. Sunday waited for him to continue, but he took too long. "Who are you?"

He chuckled. "I'm sorry. That must've been a shock."

Again, she expected him to elaborate, but he didn't. "You have nothing else to add?" she pried.

"Yeah." He cleared his throat, scratched the back of his head. "I was a…well, I knew your dad."

Sunday took another deep breath, pushed it all the way down to her toes, and slowly let it out. Still shaken from the Hound, she struggled to piece together her muddled thoughts. She wanted to ask, no, *demand* to know how Matty knew her father. She wanted to know how he had the Sight and why her dad hadn't mentioned him.

"Can I get your number?"

Sunday blinked, unraveling her way out of her thoughts and back to the sidewalk with Matty.

"Sorry," he continued, "I'm not asking in a creepy way or anything. I just thought I could introduce you to a few friends of mine. We all have the Sight and we work together on projects."

"Projects?"

"The Other Worldly kind." Matty grinned and pulled out his cell phone. "What do you say? I can give you a call tomorrow morning, see if you're up to meet them?"

Sunday imagined waking up tomorrow, her day off. She'd have a headache, leaving her in a hungover stupor. She should've had more water at the bar. Her tongue stuck to the roof of her mouth. She peeled it off before speaking.

"No," she said.

"No?"

She shook her head.

"I'm not living with the Other World anymore. I'm done."

Matty frowned. "It's part of you. How can you be done with it?"

"Just like that. I said I'm done."

"Huh."

Sunday narrowed her eyes. Was he going to argue with her? Tell her she was wrong? He was a stranger. What did he know about anything?

"You gotta pen?" He replaced his phone in his pocket and opened his wallet to pull out a business card.

Sunday dug through her purse and handed him a pen over the top of the car.

"Here's our card. London's in charge of social media and outreach, so that's her number on the front. Here's my cell on the back." He scribbled the number and then passed back the card and pen.

"I won't call you." Sunday held the card in front of her. She didn't even want to look at it.

"Your prerogative." Matty shrugged. "But if you change your mind, reach out." He put his wallet away and opened his car door again. "Nice to meet you, Sunday. Talk to you soon, hopefully."

His car rolled away from the curb before she could orchestrate an answer. She watched him disappear around the corner before walking the rest of the way home. The card in her hand made her queasy. This man had known her father, but her dad hadn't introduced him to Sunday. What about the friends Matty wanted to introduce her to? Had they known Stephen Elm too?

The two of them had shared everything with each other. Her father was the only person Sunday trusted. There had to be a good reason for Stephen befriending these other Seers and not letting her know. He must've been protecting her by not mentioning them. What danger could she be putting herself in by going to meet them? She shouldn't contact them, even if she wasn't swearing off the Other World.

Sunday unlocked her front door. The dark apartment coaxed her in, a promise of quiet and loneliness. Still not looking at the business card, she dropped it on her bedside table. As she changed and washed up for bed, she replayed the evening in her head. The dull ache in her heart throbbed. She wanted her father here, to ask him questions, to know what he knew, understand what he believed. She'd ask him why he'd hid these people from her. He'd tell her, help her decide what to do.

But Stephen was gone. He'd never answer her questions.

Should she call Matty? What harm could there be? She didn't have to go anywhere with him. She could just ask him questions, get some answers, and then leave the Other World out of her life.

Sunday crawled into bed. Before turning out the light, she picked up the card. The front read:

GHOST GURUS
Got a problem the police can't solve?
No one believes your story? We will.

She'd call Matty tomorrow, at least meet the others with Sight, and make a judgment then. The heaviness of her empty apartment lifted from her shoulders as she came to this decision. She replaced the card on the table and flicked off the lamp.

CHAPTER 7

Dr. Morris,

You suggested journaling, same as you did when I was a kid after my mom left. Didn't work for me then. I couldn't write to myself. It felt odd and, honestly, boring. I spend all my time with myself already. I don't want to write to me. So, this time, I think I'll write to you and tell you all the things I can't in our sessions. Your letters will be my journal. I feel like a teenage girl again. Private. Keep out! Okay, I'm just stalling now, I'll get into it.

You know my dad followed his faith. Never believed in organized religion, but he loved his beliefs. They were beautiful, really. All about balance, giving back what you take. Very zen. And he taught me the scientific stuff. Nothing he shared with you, I'm sure. I would've seen prescriptions for anti-psychotics if he told you the whole scope of his beliefs. He told you about the spirits, probably described them as séances. That's what he always did when talking to a non-Seer. Séances could be accepted. The Other World couldn't. If only it could be though! A world just as complex as ours with different species of flora and fauna, I'm sure. Dad theorized what plants may have existed in the Other World, but of course, neither of us had been. No one living had. Even the dead hadn't gone yet. That's where Dad liked to help.

I'll have to continue this later, Dr. Morris. Someone's here to pick me up. Not a friend, really, but a person. That's new.

•••

Matty picked Sunday up in the morning and drove to the other side of town. He pulled up in front of an old two-story house. There were multiple cars squeezed into the driveway and under the covered carport. Matty parked behind a dusty black BMW, blocking the sidewalk.

"London's in the downstairs unit." He pulled his keys out of the ignition.

She followed Matty to the front door. He walked in without knocking. Quiet voices carried from the living room. Sunday couldn't make out any words.

Three people sat around a glass coffee table. A couple of faded armchairs sat in two corners of the living room, and a green corduroy couch sat below a large window that provided a view of a wooden fence. Nothing in the room matched, instead appearing to have been pieced together from various flea markets and garage sales.

Matty introduced Sunday. London, a woman in her mid-twenties, had white-blond hair brushing the tops of her ears. Gail sat beside her dressed in a wrinkled cardigan, freckles sprinkled across her ivory skin. Jaime occupied an armchair. He rested his elbows on his knees, his hair buzzed short. His frame fought against the fabric of his T-shirt.

"This Elm's girl?" London asked.

Sunday remained standing even after Matty took a seat between London and Gail. Her eyes bounced to each face. They looked at her with such familiarity. She had never seen any of them. Another secret her father had kept from her. "You knew my dad too?"

"We all did." Jaime grinned. "Great guy."

She couldn't believe it. How could her father know all these Seers and hide them from her? They didn't look dangerous or scary. She grew nauseous. Had she really known her father, her best friend, her whole world?

"What did you guys figure out while I was gone?" Matty asked.

"Not a whole lot, unfortunately." Gail handed him two pictures. "We looked into the woman who lived in the apartment before the client. She died of heart failure at ninety-four."

"A client has called about some disturbances," Matty explained to Sunday. He grinned. "The ghostly kind."

"Could be that the poor woman is sticking around for her daughter." Gail turned a laptop around so the others could see a news article on the screen. "Her daughter, Shyanne, went missing back in the sixties. She was only fourteen years old. This article was published last year. Shyanne's mother contacted the local newspaper each year with an update on her daughter's disappearance. There hasn't been much to go on over the last sixty years."

"Why don't we pass on that information to the client?" London said. "They can tell the mother that her daughter is probably in the Other World already, and she should move on to find her. We don't need to go there and do that."

"They are just complaining about thumps in the night," Jaime added. "Not exactly heavy stuff."

"Sounds good to me," Matty said. "We'll tell them to contact us if that doesn't work."

Sunday still stood at the edge of the room, unsure where she should stand or sit. Unlike Matty, who had slid into the room with ease, Sunday didn't feel like she belonged. She was an outsider listening in on the group's work. Their conversation flowed naturally. At least as natural as a conversation about spirits could be. She crossed her arms and rested her weight on one hip.

"Sunday, have a seat." London gestured to the second armchair.

Tucking her hair behind one ear, Sunday maneuvered around the furniture and finally joined them. She sat perched on the edge of the seat, hands clasped in her lap.

"I have so many questions," London said, grinning. "I can't believe we are meeting the precious Sunday Elm."

Sunday ran her thumb over her knuckles. Her palms grew warm and clammy squeezed together. All eyes stared at her. She clutched her hands tighter.

"There's really not all that much to tell," she muttered.

"Sure there is." Gail's soothing voice pulled Sunday's eyes off her lap. "Your father had such nice things to say about you."

"He mentioned you got your Sight as a kid," Jaime added. "Only know one other person who got it young." He turned to Gail. "Your daughter's four, right?"

Sunday frowned. "That's not normal?"

"No." Gail shook her head. "The Sight tends to manifest in humans later in life, typically early twenties, but sometimes as late as your forties or fifties. I didn't get mine until after I had my second child."

"Twenty-two." London raised a hand.

"Eighteen," Jaime said.

"Same," Matty said.

"How old were you?" London leaned closer.

"Seven," Sunday said.

London's mouth fell open. "Your Sight must be powerful. Was your mom a Seer too? She must have been."

Sunday shrugged. "I don't think so. She left around that same time, though. Didn't get a chance to ask."

"She did." London nodded. "I'm sure of it."

Sunday pressed her thumb harder across her knuckles. Who were these people? These strangers knew so much about her.

"I have to go." Jaime stood up. As he walked to the door, he looked over his shoulder, waving goodbye. "Don't have too much fun without me, okay?"

"Jaime is an officer for the county police." Gail leaned over Matty to speak to Sunday. A whiff of soap filled her nose. "Helps us get jobs sometimes, the cases the police can't solve."

Sunday studied the smiling face of the teenage girl on the computer screen. The black-and-white photo showed a smiling girl with round cheeks. Her coily hair had been pinned back with shiny barrettes. So young, gone. Beside the girl was a photo of her mother, a more recent one. The old woman walked with a cane, her eyes covered by sunglasses. She never gave up, had never stopped looking for her daughter. Sunday wished she could find the spirit of the teenage girl; she didn't have a doubt in her mind that the poor girl had been killed sixty years ago. She'd tell the girl's spirit how lucky she'd been, how lucky she was to have a mother like the woman in the photo.

She thought of going home. The people around her were strangers. Her father had kept them from her for a reason. She should go home, but she couldn't bring herself to get to her feet. She couldn't convince herself that she wanted to go back to her empty apartment.

"You okay?" Gail's voice pulled her thoughts away from the computer screen.

"My father never mentioned you guys. Never mentioned any of this."

London shrugged.

"Doesn't surprise me. He never liked our hunting."

"You hunt?" Sunday frowned. "What?"

"Ghosts." London grinned.

"What do you mean you hunt ghosts?"

"There are thousands of spirits across the country causing property damage or injury to living people. We help move the ghosts on to the next life." Gail winked at Sunday.

She recalled the business card still sitting on her nightstand. Ghost Gurus.

"You guys do this together?" she asked.

"Sometimes." Matty shrugged. "It depends on who's available."

"And my dad didn't approve?"

"No." London chuckled and shook her head quickly, sending her white-blond hair dancing like a halo around her head. "He said we were going to get ourselves killed and that we exploited our Sight by selling our services."

Sunday understood. She and her father had never sold their services when they worked together. Stephen called it their faith, helping spirits and their loved ones move on. They never sought out clients, never called them clients. Her father would take her to help a friend, though never one she'd met before or would see after.

Gail's soft voice pulled Sunday closer to her. "You should join us on the next job." She watched Sunday expectantly, eyes warm and encouraging. Gail reminded Sunday of the mother she'd always wanted.

The group of ghost hunters overwhelmed her, but she had questions. Questions not only about her dad, but also about their business. Her father had taught her to use her Sight to help. Like having extra money to give to charity. If you had it to spare, help out your fellow man.

This group, though, saw their Sight as a skill, a trade like carpentry or law. They were a unique group of people who had a unique skill that they could capitalize on.

She glanced at the computer screen, thinking that perhaps the teenage girl's mother would guide her, but the screen had turned black. Her father wouldn't have wanted her to go, but he wasn't around. No one was around. She should walk away. Just the thought of saying yes made her nauseous. She couldn't handle the Other World anymore. But then what? She'd go home, watch TV, kill time until work the next day. Then what?

"Okay." She nodded. "Let's do it."

CHAPTER 8

A few days later, Sunday studied a two-story farmhouse from the back seat of Matty's idling car. White shutters and a wraparound porch made the home picturesque. A plastic outhouse and scaffolding around the wooden frame of a shed-sized building to one side of the house ruined the view.

"Seems like a big project," Gail said, referring to the construction.

Matty explained the job. "So, Mrs. Lawrence emailed us last week complaining that her closet doors wouldn't stay closed. She checked the hinges and doorknobs, but nothing seemed to be wrong with them. When she started closing them, she heard scratches behind the doors."

"Hounds?" Sunday guessed.

"I don't think so. I've never heard of Hounds being stopped by a door before." Gail rested a finger on her lips, frowning as she thought over the case.

They walked up the steps to the wraparound porch. Matty rapped his knuckles on the door.

A woman in a T-shirt and jeans answered. Her ponytail hung loose and to the side, and her shoulders slumped so low she appeared to have a growth on her back.

"You made it," she sighed. "Come on in. Are you thirsty?"

She introduced herself as Holly as she poured them each a glass of lemonade and gave them a tour of her house. She had six closets, one for each of the three bedrooms, one in the family room, and two along the hallways between the rooms. All of them stood open.

"I stopped closing them," Holly said. "The scratching scared Bella."

Holly's one-year-old daughter sat in her playpen watching them. Her eyes were bloodshot and red from crying.

"To be honest, it scares me too. My husband has been out of town for business. This house is big enough to get my imagination going, but I know that scratching is real."

Holly stood in the living room beside her daughter's playpen and staring at each of them without blinking. She was clearly waiting for the solution.

"You don't have to worry about a thing, Mrs. Lawrence," Matty said. "Did you get the hotel room like I suggested?"

She nodded, and her eyes jumped around the room. Sunday felt for the woman. She imagined that Holly wondered if she'd ever feel safe in her house again.

"Why don't you and your daughter head to the hotel? Stay there for the night, and we'll take care of everything."

Holly smiled as she pulled her daughter onto her hip. She pushed aside the playpen to reveal a pile of bags packed and ready to go. Jaime helped her with them.

"I'll grab our supplies on the way back in." He grunted as he lifted a large diaper bag over his shoulder.

Holly paused on her way out the door. "Thank you." She took Matty's hand with her free one. Her shadowed eyes were wide and watery. She stared, still unblinking. "Really. Thank you."

The front door closed, leaving them alone in the Lawrence

farmhouse to solve the mystery of the phantom scratching. Nerves squeezed Sunday's gut. She realized that she had no idea what she had gotten herself into.

"Should we each take a door?" London suggested.

"You don't want to wait for Jaime to come back with the supplies?" Matty asked.

London's smile was mischievous. "Where is your sense of adventure?"

"Why don't you and Sunday get the hallway closets? I'll get the one in the family room. Gail, check the master bedroom."

He didn't wait for a reply, instead making a dash up the stairs. Sunday and the others followed more slowly behind him.

"Is there anything I need to know?" Sunday asked. "Like tricks of the trade."

London shrugged. "There aren't really any. Every job we've done has been unique." The sixth step groaned under their feet. "Just trust your gut. You have the Sight. This isn't new to you."

Sunday looked over her shoulder at Gail who nodded in agreement. If it wasn't new to her, then why did she feel so uneasy?

London stopped at the first closet. Sunday walked to the other end of the hall and peered into another to find various coats. On a shelf above sat baskets for storage, and below were rainboots and umbrellas. Sunday felt around the doorframe, searching for a light switch. There wasn't one.

"Ready?" Gail called from the master bedroom.

Sunday turned to London who had her hand on the closet's doorknob. She gave Sunday a smileless nod.

"Ready," Sunday confirmed.

In sync, they pushed the doors closed. Holding her breath, Sunday strained to hear the scratching. Her sweaty palm gripped the doorknob.

Nothing happened. It was quiet enough to hear Jaime's footsteps walking up the porch steps again. Sunday peered over the landing. He walked in, each arm holding a bag. In his right, a sack of salt, and in his left, a duffel bag.

"Where'd you all go?" he said.

As if the phantom were triggered by Jaime's voice, vigorous scratching shook the closet door. Sunday's body jolted like she'd stuck her finger in an open socket. Her gaze leapt to London and then back to the closet. She took a step back, eyes following the sound of the scratching that began at her feet and moved up the length of the door. Halfway up, she could feel the spirit paw at the doorknob and it shuddered under the force.

"Are you guys hearing that?" London shouted from her closet door.

"Should we answer?" Matty yelled from the family room.

"No!" Sunday took another step back.

"Wait for me!" Jaime stomped up the stairs. Sunday followed him into the family room. Matty stood in front of his closet grinning; the scratching was shaking his door as well.

"I wonder what it is?" He cocked his head to the side.

"Well, let's find out. Watch out." Jaime stepped in front of Matty and poured salt across the threshold of the closet door. "Ready?" He had his hand on the doorknob when he looked back at Sunday and winked.

The door opened over the line of salt, leaving it undisturbed. The scratching stopped.

"What did you guys do?" London shouted from the hallway.

The closet was dark. Darker than it should have been, like something had sucked up all the light. Sunday, Matty, and Jaime leaned closer to try to see past the darkness.

There was a wing. It moved slowly back and forth, inching closer to them. Below the wing, a chicken leg stepped out next to the closet doorframe. Another leg stepped beside it, both close, but not passing the line of salt.

"We should have drawn a pentagram on the door or something," Jaime muttered.

It was a spirit, old. Difficult to find the human features. It had wings like a bat, chicken legs, and arms like a kangaroo. Its face was the most human aspect of its form, but its eyes were black and beady and its nose protruded like a snout.

"Man, it's ugly," Matty said.

"What is it?" Jaime said.

"A spirit?" Sunday murmured. She'd never seen one so creature-like, but what else could it be?

It looked toward her, its small black eyes narrowing.

Who are you? she asked the spirit wordlessly.

Sunday saw it all. The spirit's life played in her mind like movie clips. She no longer stood in the modern farmhouse, but on dirt, dust having worked its way between her toes through her stitched shoes. The smell of manure hung thick in the air, coating Sunday's mouth and throat.

She was *an old spirit. Early 1900s. Sunday scratched at the stiff fabric of her dress and tugged on the tight bodice the spirit wore. Beyond the discomfort of the clothing, Sunday felt it. The spirit was in love. Her heart thudded in her chest when he was near. If their eyes met, her cheeks warmed, and she giggled with the other girls behind her hand.*

He loved her too. The spirit understood his love in her soul. The way he smiled at her during his sermons. When he spoke of a righteous life, she knew he was describing their life together. It was as if they were the only two in the room. He told her, through his preaching, that he'd leave his family and marry her.

Their hands touched during tithing. She wrapped her fingers around his when he came around with the basket. When they slipped from hers, she brought her palms to her face and inhaled his scent. Perfection.

Everything was going as planned. She'd marry the pastor. They'd have a dozen children. God would smile on them and she would live happily ever after.

God's work continued when Papa's horse was spooked by a snake. The pastor offered to escort her home. They'd have time to talk. She'd been waiting for this very moment. Their souls had aligned. It was time to declare their love for one another.

"What are you talking about, Matilda?" He chuckled nervously. "You're only fourteen years old. A child!"

The anger was overwhelming. It choked Sunday, just as it must have choked the spirit.

Her hands wrapped around the top of a sack of potatoes. She squeezed the burlap, unaware of when she had grabbed it in the first place. Now in front of her home, she swung and hit the pastor. He dropped to the ground. Again, she raised the bundle of potatoes, throwing it down on the betrayal until her arms grew heavy with fatigue.

"Matilda?"

The spirit spun around to see her younger brother with his mouth hanging open. How long had he been there?

He ran home before she could catch him. The little weasel told their father what he saw: Matilda on top of the town pastor, screaming and scratching out his eyes.

"What did you do?!"

Her father shook her shoulders, but she refused to speak. She honestly couldn't remember what she'd done. All she remembered was the color red. The memory of the pastor's chuckle. His scoff at the idea of them being together.

Her father locked her in the broom closet, shouting about needing the church for guidance as he slammed the front door.

The girl shivered in the dark, not cold, but grieving.

She must have been possessed by the Devil, the church said. The Devil pushed her to attack the pastor.

When the Devil wouldn't leave her, she was beaten. She was too weak to defend herself. Too weak to continue living.

"Her name was Matilda," Sunday said.

The spirit loomed in the closet doorway. The wings flapped slowly, pushing small puffs of air at them.

"How do you know?" Jaime asked.

"The spirits don't talk to you?" Sunday asked. She'd assumed the others received a similar message.

Both men looked at her. Matty frowned. Jaime's mouth hung open.

"No." Matty shook his head. "They talk to you?"

"Well, kind of. It's more like they place their life story in my head." Sunday explained what she had learned about Matilda.

"I don't see anything, but I can hear her death." Jaime jerked his thumb at Matilda. "Not a pleasant one."

Sunday shook her head in agreement. The others still watched her, apparently more stunned by her ability to communicate with spirits than the ghoul beating its wings in the closet.

"Does everyone interact with spirits differently?" she asked.

Jaime nodded to Matty. "He's our resident Other World expert."

Matty shrugged. "Yes and no. As far as I can tell, there are slight differences in our contacts with the Other World. Mostly we get feelings off of them, occasionally snippets of the spirit's life if they are particularly strong. I've never met anyone who could actually communicate with the spirit like you."

"Lucky us, right?" Jaime said. "More insight should make this job easier."

Sunday looked to the ancient ghost again. Matilda's beady eyes still bored into her. What did that mean? London had mentioned that Sunday must be powerful. Was this the power she had referred to? Or was there more that Sunday didn't understand? The sinking feeling in her stomach forced her to admit the honest answer: of course there was more she didn't understand.

The spirit beat her wings, the gust shaking the ceiling fan above them.

"So what now?" Sunday watched the agitated light.

"How old is she?" Matty asked.

"About fourteen, lived during pioneer times," Sunday said.

"How'd she die?" Matty continued.

"Violently," Sunday said. "Beaten to death."

"Jeez," Jaime muttered.

"Sounds like a Girdwick," Matty said. "So the first thing we need to do is get her out of the house."

"Well, she's just a fourteen-year-old girl." Jaime stepped forward and dragged his foot across the salt line, breaking it. "How difficult can she be?"

Matty and Sunday shouted as Jaime's foot crossed the line. Before he had even lifted his foot to step back, the spirit flew over their heads. She loomed over them.

Sunday stepped away slowly. The spirit looked from her, to Matty, to Jaime, and shrieked. Their hands flung to their ears.

"Guys! The scratching stopped at my closet door. Did it stop at yours too?" Gail yelled from her post in the bedroom.

"Mine too!" London replied.

The women arrived in the doorway, breathless. The spirit lifted the closet door off its hinges with her chicken feet and flung it at them. They leapt through the entryway and into the room to avoid the flying door. The spirit snatched the couch and launched it in their direction. The five of them stumbled out of the room. Jaime slammed the door behind them.

"Just a fourteen-year-old girl, huh?" Matty smacked Jaime's shoulder with the back of his hand.

"Have you ever met a teenage girl?" London rolled her eyes.

The spirit raged. They could hear the furniture thumping and crashing around the room.

"What's a Girdwick?" Sunday panted.

"A gird what?" Gail asked.

"It's what Matty called the spirit," Jaime explained.

"I swear he is making this stuff up half the time." Something heavy slammed against the closed door and London jumped farther away.

"How do you know it's a Girdwick, Matty?" Gail asked.

"Sunday," he said. "She was able to communicate with the spirit and give us details about how she died."

"So what is this sucker then?" Jaime asked.

"A Girdwick is a type of spirit," Matty explained. "The circumstances of their death are so horrific that their spirit transforms. They could be called poltergeists, and they're always dangerous."

"Dangerous how?" Jaime pressed his hands on the shaking door to keep it closed.

"They need human essences," Matty continued. "That's their food."

"What do you mean, 'human essences'?" London asked.

"Like a human soul." Sunday took another step away from the door but kept her gaze fixed on it.

Her father had taught her about human essences. They varied in strength, depending on the person and their state of mind. A young woman attending college and living life to her fullest would have a much stronger essence than a man suffering from depression, for example. These essences of people gave them the colorful auras that Reap could see.

"And what happens when a person gets their essence eaten by a Girdwick?" Jaime asked.

"Death," Matty said. "It's a slow one, too. That would explain why Holly and her daughter appeared so ragged. They're slowly losing their essences."

"But why now?" Gail asked. "This family didn't just move in. Why did the Girdwick attack them now?"

Matty shrugged. "Maybe it has something to do with the construction outside. It disturbed the spirit."

"Really?" Jaime asked.

"I don't know. I'm just speculating!" A large object hit the door, cracking it. "We only have time to speculate right now."

The commotion inside the room continued. They stared at the thin crack for a moment, anticipating the broken barrier between them and the Girdwick.

"Okay, so we know she's a Girdwick. Is there any way to get rid of her without getting our souls eaten?" London asked.

"Water," Matty said.

"A little help, guys?" Jaime gritted his teeth, all his weight pressed against the door. The four of them joined him.

"What do you mean, 'water'?" Gail asked.

"You have to trap her in water. She can't swim."

They all stared at him, frowning. Sunday was beginning to think he really was just making all this up as he went along.

Matty shrugged.

"We may not like him, but the man knows his way around the Other World."

"Who?" Sunday looked to the others for an explanation. They stared back, wordless.

"My dad," Matty replied. He cleared his throat and ran a hand down the doorframe, making it clear to Sunday that he wasn't going to answer any more questions.

"Wasn't there a stream along the road up there?" London asked.

Something heavy dropped to the floor, which shook under their feet. It reminded Sunday of the horse barista who had destroyed her dining room table. That gave her an idea.

"We need to lure her out and get her to the stream, right?" Sunday glanced at each of their faces, mouths gaping.

"Doesn't sound easy." Gail raised an eyebrow as she peered at the door again.

Sunday described her idea and they developed it into a plan. One of them would be bait, and everybody else would be in charge of locking up the house. Jaime opened the duffel bag, revealing an array of tools, rope, markers, and a portable phone charger.

"What is all of this?" Sunday asked as Jaime searched the bag.

"Things we discovered we needed at previous jobs," London said. "The bag gets a little more full each time we finish a job."

Jaime handed out markers for the others to take. They used them to mark the windows with pentagrams. London and Matty were posted at the front and back doors, respectively. They spread salt across all doorways except the back door. With the windows marked and salt laid, the Girdwick only had one way out of the house. Gail held the family room door closed, waiting for the signal to invite the spirit out. The room had quieted as they were setting up. She might have run out of things to break, or maybe she waited, listening to them.

Jaime hurried around the house, marker still out. He sketched a pentagram on each of their palms.

"It'll protect you from the Girdwick," he explained to Sunday. "She'll search for a life force outside the house." He took Sunday's hand and marked it. "If she approaches you, hold up your hand to display the pentagram." He tucked the marker into his back pocket without having marked himself. Sunday understood. He'd be the essence the Girdwick would go after.

"Jaime, you take Sunday outside to help you set up there. Shoot us a text when you're ready," Matty said.

"He's the boss," Jaime said. After gathering the rope from the bag, he waved a hand, gesturing for Sunday to follow. He led the way out the back door and through the large yard to the stream.

The farmhouse stood on a large plot of land. A yard ended in a small gathering of trees. The air cooled under the shade of them and Sunday heard the trickle of the creek.

"We need to partition off a space to trap her, leaving some of the ground open, but most of it water." Jaime unwrapped the rope. Using a pocketknife he pulled from his back pocket, he cut the rope into pieces, each one a couple feet long. "You know anything about knots?"

Sunday shook her head.

"It's easy." He led her to a thin tree on the creek's edge, speaking as he wrapped a piece of rope around the trunk. "It's called a clove hitch. You wrap it around twice like this, and look, when you pull it through it creates this X across the line." His fingers traced the twisted rope, emphasizing his words. "The X represents a double barrier over the veil between our world and the Other World. You think you can tie it on another tree?"

Nodding, Sunday took the rope he offered. Jaime pointed out the perimeter they'd be mapping out. They'd mark the corners with the clove hitch, tying them to tree trunks and branches around the creek.

"It'll trap the Girdwick. We just have to get her to cross the threshold and then you'll force her into the water with your marked hand. Shouldn't be too difficult." Jaime grunted as he leapt from a rock in the middle of the creek back to dry ground, having just tied a knot on a branch overhanging the water.

"How do you know all this stuff?" Sunday asked. Her eyes bounced to the four clove hitches. How could anyone possibly know to tie that specific knot?

Jaime shrugged. "We've picked things up here and there. Gail's grandmother was a powerful Seer and taught her. Matty's dad knows a lot too. Everything else we pick up on Sight forums."

He pulled his cell phone out to text the others.

"You ready?" He grinned.

She scanned the forest and looked at the knots tied around the tree trunks and then her palm with the pentagram. Ready? She peered at the tall goofy stranger standing on the creek's edge beside her. She'd come this far already. As much as her stomach trembled with nerves, she wasn't turning back. Sunday rubbed her sweaty palms on her jeans.

"Watch that pentagram." Jaime gestured to her hand. "Remember, all you need to do is hold it up. It'll protect you."

Sunday pulled her hand off her leg. Wiping it had smeared the pentagram, but the lines remained unbroken. It was decided. She'd see this through. Jaime had *her* trust for now. Her eyes locked with Jaime's and she gave him a curt nod. She was ready.

With a wink, Jaime leapt onto a large rock in the middle of the creek and began to sing. Sunday recognized the jazz tune, the title in the first line, "For Once in My Life." His deep voice echoed Frank Sinatra, bouncing off trees, pleasant to listen to but puzzling with the Girdwick on her way.

He closed his eyes and faced the sky as he started the chorus. He was completely taken away by the music.

"Jaime!" Sunday shouted over his loud notes.

He looked down at her.

"What are you doing?" she asked.

"Strengthening my life force." A smile spread across his face. "I never feel more alive than when I'm singing my man Sinatra." He threw his head back again and continued the song.

Goosebumps flowed down Sunday's body, and the hairs on her arms stood on end. She turned her head, searching the space behind her through her peripheral vision.

The murmur of the leaves rustling in the breeze joined Jaime's voice. A branch snapped, drawing Sunday's gaze.

The Girdwick hovered between the trees, her face shadowed by her wings, her red eyes still glowing through the shade.

Her back was to Jaime now, but she listened to him continue the lyrics.

She flew at Sunday, screeching, drowning out Jaime's singing. Her chicken feet landed on Sunday's shoulders, talons digging into her like knives. What did Holly and her daughter feel while the Girdwick snacked on their souls? They couldn't see the creature latching onto them. They probably couldn't even feel the tiny chicken claws jabbing into their skin. Could they feel the draining? Suddenly, Sunday's body weakened like she'd been hit by a truck. Her whole body felt heavy and feeble and she struggled to take a full breath, each one shallow and leaving her mouth gaping. Her vision began to darken and her knees buckled under the weight.

"The pentagram, Sunday!" Jaime screamed. "Raise your hand!"

She heaved her arm up, shoving the Girdwick's wings aside. The pentagram had an immediate effect; the ancient spirit hissed.

Jaime resumed singing, bellowing over the shriek of the Girdwick.

The chicken feet launched off Sunday's shoulders and the creature hurtled toward the singing man. Sunday collapsed to her knees, gasping for breath, drained like she'd run a marathon.

Jaime shouted the next line, raising his arms as he finished.

The Girdwick crossed the clove hitches. Sunday held her breath.

Jaime's echoing voice faded. Sunday forced herself up on shaky legs, staring open-mouthed at the scene in front of her.

The Girdwick had crossed the clove hitch threshold and transformed. The chicken legs and wings disappeared. She faced away from Sunday, but Sunday assumed the beady eyes and beaked nose had dissipated as well. From her vantage point, Sunday saw a young colonial girl standing beside the creek bed.

"Use the pentagram." Jaime spoke quickly as he fished the marker out of his back pocket. "Force her into the water."

Sunday's feet crunched on dry leaves and twigs. The Girdwick's gaze snapped in her direction, revealing the soft face of Matilda. She had the same button nose and freckles that Sunday had seen in her vision, but her red eyes darkened with a frown. Matilda hissed and lunged at Sunday. She took an impulsive step back, hands held up to protect herself from the impending attack, but Matilda had been immediately forced back by the clove hitch barrier.

"She can't get to you. Push her!" Jaime stood with his feet spread as wide as they could on the rock, holding his own hand up, now marked with a pentagram.

Matilda screamed and slammed her hand against the invisible wall, snapping her teeth in Sunday's direction. Sunday pressed her marked hand forward, forcing the Girdwick back. She shied away from the symbol, hissing and spitting. Sunday came closer and Matilda cowered, stepping toward the water. Her eyes, now wide with fear, bounced from the creek to Sunday. Then the dark eyes transformed, appearing more human-like and reflecting the same pain Sunday had seen in the vision.

Sunday hesitated, her elbow slackening. The Girdwick smiled, revealing razor-sharp teeth. She licked her lips and sat up straighter. Sunday had crossed into the clove hitch perimeter. Only the pentagram stood between her and the Girdwick. Matilda extended a hand, touching the tips of her fingers to Sunday's curls while cooing. Sunday felt the urge to wrap her arms around the young girl.

She'd just been misguided.

She was only a child.

"Get her into the water!"

Jaime's shout snapped Sunday's attention back to the glowing red eyes, the razor-sharp teeth. Chicken feet talons protruded from the Girdwick's nails and scraped down Sunday's cheek. She locked her elbow straight once again and gave one final shove.

With a cry, the teenage girl stumbled into the water. It was a strange sight. The small stream appeared stronger than the Girdwick. Easily crossable by Sunday or Jaime, it dragged the spirit away like a rushing river. Matilda's hands snatched at the air in search of anything to grab hold of. Rocks and tree branches passed through her arms as she shrieked and screamed. Like a small leaf, the creek pulled the Girdwick downstream. Her screams quieted as she disappeared.

•••

Matty drove Sunday home. The sun was setting by the time they finished at Holly's house. They assured the woman that the scratching was gone, and Holly paid them with a check. Once in the car, done with the whole situation and heading home, Sunday was speechless. She kept replaying the attack of the Girdwick over and over in her head. On the one hand, she was glad to discover that she wouldn't spiral into a complete panic in such a situation like she had been reacting to the Hounds. On the other hand, though, now that everything was over and the adrenaline had worked its way out of her system, Sunday felt on edge. Her heart thudded in her chest, her agitated fingers tapping her legs. Slick with sweat, she just wanted to be home, away from…

She struggled to form her thoughts. They moved in her mind as if she were in a dream, detached from reality. She watched the familiar scenery of her neighborhood with bulging eyes, her fingers still drumming against her leg.

She looked at the people in the car with her. Strangers, yes, but she felt drawn to them. What she lacked, they had. She was timid; Matty was bold. She was reserved; Jaime was quick and witty. She was passive; London was daring. She didn't belong in this group, but they wanted her. She told herself they only wanted her for her Sight. Unlike the others, she could communicate with spirits. She'd try to enjoy it, though, even as the weight of anxiety sat on her chest. Why couldn't she just relax?

Matty pulled up to the curb in front of her apartment complex.

"So your dad taught you?" Sunday spoke for the first time since leaving the haunted farmhouse.

"About the spirit?" Matty said.

She nodded.

"He taught me almost everything I know about the Other World. I've picked up a few other things from the group."

"But Dad never taught me any of that." Sunday gestured in the direction they had just driven from.

"Your dad believed in staying rooted in our world. He confronted spirits when they were unavoidable, but otherwise he wanted nothing to do with the Other World."

Sunday nodded slowly.

She had never known anything different. Her dad would cross the street to avoid passing a spirit, or he'd leave the store if they discovered a creature in an aisle. Now that she was thinking back, it made sense.

"We usually celebrate with drinks after a success like that," Matty said. "Once the check clears, can I give you a call?"

"I don't know. All of this," she gestured between them, referring to their Sight and the Other World, "I'm just not sure it's for me anymore."

Matty frowned. "How can you stop being a Seer?"

She shrugged. "I can avoid it."

"What if I called you anyway. Will you pick up?"

Her stomach quivered. She couldn't face the Other World without her dad. The Hounds had sent her into a panic attack and a spirit destroyed her apartment, but as she'd calmed down during the car ride, she was left feeling satisfied, exhilarated. She'd confronted a spirit. This spirit wouldn't have bothered her at all if she hadn't visited the farmhouse. She'd never sought out the Other World before. It was taboo and as horrifying as she had been taught, but... She took a deep breath. It felt good. For the first time since her father's death, she didn't feel the weight of anxiety on her chest.

"Maybe." She settled on that answer.

"Sleep on it," Matty said. "You don't have to answer my call."

PRAYERS OF JAX FRASER

Lord, I understand my mission now. To have seen Your form, Your face. To have heard Your words echoed in my mind. I am unworthy to be chosen, but for this honor, I ask for Your continued guidance, God. I ask to be Your next messiah. I am Your servant and will do as You wish. My faith is great, but I pray for the strength to accept it. I pray for clarity, Lord, and an end to these headaches. I need to think clearly to fulfill this mission. Despite these hardships, I feel rejuvenated in Your presence, and for that, Lord, I am forever grateful.

CHAPTER 9

Dr. Morris,

Dad taught me that the Other World is broken into layers, like the layers of the rainforest, except there isn't a sun. You may wonder how Dad knew all that he did. I always did too. He'd talk to some spirits. Well, not actually talk. The spirits don't talk, you know. But he'd communicate. It's difficult to explain. He would just know, like a direct line between the spirit and my dad's mind. I never saw him talking a lot with the spirits, though. If he helped them, he'd ask them some questions. They didn't always know the answers because they hadn't really been there. That's what Dad was helping them with, getting into the Other World.

I asked him once. I must have been fourteen or fifteen. I asked him how he knew so much about the Other World. He said the internet. I tried my own internet search then. I just remember laughing at the ridiculousness of the sites I found. Other dimensions described from shows like Dr. Who. Bigfoot. Space aliens. It was all crap. Never did find what sites Dad must have been looking at. He always seemed to dodge my questions. Now I'm starting to understand how much he kept from me. Did he think I couldn't handle it? He's gone. And I'm meeting all these people who knew my father and knew about me. It's strange. Terrifying and oddly comforting at the same time. If I can handle this, I bet I could've handled anything my dad kept from me. At least, I think I'm handling this all right. I wonder what I can allude to at our next session to get your take on this.

•••

Matty greeted Sunday at her front door with a coffee a couple days later.

"I wasn't sure how you took it, so I just brought the cream and sugar packets." He gestured to his pockets.

"Thanks." Sunday took her to-go cup and followed Matty out the door. "So what's the plan today?"

"I thought we'd stop by my place. I could show you some of the websites we use to chat with other Seers, exchange information. I was hoping to pick your brain a bit too. Your dad knew a great deal more about the structure of the Other World. It's not just one..." he hesitated. "Division? I guess?"

They made their way to the car. Matty pulled out his keys and unlocked it.

"Dad called them layers," Sunday said. "He believed there were three."

"What the hell?" Matty frowned, looking over her shoulder.

Heavy footsteps sent a tingle down Sunday's spine. She turned around. A tall, wide man walked slowly down the sidewalk across the street. He wore a dirty white T-shirt and work boots. The blade of the large ax at his side scraped against the cement as he stomped toward them. His cold gaze remained fixed on them.

A strange sight, but surely the man didn't have anything to do with them. He continued down the sidewalk, walking closer. Probably on his way to some job, a neighbor who needed wood chopped or perhaps a contracted worker for the park behind her apartment complex. A tree could have fallen down. In the Arizona desert.

The tiny hairs on her arms stood on end as Sunday's heart beat faster, thudding against her sternum as her explanations began to unravel. Her coffee slipped from her fingers, splashing at her feet unnoticed. The man stepped off the sidewalk, moving directly toward them now. His scowl locked her in place. He raised his upper lip to reveal tobacco-stained teeth bared in an unnerving sneer as his boots clomped against the road.

"Get in the car!"

Matty's voice captured her attention. He already sat behind the wheel with the engine running. Sunday's hand scrambled for the passenger door latch. Her eyes remained fixed on the approaching man. Even at her five feet eight, he'd still tower over her. She yanked the door open and threw herself onto the seat. The door shut as the man rushed to the car. Sunday gasped. He raised the ax in both hands and swung. The car frame crunched under the blow, screaming in protest as the man dragged the ax against it. He snarled at them through the car windows, bloodshot eyes wide and wild.

"Go, go, go!" Sunday screamed, but Matty didn't need the prompting.

He slammed down the gas pedal. The wheels squealed, further disrupting the quiet early morning hours, and the car jerked forward. Sunday watched the man lurch forward with the car, hands still around the wooden handle of the ax, which was still embedded in the car. He'd lose his grip. They'd have his weapon. Sunday imagined his feet flying out from under him, his hands slipping from the handle and his body bouncing and rolling on the road as they sped away.

But he managed to wiggle the blade free. Matty pushed the car faster. Sunday turned and watched the man through the rear window.

He hunched over the blade, his back rising and falling with each breath. The blade glinted in the morning sun. Sunday stared at him, refusing to blink. The man wouldn't leave her sight for a moment. As they turned the corner, he dashed across the street again. The headlights of a truck flashed, and he climbed inside the vehicle.

Matty continued racing down the neighborhood streets. He turned sharply left and then right, not slowing down for any signs or lights. Cars honked in protest, but only a few accompanied them on the street thanks to the early morning hour. Sunday reached for the handle above the passenger door and braced herself for the ride.

Arriving on the other side of town, Matty pulled up to the curb and hit the brakes. She recognized the shopping center they'd stopped in front of. Her favorite pizza place sat comfortably between a laundromat and grocery store, a sharp contrast to the horror they'd just fled from. To her left stood a run-down Victorian house. Up the porch steps were two doors with the numbers 153 and 152 to the left of each door.

"This is my place," Matty said.

He pulled the keys out of the ignition and then rested his forehead on the steering wheel. They sat in the quiet car. Had they really just been chased away by a madman with an ax? Disbelief left Sunday speechless.

Eventually she opened the passenger door. Her body halfway out of the car, she scanned the streets. Empty. Matty stepped out of the car and she turned to him.

He stood with his grip still on the open car door. Her eyes scanned beyond Matty to the truck now blocking her view of the pizza restaurant.

"Get back!"

She shrieked her half-formed thought and scrambled back into the safety of the car. The ax man bolted at them, ax held over his head. Matty ducked. The man rammed into his door like a linebacker as Matty hit the lock. The man stumbled back, stepping wide as he lifted the ax over his shoulder. Matty fumbled with the keys, stabbed at the ignition but continually missed the hole. The ax hit the window and the man's arms vibrated from the impact. Matty cursed under his breath. Sunday pressed her body against the passenger door, getting as far away from their attacker as she could. He swung again and the impact cracked the window. She screamed. The key slid into the ignition.

"Go!" she screeched.

Matty hit the gas again. The engine roared and Sunday was flung back in her seat.

The ax blade raked against the metal surface of the car as Matty sped away. Again, Sunday twisted around to watch through the back window. The car picked up speed. The man watched them from the middle of the road.

"Did he know where I live?" Matty gasped. "Is it a ghost?"

"I don't think so. It was too solid. Had to be human." Sunday settled down in her seat.

"Then..." Matty panted, glancing repeatedly between his side mirrors and rearview mirror to check if they were being followed. "What..."

His voice trailed off as he struggled to find the words, but Sunday didn't need him to finish the question.

She shook her head. "I don't know."

She watched her small town whiz past her. Her companion drove far over the speed limit. She appreciated that.

"I think I have an idea." Matty glanced at Sunday, his eyes wide and his eyebrows raised halfway up his forehead like he was asking her permission to take the lead.

Adrenaline pumped through her body, keeping her moving at a

much faster pace. Her thoughts rolled and tumbled in her head. Who had attacked them? How did the ax man know where they lived? Who was this man who claimed to know her father? Why had she seen another Hound at the bar? Something was wrong. Would she be killed?

She grabbed the seatbelt above her right shoulder and locked it across her body. The small ritual brought her some sense of normalcy.

"Okay." She nodded.

Sunday jerked to her left when Matty made a sharp turn. He continued driving on a road parallel to the downtown strip, heading toward the industrial side of town. Here, houses were separated by greater distances of land. Sidewalks were replaced by narrow dirt pathways in front of fields. The three-lane road transformed into one lane, and Sunday watched the numbers on the speedometer increase.

Matty veered the car onto a long driveway. A large building with piping thrusting out of its top stood at the end of the private road. Past the parking lot were rows of storage containers. As they drove between them, Sunday lost sight of the piped building, the only evidence that it still stood beyond the containers was the steam dissipating in the sky above. She knew this building. Sunday had driven past the local mushroom factory before, though she typically preferred to stay far away from it. The sour, manure-like scent of the mushrooms hung permanently in the air.

Matty drove past the containers and beyond the factory. Behind the building, the grassy hills that surrounded the desert town loomed over them. The sun created long shadows off the tall grass that swayed in the morning breeze. A cabin was tucked away in the grassy terrain, a large shed built from old wood half rotted away. It looked like it would only take a strong breeze to send the whole thing down.

The horror movie scene before her made Sunday want to stay in the comfort of Matty's car. She had no plans to investigate the decrepit cabin in the woods, like so many unlucky scary-movie victims before her.

"Where are we?" she asked.

"It's a friend's house. He has the Sight too."

Matty shut off the car and stepped out. The silence pressed around Sunday. She imagined sitting in the car, anxiously awaiting Matty's return, eyes bouncing to every movement of the grass. The image squeezed her chest, forcing her breaths to shallow. Against her better judgment, she opened the car door and inhaled the smelly but crisp morning air.

The sun beat down above them, warming as it rose higher in the sky. Sunday followed Matty to the cabin, walking through the tramped-on grass like a hiking path. She wondered if she should be more scared. No one knew she was out here. She could disappear and the police wouldn't have any clues to begin their search. She kept following Matty across the field. She was trusting him.

Dried leaves and grass crunched under their feet as they approached the dilapidated cabin. Matty's claim to have known her father provided some comfort. He wasn't the one attacking her with an ax. For the time being, she'd just have to see where this horror movie scene would take her.

Matty knocked and they waited on the makeshift porch. The front door used to be a dark army green color, but the paint had long ago dried and cracked to reveal the original pine underneath. Sunday looked up at the porch roof. Planks had fallen out, giving her a view of the sky.

With her attention on the condition of the house, Sunday gasped when something brushed up against her ankles. She seized Matty's arm.

He glanced over his shoulder at her while she peered down, expecting the glint of an ax blade at her feet.

Two light blue eyes stared up at her. Well, not entirely up at her. The eyes were crossed, so they appeared to watch the tip of a nose. The small Siamese cat meowed for attention.

Sunday crouched down to pet the cat, too embarrassed by her

jumpiness to meet Matty's gaze. The cat purred and thrust its head into Sunday's hand. The coolness of death cocooned her hand as the ghost cat rubbed through her rather than against her. It walked around Sunday's legs, unperturbed by its inability to make actual contact. The cold fur seeped through her pants. Sunday stared, open-mouthed. It was a cat from the Other World.

"You can't pick her up, but she's friendly," Matty said.

The ghost cat purred and sniffed her hand.

"What's her name?"

"Her collar says Lavender." Matty knocked again. "We tend to just call her Lav."

Sunday continued to watch the purring cat; the loving feline comforted her. Matty knocked a third time.

"Is he asleep?" she suggested.

"Usually isn't. Lucho doesn't sleep much."

He tried the doorknob; it turned. Matty opened the door to reveal a one-room shack. A checkered couch sat beside an unmade bed to the far right of the shed. On the other side of the room she saw a sink and a fridge, yellowed with age. The whole shack smelled of stale beer and shit.

Sunday grimaced. She stepped into the room behind Matty. Thick hot air slapped her in the face. She gagged on the foul smell. After getting past the air barrier, her watering eyes were drawn to the rug in front of the couch.

The rug didn't catch her attention, but the man lying across it did. Or rather, the body of what used to be a man, sprawled out with his arms to his sides. His jaw had been forced out of its socket and hung by tendons to the side of his face. His left arm was bent in a right angle beside him. His torso was split open, blood and intestines spilling out on the floor. The killing blow, though, appeared to be the gash in his head. Something had hit the man, concaving his skull and leaving a matted mess of bone, blood, hair, and brain. His dead eyes stared at the wall that was in the line of sight from the front door.

Bile rose to her throat. "Is that Lucho?"

Matty nodded and stepped toward the body. Sunday grabbed his arm. Lav meowed quietly at her feet. Lucho's eyes continued to peer beyond Sunday and Matty like he was scouring the room for help.

"What are you doing?" Sunday tugged on Matty's arm. "We have to call the police."

He shrugged her off and knelt down beside his friend. His hand hovered over Lucho's mangled body before settling on his shoulder.

Lucho seized. He gasped, arms and legs lurching with one spasm against the blood-soaked rug. Then he suddenly gulped. Sunday leapt back. Matty recoiled, falling onto his bottom and then scrambling back to his feet and rushing to his friend's side. Resting a couple fingers against Lucho's neck, Matty searched for a pulse. Sunday snatched her cell phone from her pocket with trembling hands and dialed 911.

CHAPTER 10

The interrogation room didn't settle Sunday's anxious mind. The cops called it an interview room, but the walls were empty and gray. Sunday was seated in a chair beside a small table. Another chair waited on the other side for the detective who would question her. The whole setup was watched by a camera in the corner. It was an interrogation room right out of every cheesy cop show on television.

Lav's body kept Sunday's nerves at bay. Normally they wouldn't have allowed animals in the room, but seeing as how the cat was long dead and they couldn't see her, no one told her no. The cat settled at her feet, enveloping her toes with a cool aura. Sunday could almost convince herself she felt the cat's purring. She clasped and unclasped her hands on top of the table, wiggling her toes to search for the purring.

She didn't know where to begin. Did she start with the enraged man with the ax who chased them from both of their houses? That was how they ended up at the shack.

Should she start with the fact that she'd just met this guy and how he has the Sight, just like her? That was the only reason Sunday was with Matty.

And then there were the Hounds. The image of the cold eyes staring at her from under the bar table flashed through her mind. She'd never seen Hounds as often as she had over the last six months. First with her father's death and then at the bar. What were they hanging around for? At what point did Sunday need to decide whether they were hunting for someone else's pain and torment or her own?

The ghost cat rolled over on its back, relieving Sunday's feet from the cold.

The detective entered the room and introduced himself as Detective Bell. His brown hair had begun to grey around his temples, giving him a seasoned look as he sat unsmiling in the chair opposite Sunday. He dropped a manila folder on the table between them.

Sunday wanted to answer the detective's questions. She wanted to be done and go home. She'd do anything just to get up and move. Her skin crawled and she ached to run and hide. She didn't ask for this. It wasn't her fault she'd been born with the Sight. She didn't even want the supposed gift.

"I didn't know the man who was killed," Sunday said. She wracked her brain. What had Matty said his name was? He'd said it once. She had been so scared that she hadn't paid attention. "I met Matty less than a week ago."

"What were you doing at Mr. Marquez's home, then?" Bell asked.

Marquez. That wasn't what Matty had called him. Sunday squeezed her eyes shut. The bright lamp overhead gave her a headache.

"We were looking for help," she said.

"After getting away from the man with the ax?" The detective raised an eyebrow.

"Was that how he died?" She grew nauseous. Axed to death, like she could've been.

"No."

He didn't offer any other explanation. "We haven't found any evidence of this ax man, except for Mr. Merhi's car damage."

"So someone else killed Mr. Marquez?" Sunday frowned to focus. She couldn't remember the name, but she needed to keep her attention in the room with the detective.

"You tell me."

She shook her head and tears filled her eyes. "I don't know anything. We opened the door and there—" She swallowed the bile in her throat.

Lucho. Matty's friend, the dead man, was named Lucho. Lucho Marquez.

Lav leapt to her feet below the table, meowing as she hurried between Sunday's legs. Sunday watched as Lav lifted her front paws against the legs of the man who was now standing in front of the interrogation door. He carried his entrails in his arms like a baby. The hollowed side of his head made him appear lopsided. Behind him the orange striped tail of a tiger flicked back and forth as the spirit surveyed the room. His eyes met Sunday's. The same wide desperate eyes she had left in the shack behind the mushroom factory. Eyes presumably still in that shack while the spirit of Lucho joined them in the interrogation room.

Sunday reminded herself to breathe.

"You okay?" Bell's voice pulled Sunday's gaze forward once again. The detective had his hand on the manila folder on the table. He stared at her, eyes darkened by heavy eyebrows, one cocked up inquisitively.

She opened her mouth to answer, but no sound came out. Closing her lips again, she gave Bell a nod.

He grunted and opened the folder. Snapshots of Lucho's bloodied cabin spilled out. Sunday had no desire to see the details. She looked away, only to catch sight of the spirit version of Lucho. He moved around the room until he was leaning over Detective Bell's shoulder, examining the contents of the folder.

"I'm assuming you don't want to see the photos from the scene."
Bell raised an eyebrow again, eyes flicking to Sunday over the top edge
of the folder.

She bobbed her head up and down again. Bell closed the folder
and Sunday's tense shoulders fell from her ears.

He cleared his throat, resting balled hands in front of him.

"So you didn't know the victim."

Sunday shook her head. Bell watched her, patiently waiting for a
verbal answer.

"And you met Matteo Merhi recently?"

She nodded.

Her mind bounced back and forth. She could tell the detective the
truth, but would he believe her? He'd lock her up for being crazy, but if
she lied or hid something, would he suspect her?

"How'd you meet him?"

She sighed.

"I went out after work last week." Her mouth started talking. Her
mind couldn't decide, so the truth just spilled out. "I'd just met Matty
that night. At the bar. I didn't feel well, so he offered to drive me home."

Bell's eyebrow lifted again, an unspoken request for more.

"He picked me up today to meet with some of his other friends."

"Not Lucho Marquez?"

"No," she said. "And we never made it. That was when we were
attacked."

"By the ax man?"

"Yes. He showed up across the street with an ax." The words continued pouring out of her mouth. Bell's eyes widened. She didn't pause.
"He hit Matty's car. We tried to get away, but he followed us to Matty's
house. We were trying to find a safe place. That's when Matty took me
to that mushroom factory. To Lucho's."

Bell ran his fingers across the file in front of him. "And that's how you found the body."

Sunday's eyes flicked to where Lucho was still standing over the detective's shoulder. Doubt seeped between Bell's words. Lucho shrugged.

"Yes." She pressed her lips together. Fatigue washed over her. Her fried nerves weren't ready for a detective to question her story. She just wanted to go home.

Bell inhaled slowly, leaning back in his chair. He cleared his throat before sitting up straight again.

"Do you have any idea why somebody would attack you, Ms. Elm?"

"No."

Bell held her eye contact. She suspected he wanted her to speak more. Did he not believe that she had no explanation?

"Can I get some water?" she asked.

Bell sighed. "Sure."

He got up. As soon as the door closed, Sunday's eyes snapped to the bloody spirit.

"What are you doing here?" She spoke through clenched teeth.

She saw his answer. It knocked what little breath Sunday had left out of her. He wanted to warn her, keep her from ending up like him. He didn't know who had killed him, but he showed her what happened.

Lucho was alone in his shack. It was Saturday night, and he had returned from work at the factory and decided to have a few beers before showering. He got up for a fourth beer, enjoying the slight buzz he felt from drinking on an empty stomach. His nose and fingers were numb, and a calm settled over him. If he wanted to, he could stretch out on the couch, close his eyes, and go to sleep for the night. Maybe he would; it had been a long day.

A late-night talk show played on the TV behind him. Lucho turned to the screen as he shut the refrigerator. A sixty-inch television hung on the wall beside the front door. It looked out of place among the decrepit furniture and piles of empty pizza boxes and cans.

He placed the beer bottle on the edge of the sink to use the bottle opener. The cap popped off and then something knocked him against the counter from behind. Pain radiated across his face. Warm blood gushed from his nose, filling his mouth with the tangy taste. He didn't see who or what was behind him. Had he not locked the door? Had he left a window open? He was out in the middle of nowhere. He clutched the sink edge and pulled himself up, realizing that there was no one around to hear his cries for help.

Something long and hard, like a metal bat or steel piping from the factory, brought him to his knees. His attacker cracked the weapon across his back again. He choked on blood and gasped for air.

Scrambling away on his hands and knees, he wheezed. The room spun around him, lifting the floor to one side. Lucho pushed through the dizziness. He needed to get to his gun.

The lights knocked out. TV shut off. Lucho was left in black silence.

Something caught him around the foot and dragged him across the floor. The arm that was reaching for the gun safe was hit next with the same weapon that had hit him across the back. Lucho heard the sickening crunch of bones breaking, but it was quickly forgotten as his body registered the pain. The darkness turned red as a scream escaped his lips.

The scream was stopped short by a strike to the face. The blows rained down on him again and again and again.

Sunday brought her own hands to her face as if she were fighting off the blows. She was going to die. Lucho's thoughts rang through her head, meshing with her own as if she were the one being beaten to death. She was going to die alone and no one would know. Who would find her body? Someone from work concerned that she'd missed a few shifts? How long would it take? What state would her dead body be in when they finally discovered her?

She screamed, cried out for it to stop, for it all to end.

And then it did. Sunday was back in the interrogation room. Battered Lucho was standing in front of her. Again, he warned her. The thought blossomed in her head. She didn't understand how. Lucho didn't explain how he knew, what he understood. But his warning bounced off the interrogation room walls, impossible to ignore.

He warned her to be careful, to watch her back. His killer could come after her. But how did he know? Sunday shook her head, denying his thoughts. But the Hounds. They'd been hanging around her. She'd seen more of them. What if she saw another? Would she have to accept that they had followed her? They would feed off her pain. Feed off her horrible death. Her Sight bellowed Lucho's warning in her head. She couldn't ignore it.

Be careful, or you'll be next.

CHAPTER 11

It was late when Sunday got home from the police station. She had to promise she would make an appointment with Dr. Morris before the detective would let her leave. He had found her hyperventilating when he returned with her glass of water. He also promised that she would hear from him again.

Matty drove her home. She was too exhausted to be sure, but she didn't remember speaking more than two words to him after leaving the police station, and those words were "thank you" as she climbed out of the car.

She woke up feeling hungover. Her head hurt, her body ached, and every movement caused a wave of nausea. A streetlamp outside glowed orange, lighting the room dimly. She rolled over with a groan to discover two sky-blue eyes. They stared, unblinking.

"What are you doing here?" Sunday asked the small Siamese cat.

The cat meowed. Sunday pulled her arm out from under her covers and reached to scratch the cat's head. Her fingers fell through the ghost cat, the cold sending goosebumps up her arm. With a deep breath, she forced herself to sit up.

She looked around her bedroom. A chair sat beside her dresser, covered in clothes she had deemed not quite dirty enough to throw in the hamper but not clean enough to put away. Her bedside table was crowded with old dishes and books. Several pairs of shoes were discarded around the floor. The room appeared so normal. How could that be after all that had happened?

Sunday glanced at the clock. It was early. The sun hadn't risen yet. A week ago, she'd been leaving the bar. Her biggest worry was a Hound sniffing around people's feet. She wished she could go back to that unease. Now she had the ghost of a murder victim telling her she was next. She preferred the Hound.

Her mind raced and going back to sleep felt impossible. Lav snoozed between her legs. Out of habit, Sunday attempted to slip them out from under the cat gently, only to be reminded that she wouldn't ever disturb the ghost cat when her foot glided right through her. Apparently she had picked up a ghost pet in all of this. At least she didn't have to buy food or change the litter box.

She pulled herself out of bed and began her morning routine in an attempt to settle her racing heart. She showered, tidied up the bathroom, and left for the kitchen to make coffee. As she sat on the couch sipping her coffee, she had an idea.

"Reap!" She shouted for her friend Death. Sunday hoped he had some answers.

"Reap! Come on!" she repeated when she didn't get a reply. "It's my turn to vent!"

"Sunday." Reap's voice forced her to turn around. "Patience is not one of your virtues."

He was standing with his bony arms crossed over his chest beside the new dining room set. Sunday had purchased it after cleaning up the broken mess the barista spirit had made.

"Needed a change?"

"Angry barista."

Reap nodded like he completely understood the story behind those two words. His trench coat brushed over the chair as he crossed the room and sat down beside her. He pulled off his fedora, exposing the rotting flesh on the top of his head, and set the hat in the empty space beside him.

"How's it going?"

Sunday raised an eyebrow at him.

Reap lifted his hands in defense and leaned back against the couch. "Okay, no sense of humor today. Fine. I heard about the messiness you stumbled upon. It wasn't my death, but word got around."

"What did you hear?"

"It was grotesque. Those were the exact words used." He chuckled. "Man, I would have loved to see it."

"Trust me, you wouldn't."

"There are no beautiful surfaces without a terrible depth," Reap said, quoting Nietzsche again.

Sunday took another sip of her coffee, mulling over his words. "Are you saying that you know something about who killed Lucho?"

Reap shook his head.

"Did you hear anything about me?"

He frowned. "Why would I hear something about you?"

She rolled her eyes. "Are you trying to be aggravating?"

He grinned. "No, just comes naturally." He rested his elbows on his bony knees, leaning closer to Sunday. "You know why I was first drawn to you?"

She shook her head.

"You reminded me a bit of Nietzsche, alone but strong. Sure, you had your father when I first met you, but that was the extent of your support system. Despite that, though, you had this great strength inside you. You didn't make excuses; you took care of your business. You were curious about the Other World and you sought me out. I mean, you're not the perfect Nietzsche. You do indulge in alcohol every once in a while, but it's impossible to live up to such greatness."

"Nietzsche died a lonely man. He ostracized himself from all his loved ones." She had done her own Google search on the philosopher after first meeting Reap.

He shrugged. "Like I said, no one is perfect. Regardless, I'm proud of you for reaching out and meeting Seers. Just like you did with me, but these people are alive."

"You're missing the point here. Lucho was murdered. The cops are involved. They talked to me, and then his spirit visited me in the interrogation room."

Sunday relayed the vision and warning Lucho had sent her. Reap listened without interrupting, nodding his head and adding *ohs?* and *whats!?* at the appropriate times.

"The spirit said you were next?" Reap brought his thumb to his mouth and chewed on the little bit of skin still clinging to the bone.

Sunday nodded and took a deep breath, preparing herself for a hard question, but she needed to know the answer. "Have you heard anything about my death?"

Reap sat up straighter. He released his thumb from his nibbling teeth and repeatedly shook his head, his hands waving in front of him. "No! Your name is nowhere on my lists."

"What about my aura?" Sunday stood up and held her arms out, putting herself on display for him.

Reap checked her head to toe. "Still that orchid color. It's actually growing on me."

She dropped back onto the couch.

"How soon do you hear about deaths?"

"I get a daily list. It's hard to predict deaths much earlier. Too many working parts."

Sunday cocked her head to the side and frowned. She bit her lower lip like she usually did while trying to figure something out.

Reap explained. "Let's say an older man goes out for a run and has a heart attack. The heart attack could kill him, but what if a nurse in the neighborhood had decided to take her daughter out to the park and she sees the man collapse. The nurse has enough medical knowledge to keep the man alive until paramedics come. The story could have a happy ending.

"But what if the nurse's coworker called in sick that day and she had to go into work. Then the babysitter takes the daughter to the park and no one is there to save him.

"What if the man decided to pick a fight with his wife that morning about his favorite work shirt she ruined in the laundry. They fight and he is not feeling up for a run, so he doesn't have the heart attack in the first place.

"What if the wife decides she has had enough of his complaining and really lays into him. This could cause stress and trigger the heart attack anyway."

"It's all a bunch of what ifs," Sunday said, finishing the explanation. Reap nodded.

"No death is set in stone," Reap said. "There's a reason I have an editable list. Circumstances change every second."

Sunday breathed a sigh of relief. She sat back in her chair and finished up her coffee.

"So what do you know about Lucho?" she asked.

"Who?"

"The dead guy."

"Oh!" Reap chuckled again. "Not much. He had the Sight."

"Matty had mentioned that," Sunday said. "He's the guy I met at the bar the other night. Do you know him?"

Reap frowned, pausing a moment to think.

"I don't think so," he said and then shrugged. "There are so many of you guys I can't keep track of everybody."

Sunday couldn't comprehend Reap's nonchalant answers. She sat on the edge of her seat, resting her elbows on her knees.

"What do you mean there are so many of us? Up until a week ago, the only other person I knew with the Sight was Dad."

Reap shook his head. "Come on, you didn't really believe out of the billions of humans on Earth, you and your dad were the only two who had your special abilities."

"Dad had mentioned it, but I didn't really think about it," Sunday murmured.

"They're all over the world. And—wait!" Reap held up a finger and began digging through the pocket on the inside of his trench coat. He pulled out a slender tablet, a sticker of a skull and crossbones pasted on the back, and swiped his finger across the screen.

"I hadn't thought to look before," he muttered, "but now that you bring it up, I do know something more about this dead guy."

He flipped the tablet over to show Sunday a list of names and dates. He pointed to a name toward the bottom: Lucho Marquez. Beside his name was last night's date: September 6, 2018.

"Here's your dead guy," Reap explained. "This is the list of all deaths in the country, and he isn't the only one of your buddies with the Sight on my list."

Lucho's name and death date suddenly glowed red along with three other names on the list above his: Anne Marie Lincoln, Kent Brookes, and Erica Boskovich. Reap tapped an icon on the top of the screen causing all non-red names to disappear. The screen filled with the glowing names. Halfway down, Sunday's eyes found her father's name, Stephen Elm, beaming crimson with the date of his car accident. Sunday didn't acknowledge it. Reap moved on.

"I think I count fifty-six in all."

Reap flipped through a couple screens, pointing at the final name at the bottom: Karin Rosario.

"Starting with her, eight months ago." Reap pointed to the name.

"Is that a lot?"

He turned the tablet back to himself, nodding.

"I would have to go back through the decades to double check, but this *has* to be a spike in deaths."

"Do you know how they died?"

He shook his head. "I don't carry that kind of information on me."

• • •

Reap made his exit not long after Sunday looked at his death tablet. The clock read 5:15 a.m. Sunday peered out her second-story window. The sun was just beginning to rise, giving the horizon a pinkish-orange shade. Beautiful time for a run.

One of the selling points of the apartment complex she chose to live in was the city park right in her backyard. Grass was laid down over a small hill; at the bottom was a tanbark playground. Past that was the flat expansive pebbled beauty of Arizona. Trails that looped around the park had been carved out of the weeds and dirt. Sunday had a few favorites, but in the early morning she liked to take the trail that moved up. It ended after a mile at the top of a hill. It wasn't the Grand Canyon, but it did give her a view of the town and the sunrise.

Sunday kept her breath even as she trekked up the hill. She watched her feet pound on the dry dirt. Lizards scampered across her way, running from one hiding place to another. The sun was rising enough so she could begin to make out the individual grasses of the weeds surrounding the trail. The cool air opened up her chest and allowed her to take a deep breath, something she hadn't been able to do since leaving the police station.

On her way down, it was apparent that the rest of the world had begun to wake up. She spotted a few other joggers along the trails. Cars were beginning to drive more regularly across the street between the park and her apartment. Sunday was just reaching the playground again when something caught her eye.

She turned to her left. It was a spirit. Not an unusual sight, but this one seemed to shimmer. Sunday could almost hear the angel choir singing as a woman stood at the edge of the grass, facing her.

Sunday's feet slowed until they stopped altogether.

The woman wasn't wearing any clothes. She had dark cinnamon-colored skin and perfectly round breasts that Sunday found difficult to look away from. Long horns that curved like a bovine's emanated from her long black hair. Cow ears protruded on either side of her face. Her bright eyes glowed, two shining lights in place of irises and pupils. They stared in Sunday's direction, her gaze stopping her from moving.

The Cow Woman raised her arms toward Sunday and a wave of calm washed over her. She was still aware of Lucho's warning and the mysterious deaths of people with the Sight, but she was no longer worried she couldn't handle it. She felt strong. She had the will to overcome.

The woman lowered her arms. She turned around slowly and walked in the direction Sunday had just been running. A light shone behind her, bright and blinding like another sun was rising above the playground horizon. The Cow Woman stepped into it and the light grew brighter, swallowing her up.

Sunday's calm high carried her the rest of the way home. She dropped her keys on the shelf beside her front door and floated to the shower. A small smile never left her face. She didn't even care who the Cow Woman was; she just enjoyed the feel of the water running down her body, the scent of her lilac shampoo, and then the soft, cushioning feeling of the towel across her body. Rubbing down her arms and legs left her buzzing like she'd had great sex. She ended up lying on her bed still wrapped in her towel, swept away in the euphoric hug that enveloped her. Lav crawled over and curled up against Sunday's side, meshing their bodies together.

And then there was a knock at her door.

Part of Sunday considered answering the door in the nude. She was so comfortable. Why should she put on pants that were too tight around her waist and a bra that dug into her flesh? She settled on an old pair of college sweatpants and a concert T-shirt and shuffled to the door.

Matty stood in her doorway, wiping the last of her euphoric calm away. He leaned against the doorframe; dark circles had formed under his eyes and his hair was greasy and pushed back like he had been constantly running his fingers through it.

"Jeez," Sunday said.

He brushed past her and entered her home.

"I know." He ran his fingers through his hair again. "I've barely been home. Haven't had a chance to sleep."

"No, no." Sunday rolled her eyes and muttered under her breath as she closed her front door. "By all means, come on in. Make yourself at home."

Not hearing the comment, Matty sat down on the couch and pulled photos out of his jacket pockets. They were crumpled and grey, like he had cut the pictures out of a newspaper.

"Something's wrong, Sunday. After leaving the police station, I visited a couple other friends of mine who have the Sight."

Sunday sat down and examined the pictures. They were all smiling faces of men and women. Underneath were names and dates. She recognized one of them: Erica Boskovich. The smiling face of a beautiful blond-haired woman stared back at her.

"They already knew about Lucho's death. He had visited one of them and warned him."

Lucho had apparently made himself busy in his afterlife.

Sunday picked up another photo: Tim Yeats. He looked like he could have been a dad, probably coached his kids' sports teams.

They were all dead.

"Something's targeting us. It's all across the country. I don't know how far this goes back, but—"

"Eight months," Sunday interrupted.

"What?"

"There have been killings for eight months."

Sunday went on to explain everything she knew. She told him about Lucho's visit to her in the interrogation room and Reap's visit and discovery.

He interrupted before she could mention the weird encounter she had with the Cow Woman. She wasn't sure she wanted to share that anyway.

"Your dad mentioned you were friends with a Grim Reaper. That's pretty cool." Matty grinned. He gathered up the photos he had just laid out. "You have a pen?"

With the felt-tip pen Sunday was able to dig out of her junk drawer, Matty began writing on the backs of the images:

William (Bill) Preston: shot in the head
Jacqueline Draker: drowned in her bathtub
Erica Boscovich: stabbed
Tim Yeats: poisoned

"These are the causes of death listed in their articles," Matty explained. "I want to look into them more, try to find a pattern. Nothing stands out right now."

He had fifteen photographs labeled.

"I'm sure that this isn't all of them," he said.

Sunday shook her head. "Reap had a list of fifty-six. He believes the first one was a woman named Karin Rosario. You don't have her on your list. And…"

She stood up, leaving Matty without an explanation. She went to her room and pulled a photograph out of a shoebox she kept on the top shelf of her closet. She hadn't opened the box since her father's funeral. Inside were a few pictures of her family, a necklace with a small cat charm given to her for her birthday last year, and salt packets. Packets like these were constantly littering her apartment when her dad was alive. He would collect them whenever he was at a café or restaurant and bring them to her, just in case. He never wanted her to be left without protection. After his death, she couldn't look at the packets without crying. She tucked them away in her shoebox and kept a sack of salt by her door, still always protected.

The photo she pulled out of the shoebox was an old one of her father in the Navy. He was dressed in his uniform, smiling at the camera. His face reflected a clean-shaven, wrinkle-free twenty-two-year-old version of himself. In the picture he was younger than she was now. She smiled at it, then carried it back to the living room.

"Here."

Sunday took the pen from Matty's hand, wrote *car crash* on the back of her father's Navy photo, and added it to the pile.

"You don't think...?"

She nodded. "It can't be a coincidence that he died within these last eight months. I think more happened in the accident than we know about."

Matty finished gathering up the pictures. He shoved them back into his jacket pocket and stood up.

"So what now?" Sunday said.

"Why don't we meet with the gang?" Matty suggested. "They can help us sort this out."

CHAPTER 12

Matty studied the obituary photos on the way to his car. His thumb pressed against the paper, wrinkling the clippings. "This can't be a coincidence," he said. "I don't know if the threat is part of our world or the Other World, but it's a very real threat."

An image of Lucho in his cabin flashed through Sunday's mind. She closed her eyes and ran her thumb over her knuckles to settle her nerves.

"I know." She spoke through gritted teeth.

"We gotta stick together." He folded the pictures and tucked them into his pocket. "We need you, Sunday. You're the only one who can truly communicate with the spirits. That paired with our knowledge of the Other World—" He sighed. "I don't know. Maybe we'll have a fighting chance."

She nodded. Matty's lights flashed when he unlocked the car, and she opened the passenger door with a shaking hand.

"Ms. Elm," a voice called from the sidewalk.

Sunday recognized the gravelly voice, the no-nonsense tone. If it wasn't the spirits or the mysterious killer disrupting her life, why not the detective from the night of Lucho's murder?

"I just have a couple follow-up questions." Bell hurried to Sunday's side. He glanced in the car and raised his eyebrows. "You're saving me a trip. I planned to visit Mr. Merhi next. I thought you'd said you just met?"

"I did." Sunday glanced at Matty who watched from the driver side, his face unreadable.

"And here you are with him again?"

"We've decided that we get along." Matty rested his elbows on the car.

Bell nodded, one eyebrow still cocked. He pulled a notebook and pen from his pocket.

"I've been investigating Mr. Marquez and discovered that you do have a connection to the victim."

"Me?" Sunday frowned.

Bell nodded. "Through your father, Stephen."

He waited for a response. Sunday waited for him to continue. Matty cleared his throat and opened the driver's side door.

"I'll be with you in a moment, Mr. Merhi. I have questions about Stephen Elm for you too. But first, Ms. Elm, I found that Mr. Marquez and your father made regular transactions over eBay, often discussing the merchandise over their personal emails."

She hugged her arms tighter against her chest. "My father sold antiques on an online store. He could have been buying from Lucho, or Lucho could have bought from Dad."

"I figured that much. It wasn't the transactions I had questions about. It was the encrypted emails. I can't imagine they were discussing turn-of-the-century furniture in those messages. Know anything about them?"

She could speculate. Knowing now that Lucho had the Sight, he had undoubtedly talked to her father about their shared ability through the encrypted messages, but she didn't believe Detective Bell would be receptive to her conjecture. She shook her head.

"No?" He turned to Matty. "What about you, Mr. Merhi? You also sent and received encrypted messages to Stephen Elm. Care to explain?"

Matty shrugged. "Stephen preferred to keep those conversations private. Nothing illegal was happening because of those emails, so I'll keep that trust."

"Stephen Elm has passed, has he not?"

Matty nodded. Sunday hugged herself.

"I'd like to keep those conversations private as well. Again, we haven't done any law breaking."

Bell pressed his lips tight. "Very well. Expect to hear from me." His cold eyes met Sunday's and Matty's. "Each of you."

They watched Bell walk away. About half a block from them, he pulled a phone out and pressed it to his ear. A dark sedan beeped when he unlocked it. The detective climbed in and drove away.

"You ever been involved with the police like this before?" Sunday asked.

Matty shook his head. "Jaime typically takes care of small problems with his job, but never as much as a murder. He won't have any pull here."

Sunday inhaled, pushing down the anxiety knotted in her stomach. She kept her arms crossed tight against her chest, keeping the trembling at bay. Murder. The word spoken aloud sat heavy between them. Could she do this? Did she have a choice?

"I need to rest before work tomorrow." She jutted a thumb toward her condo. "Why don't you meet with the others without me."

"Oh—uh, okay." Matty scratched the back of his head. "Are you sure?"

She nodded. The knot in her stomach loosened.

"Yeah, sure." He climbed into his car. "I'll give you a call, okay? Keep you in the loop."

"Thanks," she muttered.

•••

A headache had erupted across her forehead and behind her eyes as she watched Matty drive away. On her walk back to her condo she spotted the Cow Woman, her eyes watching Sunday from the park across the street. Sunday stopped at her door to stare back at the spirit woman, embracing the now-familiar wave of bliss. Her chest loosened, allowing a full breath to fill her lungs. Her arms dropped to her side, heavy and warm. Sunday still hadn't mentioned this spirit to anyone. She wondered what she was; obviously not a typical spirit, but also not a Girdwick. But what could have such an effect on her, and why did she appear to Sunday? Eventually Sunday unlocked her door and stepped through the threshold. She felt the gaze of the Cow Woman on her back, a comfort as she walked into her home.

Back in her living room, Sunday settled on her couch. Her mind wandered to her father. Detective Bell had just reminded her again of how much she did not know about him. Had Sunday even known her father? They were close. They'd worked side-by-side not only to move on the few spirits they did confront, but also with his business. Now gone, he was a mystery. It broke her heart.

The quiet began to feel suffocating. She switched the television on, thumbing through the channels. One actress's haircut reminded her of Gail. Another show was doing a special episode that took place in London. Every time a cop strode across the screen, she thought of Jaime sauntering off to work. She thought she'd be safe with a rerun of *Scrubs*, but the banter between the characters brought Matty's carefree attitude to mind. She tossed the remote on the couch beside her and sat back, happy for a commercial break.

She wasn't alone now; she wouldn't become Nietzsche as Reap had suggested. Seers, four of them, had beckoned her into their group. Four. Sunday didn't think she'd ever had four friends at one time. Matty and his club fascinated her and made her nauseous. She understood why her dad found their work to be dangerous, but they were so knowledgeable. In her world, spirits and creatures were to be avoided in everyday life. She never had the opportunity to learn. Did her dad know about the Girdwicks? She wanted to believe that if he had, he would have taught her. Did working with Matty and the others mean she was letting down her father?

She sighed. There wasn't a point in questioning it. Her father was dead. Lucho was dead, along with so many others. She'd been attacked. She could refuse to work with the Ghost Gurus, refuse to acknowledge the Other World, but then what? She'd join the list of names on Reap's tablet. She didn't have the luxury to even hesitate. How could she have been so weak to come home? She should be with Matty trying to figure this out, to save her life, all their lives.

Her phone pinged, notifying her of an email. She didn't recognize the sender: seergroup@webmaster.net. It read: *thought you would find this interesting. –M*

Attached was an article from Monterey, California. Sunday's eyes whizzed across the screen:

The body of Janice Woodbridge, a young marine biologist, was found washed up on the beach early yesterday morning. Woodbridge was reported missing a week ago by her roommate. The unnamed roommate told police that Janice had been acting strange before she disappeared. Janice claimed someone was after her.

The roommate told police, "She said that if anything were to happen to her, it wouldn't be an accident. She was very persistent, saying even if it looked like an accident, it wasn't."

Law enforcement suspect foul play beyond the roommate's tip. The details of her death have not been released, but the case is being investigated as a homicide.

As the investigation continues, residents of Monterey are asked to be aware of their surroundings and to stay safe.

A memorial for Woodbridge will be organized by the Monterey Bay Aquarium. Her research in marine biology had a significant impact on the aquarium and they want her to be remembered as an excellent scientist and caring friend. If you are interested in attending the memorial, details will be posted on the Aquarium's website.

A picture was included below the article. The woman wore a dark collared shirt with the aquarium logo embroidered over her chest. Her dark hair had been twisted in two braids that rested over her shoulders. She beamed at the baby otter in her arms, cradling it like it was her own child.

Sunday frowned. Another Seer?

She exited the attachment and shut off her phone. The show had returned from the commercial, but she'd lost interest.

•••

Work usually made Sunday feel in control. The restaurant was a second home to her, one that she was in charge of; it was safe. But today when she walked in through the back door and made her way to the kitchen, she was on edge.

In the dining area, she found Shelly at the entrance greeting guests and putting their names down for tables.

"Hello, fearless leader." Shelly winked. "Did you end up getting sick the other night?"

Sunday frowned and racked her brain, trying to figure out what Shelly was talking about. Then she remembered her freak-out at the bar. To anyone without the Sight, it must have looked like Sunday had too much to drink.

"No, I didn't." She studied the list of wait staff scheduled to work that evening and where they would be assigned.

"Well, good!" Shelly squeezed Sunday's arm. "I got his number." She giggled.

"Who?" Sunday barely glanced up from the schedule.

"The guy from the bar." Her smile grew and a small squeak snuck past her exposed teeth. "Matty. Wasn't he cute!?"

It felt strange hearing Matty talked about in such a normal setting. From the moment Sunday had met him, he had been wrapped up in her secret world. He knew about her Sight. He taught her about Other World creatures. All while people were mysteriously killed. The idea that Matty was passing out his number to girls at the bar felt too normal. Sunday didn't know how to react.

"Didn't you think he was cute?" Shelly apparently took Sunday's silence as disagreement.

She shook her head. "No, he was cute. Good for you."

Was Sunday jealous?

The thought crossed her mind, too large to even contemplate. Who was she jealous of? She couldn't possibly be thinking about dating when she was working so hard just taking care of herself. The Hound gave her a panic attack. She often woke up in tears, dreaming of a never-ending search for her father. What were his last moments like? Did he die in pain? Functioning every day drained all of her energy. She didn't need to think about dating.

Sunday turned around, leaving Shelly to greet guests. As she stepped toward the kitchen, something tangled up at her feet. She stumbled forward, catching herself on the chair behind the hostess stand. Looking back, she saw twine stretched across the room, starting at the handles of the front door and tied to the kitchen door. It cut across the whole room, set up to trip whoever was walking across. She looked past the twine and saw Shelly's Toko sitting next to a woman in a bright pink polka dot dress, like it was waiting to be seated. When Sunday made eye contact with it, it smiled its evil grin.

"Are you okay?" Shelly took Sunday's hand as she righted herself. She scanned the floor for the source of Sunday's fall, but the twine had disappeared.

"I'm fine." Sunday straightened her top. "Must be tripping over my own feet."

She walked to the kitchen, and the Toko jumped down from its seat. Sunday glanced continually over her shoulder. The trickster spirit was behind her the whole time. She stopped in the back storage room. They were alone.

"What's your deal?" she asked the Toko.

It stared at her with eyes gleaming like a child excited to open presents on Christmas.

"So you are attached to me now?"

It continued to stare. Sunday threw her arms up in frustration.

"Fine!"

The Toko followed Sunday through her whole shift, continually tripping her or causing others to bump into her. It dumped food and plates off the shelves so they would land on her. The staff couldn't believe Sunday's bad luck as she ended the night covered in coffee, wine, cake, and something she couldn't even identify. They didn't see the spirit rolling on the floor laughing while she picked fish out of her hair.

"You fucking suck," she hissed at the Toko. She felt foolish cursing at the spirit, but then she caught a whiff of the fish coming off of her and she was ready to strangle the tiny creature.

She braced herself as the last customers left and the doors closed. Was the spirit actually attached to her now? Was it going to follow her home? Banished from the kitchen at that point because the staff didn't want yet another mess to suddenly occur, Sunday worked on closing the register. She counted the money three times to make sure it was accurate. It would be no surprise, though, if she heard the numbers were off the next morning. The Toko sat on a chair beside her, picking dirt out from under its nails and flicking it on the floor. Its feet kicked gleefully in front of it and it bobbed its head while it hummed. She glared at it.

"You have any big plans tonight?" Shelly asked as they were gathering their belongings from their lockers.

"Not much." Sunday eyed the Toko standing between them. It grinned back.

"Me neither. I'm looking forward to putting on my sweats and curling up on the couch to watch TV."

Shelly tossed her purse over her shoulder and led the way out the door. Sunday waited for the Toko to follow her, but it remained stubbornly at her side; she groaned and exited first.

"What are you going to watch?"

Sunday wasn't really paying attention to the words coming out of her mouth. They had to walk about a block before they reached Shelly's car and Sunday continued on to the bus stop. The Toko followed behind them, smirking and humming. It knew why Sunday was watching it and enjoyed her anxiousness.

"I was going to see what new movies are on Netflix."

Shelly hit the unlock button on her car fob and they both slowed their pace. Sunday couldn't breathe as she watched the waitress place her purse on the passenger seat and then walk around the car to sit behind the wheel. She put the keys in the ignition and waved at Sunday through the windshield.

The Toko stood on the sidewalk, chuckling.

"You're getting in, right?" She gestured to the car.

It laughed again. Sunday couldn't tell if it was shaking its head no or nodding yes. She suspected it was just waving its head around to screw with her. She was nervous enough without a Toko messing with her, but now she was really going to end up in the nuthouse with that demon attached to her. She mentally prepared herself for her fate.

Shelly started the car; the brake lights flashed. Wiping tears from its eyes, the Toko jumped through the back seat door and waved through the window.

Sunday's knees almost gave out when she finally released the breath she'd been holding. She leaned her hands on her thighs, needing the support.

Shelly thought Sunday was crouching down to talk to her through her car window. She rolled it down and waited expectantly.

Sunday smiled. "Maybe skip the scary movies tonight, Shel."

Shelly laughed. "You know I always do!"

Sunday stood back up and waved at Shelly's car as she drove away. Then she turned back towards the sidewalk and enjoyed her solitary walk to the bus stop.

On the bus, Sunday's eyes fell closed. Any workday was draining, but between dodging the Toko and then panicking when she thought it was going home with her, her energy was gone. As she dozed her thoughts drifted. She kept seeing the red eyes of the horse barista which then transformed into the red eyes of the Girdwick. The evil grin of the Toko would replace the eyes, and then images of the Cow Woman flashed through her mind.

The squeaking bus brakes pulled Sunday out of her doze. She sighed and pulled out her phone.

Working with her dad had isolated her. Even after graduating high school, when Sunday was expected to spread her metaphorical wings, go off to college and experiment with alcohol and dating, she'd remained alone. It was her choice. She didn't want to go to college; high school had been difficult enough to juggle along with her Sight. Now she was twenty-seven. Her dad had passed, and she rarely had any phone calls. She clicked the screen on for the first time since her shift had started that afternoon.

There were several emails, all from unfamiliar addresses. The only emails she typically received were newsletters from her old high school and ads based on her Google searches.

The senders' email addresses all had names that she recognized: katLondon62@yahoo.com, Matteo.Merhi@hotmail.com, gail_hannigan@gmail.com, and jlopez@yahoo.com.

Sunday looked through the conversation going back and forth. They were discussing the article she had received that morning. London and Gail knew the woman who had died. She was another person with the Sight, and now another death added to Reap's list.

Sender: jlopez@yahoo.com
I say we just go to Monterey. Get the answers ourselves.

Sender: gail_hannigan@gmail.com
Oh ya, let's just up and buy a plane ticket to California, like we're all made of money.

Sender: jlopez@yahoo.com
I imagine we would drive there. No need to be an ass.

Sender: katLondon62@yahoo.com
I agree with Jaime. We won't get any information sitting around here and we can't get close to Lucho's death without making the cops suspicious. We don't have the same connection to Janice Woodbridge. No one would know us from Adam.

Sender: jlopez@yahoo.com
So are we all really going to California?

Sender: Matteo.Merhi@hotmail.com
I've always wanted to go. Let's do it!

Sender: gail_hannigan@gmail.com
I can't leave Rose and Jacob. I'm out guys.

Sender: jlopez@yahoo.com
Haven't your kids grown up yet? One was born a whole two years ago. Jeez…

Sender: katLondon62@yahoo.com
I can try to get the time off of work. How long do you think we'll be there?

Sender: Matteo.Merhi@hotmail.com
Until we get answers! I would plan on a long weekend.

Matty's email was the last in the feed so far, sent sixteen minutes ago. Sunday scrolled through the thread again. They were planning on going to California, and it appeared she was invited. The idea of driving to another state to investigate the mysterious death of a marine biologist left Sunday's breath short. Her tongue latched onto the roof of her mouth; she craved the water she'd left in the car. Tucking her phone back in her purse, she closed her eyes to focus on alleviating the anxiety.

Her stop arrived quickly; she'd been distracted by the emails. Sunday stepped out of the bus on shaky legs, digging around in her purse for her keys.

Her breathing quickened as she unlocked her front door. It felt like someone squeezed her heart and lungs, keeping the heart thudding against her sternum and shortening. She pulled the herbal tea from her cupboard; the box advertised its relaxing effect.

She'd never been to California before, though she imagined she wouldn't do much sightseeing if she joined Matty and the others on their trip. The thought wrapped her stomach in knots. Sunday cradled the warm mug in her hands and sat on the couch. She sipped the tea, fighting the same panic she'd felt around the Hounds. Could she do this? It was just her, no Dad. She had to decide alone. But did she even have a choice?

Sunday tried to remember her life before anxiety. She hadn't appreciated the carefree feeling. It was safe. She would have leapt at the opportunity to chase this mystery to California. Dad was her safety net if something went wrong. He always knew what to do.

She stood up to reheat her tea, wiping a couple tears away. Her dad was gone. No more safety net, no more leaning on him to make these big decisions. With the mysterious deaths forcing her hand, she'd do it on her own. She took her heated tea back to the couch. The warm mug felt nice against her cold fingers. Seated, she recalled Reap's list, the glowing red names. Her name wasn't on his list, but that didn't mean she was safe. There were too many what-ifs. What if she worked with Matty and the others? What if she ran? What if she stayed home? The man with the ax knew where she lived.

Her eyes flicked to her front door. Locked.

She pulled her mug to her chin, cradling the warmth to melt the icy chill running down her spine. She couldn't control all the what-ifs, but she could decide to take the offensive. The others were going to California to investigate Janice's death and learn what might be behind all these Seer deaths. Sunday finished her tea and then double-checked that the front door was locked. She'd join them. Together, they'd find a way to save all of their lives.

CHAPTER 13

Dr. Morris,

Most of the creatures don't want to be in our world, and the ones that do get into our world rarely make it. At least, that's what Dad taught me. The Tokos are enslaved, forced to do the bidding of the one who summoned it out of the Other World. There are also the Gowrows, large lizard-like creatures that stumble into our world. They're a two-ton toddler that just dawdled in the wrong direction and can't find their way home. They howl. The howl is so strong that sometimes non-Seers can hear them. Legends of sorrowful ghosts, like mothers who snapped and drowned their children only to realize what she had done and kill herself, are caused by Gowrows. It's a heartbreaking sound; I can understand the jump to such a morbid story. The Gowrow's fate isn't much better. If it can't find its way back, our atmosphere becomes too much for the creature and it dies. That happens often. Dad and I could never figure out how to help Gowrows find a way back to the Other World. We didn't understand how they slipped into our world in the first place.

I'm going to do it, Dr. Morris. I already followed this group to a Girdwick, so why not go with them to California? I've always wanted to see the beach. Dad talked about taking a trip with me. I suggested we could go when a buyer or seller reached out to me from the coast. That never happened, though. Time got away from us. How long ago had we decided to find an excuse to go to a beach? Has to be less than ten years. Now I'll go without him. I hope I can walk barefoot in the sand.

• • •

They left late the next afternoon. That gave them the day to get ready. Sunday was done in an hour, so she was left with a day of worrying followed by a long car ride on the edge of panic.

"Can we stop to get snacks?" Jaime buckled his seatbelt in the back seat.

London shoved the duffel bag between them over, pressing him against the car door with her elbow. "Quit manspreading. There's barely enough room for all of us back here as it is."

"Of course." Matty pulled away from the curb. "What's a road trip without snacks?"

Sunday envied them. From the passenger seat, she felt nauseous, nervous about the drive, the investigation. The thought of munching on chips hadn't even crossed her mind. The others didn't seem bothered. After a stop at the gas station, the smell of Jaime's Doritos wafted through the enclosed space. London reached into the bag. He jerked it away.

"Now you're not sharing?" London raised an eyebrow.

"What did you get to trade?" Jaime scoffed at her yogurt-covered pretzels.

"I'm happy to share," London said.

He turned the bag's opening to her. "You've got the worst taste in road trip snacks. What'd you get, Sunday?"

"Nothing." Sunday raised a water bottle over her head to show him.

"Animals." Jaime shook his head.

London winked at Sunday and stuffed a chip into her mouth. Sunday smiled, cheered up by the banter. As they settled in with their snacks, Matty switched the station and turned up the radio. He took a sip of his energy drink and then replaced it in the cup holder.

"So." Sunday twisted and untwisted the cap on her water, wanting to get to know the people in the car. "You have any siblings, London?"

"Two," she replied. "Both older brothers. Ones in the Marines, the other's working in Washington, manages a sawmill."

"He still with the same company?" Jaime asked.

"Yup. Still claims the place would fall apart without him."

"And you, Jaime. Siblings?"

"A few half siblings. It was just my mom and me growing up. My dad moved down to Texas and started a new family. I don't know them that much."

"I'm an only child," Matty said.

"I knew there was something off about you," London teased.

Sunday craned her neck to face the two in the back seat. "Do your siblings have the Sight?"

"Dru has it," London said. "He's the one up in Washington. Marc hasn't gotten it, but I guess it's possible he'll get it late."

"It works just like any other trait your parents pass on," Matty explained to Sunday, "just like you would get brown eyes from your mom or blue from your dad, unless they both have the same trait. Like mine. Both Mom and Dad had the Sight."

And hers too? She'd always hesitated bringing up her mom around her dad, didn't want to make him sad. But now she couldn't ask.

"But both of your parents don't have the Sight, right?" Matty asked London.

"No, just Dad." London gathered another small handful of Doritos from Jaime's bag. "Mom loved it. She called herself a witch, and my father her divine grace. Made for one-of-a-kind holidays at home."

"Your mom was a witch?" Sunday frowned. Did they exist too?

London chuckled. "Not like the Halloween witch. She practiced Wicca, had an inner power that she harnessed to cast her spells and blessings. If I'm being completely honest, I don't know how much she actually believed in the stuff, more like it was just a fashionable thing to do with her friends. She never truly believed in a connection with nature. She'd use Dad's Sight like a parlor trick, then mine and Dru's when we developed it."

Jaime pulled his bag of chips away when London reached for it again. "Don't think my brothers and sisters have it. But my mom was the one with the Sight, not Dad."

"Can that happen?" Sunday asked. "Can someone spontaneously develop the Sight?"

"I haven't heard of anyone like that." Matty shook his head.

"You were seven when you started seeing Other World creatures, right?" Jaime leaned forward to face Sunday.

She nodded.

"You have any childhood friends from the Other World?" London grinned. "I always imagined those kids in thrillers that talked to ghosts having the Sight. Would've been so much fun freaking people out."

"I had an imaginary friend growing up," Jaime said. "Actually imaginary. Named him Ciro, a mouse. Played with him for a couple years until Mom told me mice only lived for two or three years. Then Ciro died."

"That's an uplifting story. Loved it," Matty spoke into the rear-view mirror.

"I think your mom just didn't want you talking to an invisible mouse." London giggled.

"According to my dad," Matty said, "men and women develop the Sight differently. Women are more consistent; their hormones keep them more regulated. Men are all over the place. Sometimes it emerges when they're children, usually when they're young adults, but sometimes older, even middle aged."

"That must be freaky," London said. "You go your whole life thinking the world is one way and then you're forty and your world gets flipped upside down and you're getting a crash course in the Other World."

The men nodded in agreement. Sunday followed, rapt. She'd never heard so much about others' experiences with the Sight. Questions whirled through her head. What did their parents do? How did they help them with the Sight? Where did they meet? How did they learn about the Other World? She didn't know what to ask first.

"We should talk about Monterey." Matty changed the subject. Sunday's nausea came thundering back.

Jaime leaned forward again. "I was thinking that you, Matty, should search Janice's apartment with Sunday."

"Do we have a key?" Sunday squeaked. She knew the answer already, but she had to ask.

Jaime raised his eyebrows. "No." When no one objected, he continued, "London and I are going to check out the crime scene. Her body washed up on the beach, but I doubt that's where she was killed. We'll take a quick look and then head over to her work to ask questions."

"We'll all meet back at the motel," Matty finished.

The car fell silent as they sped on the freeway. Sunday found it ironic that Jaime, the cop, organized their break-in. The sun sank towards the horizon behind them. Sunday lay back against the headrest and closed her eyes.

The weather in Monterey was cool and crisp. She took a deep breath in, smelling the ocean. It was a change from Arizona's dry heat; the ocean breeze was uplifting. The cold air filled Sunday's lungs, clearing away the suffocating tightness for the first time in days. She leaned out of her opened window as Matty navigated the streets.

"Her apartment is around the corner," London said, studying the map on her phone.

He followed London's directions, pulling into a parking lot. The apartment was a refurbished Victorian home which stretched across half the block, and, according to the numbered parking spaces, was broken into twelve units.

"What number is she?" The car idled in the middle of the lot while Matty searched for the space.

"Eight," London said.

Matty pulled into parking spot eight.

"It's not like Janice is using it." He shrugged and pulled the keys out of the ignition.

Sunday climbed out of the car, taking a moment to stretch her legs. It had been a long drive. She was impressed. Matty had driven all night, getting them to California by mid-morning.

She scanned the view. It was beautiful. Everything around them was green. The houses around the apartments were well-kept, with gardens and aquatic lawn statues decorating many of the yards. A few neighbors were out for a walk. She thought she heard the soft sound of the waves crashing against the beach, but it might have been her imagination. She peered past the trees behind Janice's apartment building, wondering how far the beach actually was.

Jaime climbed into the driver's seat to take London to the crime scene and the marine research center Janice worked at. Sunday and Matty crossed the quiet parking lot.

They found the door. Matty jimmied his way in and stepped into the dead woman's home. Sunday stayed in the doorway, peering inside. Her leg had bounced incessantly during the drive to Monterey, her worried thoughts keeping her from sleeping. Now that she was here and breaking into Janice Woodbridge's home, the thoughts continued, leaving her dizzy and nauseous. She forced a deep breath through her nose and followed Matty inside.

The apartment was carpeted so their steps were quiet. The front door opened into the living room. The television hung to their right and the couch sat against the wall with the door. A large poster of Audrey Hepburn hung over the couch. The coffee table still had a used mug. The dirty dish reminded Sunday of something she had read in the article. Her heart leapt into her throat. She held her shaking hands against her stomach to keep from panicking.

"Uh," she whispered. "Doesn't she have a roommate?"

"At work." Matty spoke out loud, obviously not worried. "I checked before we got here."

Sunday frowned. "How?"

He turned to her and winked before continuing deeper into the apartment.

They explored each room. There was nothing fantastic or unique about the apartment. It could have been Sunday's place. The walls were sporadically decorated with photos of friends and family and pretty pictures of Paris and flowers. The kitchen was mostly clean but for the few dishes in the sink, days old. It was a two-bedroom apartment. Sunday felt it safe to assume the room with the made bed and a picture of Janice with a dog on the nightstand was the bedroom they were looking for.

It was strange opening the dresser drawers, like she was invading Janice's privacy, but the woman was dead. Was Sunday any worse than the police who had undoubtedly already searched the room?

She rummaged through a wooden dresser. The top drawers contained clothing, socks, underwear, jeans. The bottom drawer was heavy. Sunday yanked the handles, forcing it open. It was a space dedicated to Janice's Sight. Inside were printed articles on the supernatural, along with a couple books about mythology and folklore. She pulled a clipping of blond hair tied together with twine out of the drawer and wrinkled her nose. Underneath the hair was a capped mason jar with dried flowers inside.

"Are these orchids?" Sunday pulled the jar out with her other hand, keeping the hair between her forefinger and thumb and her arm stretched out away from her.

"Looks like it." Matty agreed after examining it. "I've read about orchids being a good luck charm against curses and other bad luck. I never thought much of it, but I guess Janice believed it."

"And the hair?"

"Hair and nails are supposed to contain the essence of people." He shrugged. "Maybe it was a keepsake?"

She placed the jar back in the drawer and set the hair back on top of it. Beside them was a hardcover book with blue spine and no title. She pulled the book out and opened it. "I found her diary."

"Flip to the end." Matty squatted down next to her to read over her shoulder.

They read her entries backward. In the last entry, Janice wrote about her fears, the same suspicions her roommate mentioned. She was afraid something was going to kill her. Not someone, some*thing*. As they continued traveling back in time through Janice's journal, the threat disappeared. The first remark she made about a potential threat caught Sunday's attention.

Janice wrote about being scared over six months ago. She said she began feeling threatened by the spirits around her.

FEBRUARY 15

I pass a Kappa every day on the way to work. It lives in the sewers, and watches the people go by through the drainage on the curb. Normally, it leaves me alone, since Kappas prefer to target children, but today it grabbed at my feet. I fell face first on the road! A few people stopped to ask if I was all right. A man helped me to my feet. They must have either thought I was a total klutz or a drunk and unable to stay on her feet at eight in the morning. I turned around and the Kappa was staring at me. Its little lizard eyes bored into my soul; it might've killed me with that look. And this has continued to happen! A Toko has begun picking on me when I cross its path. A spirit of an old car salesman yells at me and throws branches at me in the park. I don't understand what's happening. Why is the Other World attacking me?

Just like Shelly's Toko. The Other World was attacking Sunday too. Not long after Janice began noting the strange threats from the Other World, a name showed up.

FEBRUARY 20

Stephen Elm reached out to me. I'm really glad he answered my email. I know he doesn't like to get involved with people who have the Sight, but he said he's having the same problems and is investigating. I'm worried about continuing over email. Those of the Other World seem to have the power like Big Brother. I'm going to write to him from now on.

"Are there letters in the drawer?" Sunday scanned the entries again as Matty shuffled through the drawer's contents. Her heart thumped in her throat. This woman knew her father. She had information about him. Maybe information about his death. Why hadn't he mentioned any of this to her?

"There are a few here." Matty fanned out sheets of paper folded into three parts and unfolded the one on top.

FEBRUARY 25

Janice,

I have a few theories about what it could be, and none of them are good. This has to be done by humans. There is no way that beings from the Other World could be hurting so many people. Not just hurting, killing! It's just not possible. I haven't come across an Other World creature who has that much power in our world. But the Other World has to be behind this. What would the human motive be? Most humans don't even know we or the Other World exists. I really don't know. None of the others I've talked to know either.

I can't make it out to California. It would put Sunday in danger. Do you have anybody else you can reach out to? What about a group more local?

Stephen

The next one read:

MARCH 2

Janice,

I am scared for your life and mine. They know I can see them. Whoever is killing us knows I exist. You NEED to go into hiding. Leave without telling anybody. Leave the state at least.

I am going into hiding too. I'm leaving the country. If I drive south, there won't be much record of where I went. I can't take Sunday with me and it breaks my heart. They don't know she has the Sight. She's safer without me. I invited her over for one last dinner tomorrow night. An unspoken good-bye. I hope she'll forgive me. I don't want to leave her, but I can't protect her if I'm dead.

Janice, am I doing the right thing?

Stephen

The final one:

MARCH 3

Janice,

I've been doing some research on Horus that I thought you would find interesting. I don't want to put it all in writing, but read about his war with Set.

Could that be where it all started? I've traced my family back to Egypt. I believe I've found connections to Isis. You do your own research, Janice. What can you find?

Stephen

Sunday's palms were sweaty. She struggled to get a full breath in. Her vision blurred until she couldn't make out the letters on the page anymore. She closed her eyes and listened to the blood rushing in her ears.

"Are you okay?" Matty said.

She kept her eyes closed. "No."

She felt his hand rubbing her back. Her father's words bounced in her head. Words that were written right before his death. Words about her. Further proof that her father had been hiding secrets from her. How could he? He was her best friend. She'd trusted him with her life, and he'd been lying to her. How could he?

And she was left to be comforted by a man she barely knew, a man who'd known her father better than she had.

She opened her eyes. Not only had he known her father better, he knew her better than any living person. The small scope of Sunday's world had never been so clear to her as she looked at him. She made a decision, one that she hoped wouldn't turn around to bite her in the ass.

She decided to trust him.

"I've been having a hard time ever since my dad died." She brushed tears away with the back of her hand. "Those letters—"

She couldn't find the words. They were tangled up in her head, all there, but unreachable.

"The last one was written the day he died." She ran her fingers over her father's words, mesmerized by the ink on the paper.

Matty nodded. He slipped the letters out from under her fingers and placed them back in their spot in the drawer before helping Sunday to her feet. Her legs trembled under her weight. Her whole body quaked like a small dog shivering from too much stimulus. Without another word, Matty took her hand and led her out of the apartment.

"Janice was into some weird shit," Jaime announced.

The group had met back at the motel that evening. They'd dropped their bags between the two rooms, gathering in room 5b where Jaime and Matty were sleeping for the night.

London dropped a manila folder onto the thin geometric-printed bed cover. She opened it up to reveal a stack of printed web pages and emails. The page on top was titled in large cursive print: *Meet the*

Egyptian Gods. Underneath was text and pictures of ancient Egyptian wall art and hieroglyphics.

"Most of the web pages we found in Janice's history at work had to do with ancient Egypt mythology, but there were other websites on folklore all over the world." London showed them the printed pages she was talking about.

Matty glanced at Sunday. She was exhausted. The Egypt connection London and Jaime had found only made her want to crawl into bed and never leave. This was more than she could handle. She didn't even attempt to figure out how they'd managed to get onto Janice's work computer and print out the web pages.

"We found letters about Egypt also." Matty explained their search of the apartment. "Janice really was running away from something." His gaze flashed to Sunday, waiting to see if she was going to interrupt or ask him to stop. She didn't. "She was in contact with Stephen. He felt like he was in danger too."

Sunday had suspected that her father's death wasn't an accident, but Janice's letters confirmed it. It was a strange feeling knowing her dad was killed. It didn't seem real, like the tragedy had happened to someone else. Seated on the bed beside the printouts, she laid her face in her palms. Her skin was clammy but cool, and the darkness settled her buzzing mind.

How was she going to function?

CHAPTER 14

Driving back to Arizona settled Sunday's anxiety. The familiar desert landscape comforted her. She knew the grassy hills and rocky terrain. Back home, she inhaled the familiar scents of the herbs she had growing on the window sill in the living room and the air freshener plugged into an outlet in the kitchen.

Images from the past week flashed through Sunday's mind, disturbing her sleep. She saw the Hound in the bar, the murderous ax man, Lucho's body, Lucho's ghost, and the Girdwick. It never ended. She lay on her back, staring at the dark ceiling. Shit had hit the fan this week.

When she finally fell asleep, the Cow Woman appeared in every dream. Sunday found herself back in her old middle school building. She'd walked those halls with her eyes on the ground, blocking out the voices and images of Other World creatures roaming the halls with the other students. In the dream, Sunday walked into a science classroom; the Cow Woman stood in the corner of the room. Her bright eyes, framed with black eyeliner, followed Sunday as she crossed the room.

The classroom transformed into the restaurant. Sunday stood in front of the large metal door to the walk-in freezer. The handle cold against her fingers, she unlatched the door. Blood pounded in her ears as the door creaked. She sensed the danger behind the door. The knowledge sprung the tiny hairs on her body on end. What creature from the Other World waited for her? It breathed heavy, still out of sight. What would be her end? She squeezed her eyes closed as she yanked the door open.

Sunday rocketed off her pillow. Her body was sleek from a cold sweat, and her eyes darted around the room searching for the source of the panic that enveloped her. The clock shone, displaying the early hour. She wanted to crawl into a hole and never leave, but just the thought of closing her eyes again brought her back to the suffocating terror of her nightmare. So she dragged herself out of bed, tugging at her T-shirt. A shower would wash the nightmare away.

"Bad dream?" A voice stopped Sunday with her arms in the air and the shirt over her head. She spun around, startled and struggling to cover up.

"Reap!" Her hand found a pillow and threw it at him. It went right through him, of course, and hit her bedroom door. "You can't just show up in someone's room like that."

Reap shrugged. "You okay?"

"I don't know. The whole life-threatening mystery makes it difficult to tell."

Reap nodded. "I'm here for a reason." His skeletal hand disappeared inside his cloak and reappeared with his tablet. He tapped the screen several times before handing it to Sunday.

A new list of glowing red names lit her face.

"I did some digging," Reap explained. "Those are people around the world with Sight. All of them have died over the last two months. That's an outrageous rate, something I would assume was caused by war or a plague, but it's only targeting people who can see the Other World."

"This isn't a plague." Sunday handed Reap back the list. "What do you know about Egypt?"

Reap frowned. "Country in Africa. Borders two seas. Rich mythology. What kind of information are you looking for?"

Sunday explained the cryptic information and connections they'd made since going to California.

"You're all from Egypt." Reap shook the list in his hands.

"What do you mean by all?"

"Everyone with Sight." He spoke so matter-of-factly, as if he were explaining 1+1 to a kindergartner. "It originated with the Egyptian gods."

Sunday shook her head. "Back up. Gods?"

Reap sighed. "I hope you paid attention to mythology in school. It's your family history. The Egyptian gods began passing pieces of their souls on to humans after the war between Horus and Set. They left this world but didn't want to leave it unprotected, so their souls kept the humans connected with the gods from the Other World."

Sunday raised her eyebrows and cocked her head to the side. She had paid attention to mythology in school—what kid wouldn't enjoy the magical stories? That's what they were, though: stories. They were believed by people who used to think that when the sun set it wasn't coming back.

"You're shitting me, right?" She chuckled.

"No." Reap frowned. "Why would I make this up?"

"So you're saying that anyone with the Sight is connected to an ancient Egyptian god?"

"A simplified explanation, but yes."

Sunday walked to her bedroom door, no destination in mind, but she needed to move. In the kitchen, she pulled a glass from the cupboard, then stopped on her way to the sink when her eye caught the bottle of Scotch on the counter. She poured the liquor into the cup instead and found Reap in the living room, reclined on the couch.

"Fuck." She collapsed in the armchair opposite him and took a swig. "Why didn't you mention any of this before?"

Reap shrugged. "Honestly, it never occurred to me. It's not something that comes up in normal conversation. I mean, do you talk to your friends about how the Earth is round?"

Sunday took another gulp out of her glass. "Okay." She took a deep breath. "So what god am I descended from?"

"That I don't know." Reap sat up. "That is a *very* large family tree that started thousands of years ago. It would take a lot of backtracking to figure that out."

"Do you have any idea what this has to do with people being killed?"

He shook his head. "I wish I did. The descendants haven't been threatened like this since there were kings and pharaohs, and that was a war for power. I don't know why you guys are at war now."

"Is it human?"

"I think so. It has to be. We can't affect humans this much from the Other World."

"That's what I guessed too. Something from the Other World must be helping whoever is causing the deaths, though. Humans don't have a list of descendants."

"Probably not."

Sunday finished her Scotch.

She wanted more but decided against it.

"I have to talk to everyone else about this. If we can figure out who we are descended from, maybe we can figure out who's trying to kill us."

Sunday sent out an email with the subject line: *Death Lent Us a Hand*. She smiled, enjoying the weird nature of her friendship. The group agreed to meet at Matty and Jaime's house so Sunday could share in person what she learned about Egypt. They took Janice's worry to heart, keeping everything limited when talking over the internet.

•••

"So you're saying that I am related to a god?" Jaime grinned.

Matty and Jaime's townhouse was minimally decorated and darkened by the drawn curtains. They crowded into the living room, Sunday perched on the edge of the couch with Gail and Jaime. London had pulled a dining room chair from the other room and sat across from them while Matty took the armchair at Sunday's elbow.

London rolled her eyes. "Great. His head wasn't big enough."

Sunday rubbed her neck. The restless nights were taking a toll on her. Her eyes felt swollen and heavy, her body was sore, and the tightness in her chest persisted. She took a deep breath to force space into her lungs.

"I get it," Gail said, "but what does it all mean? Is this just our origin story, or does this really have to do with what is killing people like us?"

"That's what we need to figure out," London said.

The rest of the group continued to talk in circles about the possibilities behind the ancient Egypt connection. Sunday couldn't follow the conversation. Her eyes fell on the water-ring- riddled side table beside her.

"You okay?" Matty whispered to her.

Her gaze still on the table, she shook her head.

"You can go lie down." He gestured toward the hallway behind her. "My room's the one on the right. And you're in luck! The sheets were recently cleaned."

Sunday cocked her right eyebrow. "What does recently mean?"

Matty smirked. "Do you really want to know?"

She took him up on his offer. Even if she didn't manage to fall asleep, she'd at least close her eyes. She desperately needed a break.

The voices were muffled by the closed bedroom door. Sunday suspected that the tidy room had been pulled straight from a dorm catalog. He seemed like the type of guy who would buy all of page 16. Everything he needed was there, in black, so it all matched.

She plodded to the bed. Having no energy to take them off, she lay down with her shoes hanging over the edge.

The muffled voices continued. Sunday wondered what else they could possibly be talking about. If anything, she thought they could take a trip to the library, read up on their Egyptian mythology. She'd suggest it after her nap.

• • •

Sunday stood face to face with the ax stranger. He stood tall over her, ax resting at his side. He grinned at her, his face morphing into Lucho's. Grunting, he raised the ax over his head.

She ran.

There was no way she could outrun the man's large strides, but she couldn't stand still to be butchered. Her feet felt encased in cement blocks. Willing her legs to move faster, she glanced over her shoulder.

The ax stranger transformed into a Hound, sending Sunday's heart into her throat. It snarled, having discovered her secret. She could see it; now she had to be killed.

Her mouth fell open, but no sound came out.

The Hound's breath engulfed her heels. Sunday attempted to run, but the weight grew heavier. Her knees crashed to the floor. She flipped over. Accepting her fate, she faced the beast.

Instead of the Hound's jaw clamping onto her throat, legs straddled over her. Sunday's eyes trailed up the appendages above her.

She scrambled out from under the legs and stood back up.

The Cow Woman stood between Sunday and the Hound. The beast cowered at the woman's feet. Sunday didn't blame it. The terrifying glare would have sent her running again.

Sunday's eyes shot open.

She felt heavy from waking up so abruptly from a deep sleep. She lifted herself onto her elbows.

Where the hell am I?

The room was unfamiliar. It took her a minute to remember why. Matty's room. Her nap. It slowly came back to her.

The voices outside the closed door had stopped. Maybe they had actually gone to the library.

And then she heard the scream.

● ● ●

"Fuck. Fuck. Fuck. Fuck."

Jaime ran past Sunday. He'd come through the back door just as she stepped into the hallway to investigate the scream.

"Jaime!" she called after him.

"Standoff outside! Getting gun!" he called over his shoulder without stopping, turning to the left into a room Sunday assumed was his.

Was his T-shirt tied around his face? Sunday went down the hallway into the living room. Standoff? What did Jaime mean? Why would he need a gun? Her stockinged feet dragged against the carpet as her breath caught in her throat.

As she entered the living room, a cough pushed the rest of the air from her lungs. She gasped for another breath while wiping her burning eyes. Through the gathering tears, she noted the hazy smoke around the room. The air burned her nose and throat. She pressed her palm over her mouth and rushed to the front door. The door knob twisted in her hand, but it remained closed. A small sob escaped her lips as she rammed her shoulder into the door. It should open. Why wasn't it opening?

Spinning around, she hurried across the living room again toward the open sliding door. She ached for the clear air outside. Tears rolled down her cheeks, saliva and mucus down her neck. In her dash to the door, she searched the room for anyone else. Empty.

Her foot slipped out from under her. With a gasp she fell to the floor, pushing a wheezing cough past her lips. At her feet, a metal canister lay on the carpet. She must have slipped on it. "Riot Control" was printed across the can in large block letters. Sunday scrambled to her feet. Was that what was in the air? Some sort of pepper spray or tear gas? Why would riot control spray be released in Matty's house?

She stumbled the rest of the way to the sliding door, forcing her feet to propel her out of the poisonous air.

"Get down!" Gail's scream whipped her attention to the right.

Gail flung her arms, gesturing for Sunday to crouch down. London, Matty, and Jaime squatted around her, all of them hiding behind a stack of outdoor lounging chairs. Why? Her burning eyes and blazing lungs slowed her thinking. She couldn't focus while she still inhaled the gas.

"Get! Down!" Gail screamed again.

Sunday dropped to her knees. She scanned the yard, her new friends hiding on the porch. Jaime peeked outside of the barrier, pointing a Glock toward the yard. A couple of trees provided shade along the fence line. He shot at them, aiming for the burly figures taking cover behind the trunks.

"Sunday! Get over here!" Gail now waved her over.

Behind the barrier, the air cleared. Sunday gulped the clean air, leaning against the stacked chairs to keep from collapsing. Closer to the others now, she saw the effects of the gas on their red faces. Had the gas been used to draw them out? The front door hadn't opened for Sunday. Had the others attempted to escape through there too? Had they been forced into an ambush in the back yard?

Jaime's gun boomed at her side. Return fire ricocheted off the chairs and the pillars around them. Sunday sank low. Gail's body draped over hers.

"What's happening?" Sunday shrieked in her bent position.

"They started shooting at us. We haven't been able to get away." Gail howled over the gun fire.

"They?"

"We don't know who they are. They just started attacking us."

The stranger with the ax flashed through her mind.

The guns quieted. Jaime jostled Sunday as she fell back behind the barrier.

"I'm trying to save the ammo, but we only have what was in the gun." He checked the gun. "We've got six rounds left."

"We can't just stay here," London hissed. "I feel like a sitting duck."

Gail crawled off of Sunday, allowing her to lift her cheek off the cold cement.

"Sunday, do you have your phone on you?" Matty asked.

She patted her jean pockets, then remembered that she'd dropped her phone on Matty's bedside table before napping. "No."

"Fuck!" London leaned against the barrier.

"Someone must've heard the gunshots. They'll call for help," Gail said.

"Hold up. They're too quiet over there." Jaime crawled to the side of the barrier again, holding the Glock ready. He squeezed the trigger. Sunday felt the explosion of the bullet in the pit of her stomach. "Got him! You guys need to run! They're closing in."

London leapt from their spot first, stooped over and dashed to the side of the house. Sunday followed behind Matty, Gail's hand pushing her forward. Shots rang in her ears, disorienting. Which were Jaime's? How many were attacking them?

She peered over her shoulder. Two men found shelter behind the rest of the yard furniture, one huddled behind a stone fire pit and the other behind an outdoor couch. Jaime panted beside her. His presence made her feel safer. He was a cop; his expertise had kept them alive so far. He'd guide them to safety.

Another shot rang out. Sunday's eyes jumped to the gun in his hand. Had he shot? The seconds slowed. The moment halted.

He grunted, his body falling to the ground with a loud thump. Gail screamed. Matty and London spun around. Another shot. Gail collapsed beside Sunday.

"Down!" Matty yelled, pushing Sunday's shoulders. They fell to their knees beside Jaime and Gail's bleeding bodies. London snatched Jaime's gun and aimed at the men hiding among the yard furniture.

Matty crawled past London, grabbing Jaime's pant leg and pulling him out of the line of fire. Sunday watched his limp arms being dragged across the cement, a chill enveloping her body. Gail groaned behind her; she turned to the woman who had protected her the moment she stepped out of the gas-filled house. Sunday searched Gail for the bullet wound. Blood ran down her arm from a hole in her shoulder. Hope warmed Sunday; Gail would live.

"What do I do?" Sunday muttered under her breath.

Should she carry Gail back to their chair barrier? Attempt to run her down the side of the house? Her wide eyes searched the yard for an answer. Matty continued to lug Jaime's inert body, moving him behind the protection of the chairs.

London lay on her stomach, eyes glued to the men, finger on the trigger. She squeezed. Her shot caused a cry from behind the metal couch. She squeezed again. A grunt from behind the fire pit; the man pulled his legs from view. Sunday wrapped a protective arm around Gail who buried her face into Sunday's T-shirt. The attackers lowered their guns, retreating. London pushed herself up, gun still raised in their direction.

"Turn toward me at all and I'll blow your head off!" She pressed her lips tight, both hands wrapped around the Glock.

The men continued their retreat, leaving their third bleeding in the yard. The back gate slammed behind them. London finally lowered her arms. Sunday's eyes jumped to Jaime. Matty had laid Jaime's head in his lap and smoothed his hair off his sweating forehead. Jaime stared wide-eyed at the overhang. His chest heaved up and down. He coughed. Blood trickled from the corner of his lip.

London ran past them, gun hanging at her side and one arm draped over her face like Dracula hiding behind his cape. She bolted inside, returning red-faced once again, with her phone against her ear. Out of breath, she dropped to her knees beside Jaime and Matty.

"I'm at 775 Shea Boulevard," she sputtered. Filled with tears, her eyes fell on Jaime's gasping body. "He's been shot. Hurry! We need help!"

THE APOSTLES OF THE LORD
MISSION STATEMENT

The wages of sin is death. The gift of God is eternal life. Warriors of God will be rewarded, those who go to battle for Him. His light will shine in the darkness. The darkness will not overcome. The servants of God would not allow it. In this modern world, a world of television and internet, a world where temptation is there with a tap of a screen, a world where God is lost in the mix of tweets and memes. We can't accept God's fall. We would be worse than the sinners. It is our duty as servants of the Lord to fight back. This is a war, apostles! We are at war with the non-believers! They will not be satisfied damning their own souls to Hell, but will take us all down with them! They want to ravage our Faith, maim our Savior! He has spoken to me. He has described His mission and has ordered us to fight back! Be strong and of good courage; be not frightened, neither be dismayed. The Lord, Set, your God, is with you wherever you go. Follow us and you too will see His light!

theapostlesofthelord.org/missionstatement

CHAPTER 15

Right after the ambush, the paramedics arrived at Matty's house and immediately treated Gail before placing her in the ambulance.

Jaime had collapsed on the ground. His mouth hung open and his eyes stared up at the sky, unmoving. Blood had dribbled down his cheek, collecting on the cement beneath him. His hand lay limp in Matty's, but Matty maintained his vigil over his friend even after Jaime stopped breathing. Sunday sighed as the paramedics draped a sheet over him.

Reap had one more red glowing name on his list.

At that thought, Sunday looked around the backyard. The once-green lawn had transformed into lumps of grass and debris. Furniture had been upturned, and shards of the surrounding fence littered the ground. She wasn't assessing the damage, though.

Shouldn't Reap be here to collect Jaime's spirit?

She didn't see Reap or Jaime's ghost. There were limitations to her Sight, but she ached to see Jaime moving on to the next life. Did he walk into the Other World singing Sinatra? If she didn't see him move on, did that mean he'd become a spirit trapped in this world? Sunday closed her burning eyes. The image of Jaime's body gasping for breath would haunt her nightmares forever.

But maybe not. She whimpered. What other horrific sights were in her future? Would they all be seared into her head, a plethora of terrifying images, ever changing and unending? Or would they all mesh together into a glob of terror?

Sunday shivered, despite the warm evening.

"Miss."

Someone touched her shoulder. While she stared at Jaime's covered body, the others had walked away from the scene. She was left with a couple strangers, one photographing the yard and the other standing over her.

A young police officer, his name tag reading *Donk*, watched Sunday with concern. He held out a hand to help her to her feet.

"Will you come with me?" He indicated the side gate. "We want to ask you some questions away from the scene."

Sunday followed him into the front yard. She dropped onto the curb in front of the house, catching sight of London and Matty sitting on the front porch before burying her face in her hands. If she couldn't see the cop beside her, would he disappear? She didn't want his questions. Answering questions would make all of this real. It couldn't be real.

Officer Donk cleared his throat. Sunday didn't move.

"Um," he said hesitantly. "Can you tell me what happened?"

What happened? Seemed so straightforward. A question you were asked in elementary school when Sally cried and Hannah sat off to the side with her arms crossed, angry.

What happened? An inappropriate question when armed men appeared in a suburban neighborhood and shot down her friend.

Tears filled Sunday's eyes. She wanted to call Jaime her friend. They'd vanquished the Girdwick together. He'd defended her and the others in the ambush, ultimately causing his death. In reality, though, she'd just met him. She didn't have time to get to know him.

Having no idea what else to do, she told him the truth. How else could she explain the bullet-riddled back yard and dead body? She left out details about the other deaths, their theory about the Seers being targeted and ancient Egypt, but she gave Officer Donk the play-by-play of what happened to Jaime Lopez.

The man standing over her appeared even younger than Sunday. Did he even need to shave?

When Sunday finished telling the story, he stared at her with narrowed eyes, pen still hovering over his notes. A quick glance at the pad showed that he stopped writing after Sunday described the smoke-filled living room.

Sunday shrugged. "Hard to believe, right?"

Officer Donk cleared his throat. "Yeah, um, I mean…"

He excused himself and retreated. He would have to believe her. Sunday dared him to come up with another explanation.

The detective from the night of Lucho's murder approached her after Officer Donk ran away. He re-introduced himself as Kincaid Bell.

Sunday pulled herself to her feet to accept his outstretched hand. Did he recognize her? Bell's eyes flickered in her direction before moving back to the notebook in his hand. He waved London and Matty over. London wrapped her arms around herself, her cheeks stained from crying. Matty glared at the ground, teeth clenched and accentuating the muscles of his jaw. His fists were balled at his side.

"I don't quite understand what's going on here." Bell made one last note in his notebook before tucking it back into his pocket. He made a point of establishing eye contact as he spoke. Sunday forced her gaze on him; the second he looked away, her eyes jumped to the others. London shrugged, tears still in her eyes. Matty gave him a quick glance before looking back to the street.

More distinguished than Officer Donk, Bell's face showed the early signs of wrinkles around his eyes. These should have made him appear warmer and more welcoming, as if his eyes were permanently smiling, but the hard line of his mouth told another story.

"We're here again, Ms. Elm and Mr. Merhi. Are you ready to share the truth now?"

Sunday could see Matty's jaw moving as he ground his teeth. He crossed his arms. She nodded to answer Bell's question. The detective pulled the small notebook back out of his pocket again and flipped through a couple dozen pages.

"You told my officer that a small militia attacked your home. Bombed the house with tear gas to get you outside? There, they shot at you? And you have no idea who these people were and why they attacked you?"

"Yes, sir," London replied.

Bell studied them, glaring down at them and their unbelievable story. Sunday controlled the muscles of her face; she didn't want a tear or twitch to bring more suspicion on her.

He exhaled. "Ms. Oliviera, you're going to have to come with me while we get this all sorted out."

"Am I under arrest?" London's eyes widened.

"Not if you come voluntarily. You shot those men, we need you to come in for questioning."

She agreed and Bell turned back to Sunday and Matty, reached into his pockets again and pulled out a handful of business cards. He fanned them out and offered them.

"Your life'll be a lot easier if you tell me what you're hiding," he continued as each of them took a card. "Either way, I'll find out. Finish giving your statements to Officer Donk, and then you are free to go. I'll be in touch."

At the hospital, they all sat in the waiting room, silent. Matty's knee bounced while his head rested in his hands. Gail's husband, Gin, held their daughter in his lap. He was a tall Japanese man. He slouched lower in his seat as they waited for news. He rocked the young girl and watched the sleeping toddler in the stroller beside them. Sunday paced the waiting area, anything to avoid watching Matty's incessant bouncing or listening to Gin's nail biting. The waiting room felt surreal. The lights shone too bright; the ringing of the receptionist's phone echoed. Her limbs even felt disconnected from her body; she was shocked her legs moved while she paced.

The adrenaline no longer pumped through her body, leaving her weak. She forced the tears away, though she could easily sit down and cry. Instead, she wrapped her arms around herself and watched the carpet under her feet. She focused on the breath moving in and out of her body.

Gail's daughter wiggled in Gin's lap. With her arm latched around his waist, she leaned forward, her little arm stretching, fingers extended towards her sleeping infant brother.

"Don't," Gin muttered, giving the little girl a jolt.

She crossed her pudgy arms and sat back against his chest again. She had the same haircut as Gail, the same golden-brown hair chopped at her shoulders. She even tucked strands behind her ears like her mother. She pressed her lips tightly together, accentuating her round cheeks.

"He's sleeping, Rose," Gin said to the four-year-old. "Leave him alone."

Her arms squeezed tighter against her chest. She pressed her chin down, and her eyes searched the room, looking everywhere but at her father. The child's large dark eyes eventually found Sunday sitting across from her.

Gin rocked her gently in his lap. He laid his head against the back of the chair and closed his eyes.

Rose relaxed her arms. She leaned against Gin's chest, melting into him, but her eyes stayed on Sunday. Sunday's gaze shifted between the child's curious eyes and the rest of the waiting room. The tall fig tree and a wall plastered in donor plaques couldn't distract her from Rose's stare.

"Do you see the animals too?" Her voice was high and childlike, but her words were enunciated as good as any adult could speak.

"Animals?"

"She means the creatures from the Other World." Gin spoke with his eyes still closed.

Sunday's jaw dropped. The toddler saw the Other World?

"Do you?" Rose repeated.

"Yes," Sunday whispered. Her eyes jumped to Matty, his face still hidden in his hands. "You see them?"

Rose sat up tall, her chin raised higher when she nodded.

"But…"

"I got my Sight younger too," Gin explained. "Not as young as Rose, though. Shocked me when I first heard my four-year-old talk about her friend the Gowrow."

"His name is Emmett." Rose twisted her body to Gin. His head rested against the back of his chair, but he patted the girl's shoulder in response.

"What's your name?" she asked, turning back to Sunday.

"Sunday."

Rose wrinkled her nose. "That's weird. Your name is a weekend."

Gin frowned. "Well, your name is a flower, and mine is a type of alcohol. They're weird too."

Rose shook her head. "Flowers are pretty, and Mama says your name means silver, like your hair." She ran a pudgy finger through his salt-and-pepper locks and then asked Sunday, "Why a weekend?"

Both Gin and Rose watched Sunday for an answer.

"My mom chose my name. She used to tell me that I made every day bright, like the sun."

"That's sweet." Gin smiled, but it didn't reach his eyes.

Not bright enough to keep her around. Sunday kept her thoughts private. She grinned. Rose lost interest and reached for her brother again. Gin pulled her hand away. Tears filled the girl's eyes when a nurse dressed in navy blue scrubs approached them.

"Gin Sato?" the nurse questioned.

"That's me." Gin scooted to the edge of the chair.

"Gail is asking for you."

He lifted Rose off his lap. The girl clung to his leg, wiping her runny nose on his slacks.

"You're going to stay with Uncle Matty and Aunt Sunday for a few minutes, okay?"

Rose blubbered.

He pulled her chubby hands off his leg. "You need to help them take care of Jacob for me. Neither of them know his lullaby song, so they'll need help getting him back to sleep if he wakes up."

Matty wrapped an arm around Rose's waist.

"No!" she sobbed and reached for Gin.

"I'll be right back," he promised.

Rose whimpered, and reluctantly allowed Matty to sit her in the chair next to him. Her eyes followed her father being led through the hospital doors. As the doors swung closed, she jumped off the chair and shuffled on her knees to her brother's car seat.

"Rose…" Matty sighed.

"I'm just watching him!" she argued. Her face, red and blotchy from crying, turned up to Sunday. "Mommy says I'm the best big sister." She gently touched the baby's cheeks with the tips of her fingers. "She says I'll be the one to show him that the animals aren't scary. They're not, you know. They're just scared because they're not home with their mommy."

Sunday watched as Rose traced the tips of her fingers over her brother's face. He wrinkled his nose and sighed. Unlike his sister, Jacob had inherited Gin's black hair.

"Do you miss your mommy, Aunt Sunday?"

She choked on her breath. Her eyes jumped to Matty who looked back at her, his lips pressed together and his eyes half closed. The child had to be asking because she missed her mother. She didn't know how Sunday's mother had left them. Did she?

"Yes, Rose, I miss her."

"I miss my mommy too." She dropped her hand in her lap. "She'll be okay, right?"

Sunday didn't know how to answer, but Rose didn't wait for one. Jacob's eyes opened and his sister cooed over him. Gin returned less than ten minutes later.

"She's resting," he announced. Rose latched onto his leg again. "The doctors want to keep her overnight to make sure the wound doesn't get infected, but otherwise she's on the mend." He tucked Rose's hair behind her ear. "I'm going to take Rose and Jacob for a visit before taking them home. Did you guys want to see her too?"

Matty shook his head before Sunday could turn down the invitation.

"She should rest. Tell her to call when she's feeling up to it." He pressed his hands against his knees to stand up. "Do you agree?" he asked Sunday.

She nodded. Gin gathered his two kids. Rose waved good-bye to them as they walked through the swinging doors. They disappeared and Sunday followed Matty to the elevator.

"Need a ride home?" he asked. They had the elevator car to themselves.

Sunday pictured sitting in Matty's passenger seat, the forced conversation. Empty words. She replayed the afternoon in her head. Where had it gone wrong? What would they do differently? She wanted to be home, but would she be safe?

"No, thank you." She shook her head.

The bus called to her as they stepped out of the hospital. The sun had sunk below the buildings, giving the sky a purple hue and allowing the afternoon air to cool. She needed the travel time, a time where her only job was to sit in her seat and wait. The in-between time would give her a chance to breathe, to collect her thoughts. The comforting scene outside the bus window blurred past her as she rested her forehead on the window. It drove through downtown, passing Bokka's. The heat lamps flickered along the edge of the restaurant's outdoor seating. Patrons ate, living in a different world from her. The window wasn't the only barrier between her and those enjoying their dinner out.

The bus dropped her a few blocks from her condo complex. The air outside had cooled now that the sun was down. Chirping crickets and croaking frogs accompanied Sunday on her walk home. She crossed her arms and watched her feet carry her along the sidewalk. She expected tears, thought she would be suffocated by panic and grief, but she was content watching her feet pound on the pavement. Her molars ground together until her jaw ached. She raised her eyes and watched her apartment building move closer to her, the rest of the neighborhood just a blur in her peripheral vision.

Her father had taught her about the Other World when she was a little girl. He had sat her down on the couch after dinner, clearly wanting a serious talk. Crouched down in front of her, he had pulled off his wire-rimmed glasses and allowed them to hang from his finger. Sunday had watched them swing slightly, nervous.

"You're pretty lucky, you know that?" He had smiled, a contagious one that Sunday couldn't help returning.

Of course she was lucky. Sure, her mom had left her, but she had her dad. He was all she needed.

He had continued. "I don't think you understand why you are lucky, though."

Sunday had waited patiently for him to continue. They had never had a talk like this before. Should she ask questions or listen quietly? She had become acutely aware of her hands. Where did people place their hands during talks like this? She had looked to her father's. One rested on his knee, glasses hanging between his pinky and empty ring finger, and the other hung limply between his legs. She had rested hers on her knees.

"You're lucky because you have a gift." His smile had widened. "You have the privilege to see into a whole other world. To see and meet creatures you couldn't even imagine."

Sunday's nose had wrinkled. Creatures?

"Like trolls?" she had asked.

"Well," he had shrugged, "kind of. Some of them may be a little scary, which brings me to my point. Your Sight is a privilege. The Other World is not yours, and you have to respect the creatures that come from it, like you respect your friends' houses when you visit. Does that make sense?"

She had nodded.

"And if anything does scare you, remember, if you leave them be, they'll leave you be. Just like if you see a snake while hiking."

Now, walking home, Sunday swung her leg, aiming for a pebble in the middle of the sidewalk.

They'll leave me be, Dad?

What was he thinking? Did he forget to take off his rose-colored glasses?

The ground beneath her feet disappeared. She stumbled forward, landing on her knees with a thud that rattled her. She turned back, seeing a scaly arm recede into a storm drain. As she stood back up, the creature hissed and snickered.

She took a couple steps back to the storm drain. The small claw reached out again, grasping at the air, searching for her feet. She knew of the brute connected to the arm. Part fish, part human, Kappas walked like a person, crawling out of rivers, ponds, or sewers to pull children into their watery dens. Sulfur warded them off. Sunday recalled the words from Janice's journal:

Normally it leaves me alone since Kappas prefer to target children, but today it grabbed at my feet.

"You have got to be fucking kidding me!" Sunday stomped her foot, aiming for the arm waving out of the drain again, but missed. She looked to the sky, chuckled, and shook her head. "You're literally kicking me while I'm down." Spinning on the balls of her feet, she continued the walk home. She thought of the Toko and the Kappa, the stranger with the ax and the men who had ambushed them. She'd been the victim, threatened and attacked, but she was done. "Fine. If you're not going to leave me alone, I'm not leaving you alone."

CHAPTER 16

Sunday's heart leapt to her throat when she opened the front door. The light from the evening sun dimly lit the room, but the figure perched on the couch remained in shadow. Sunday flashed back to the barista spirit. Was she back? She'd only cleaned up the salt line along the front door, but that had been a way back in. Did the spirit think Sunday would change her mind and decide to help her? She couldn't. What would the spirit do this time?

Sunday flipped the light switch by the door, turning on the lamp beside the couch.

The spirit was young, only fourteen or fifteen. She stared at Sunday with silver eyes. Each breath in and out fluttered the gills on her neck, and her stringy hair dripped on the carpet. A smile crept across her lips and she gave Sunday a wave with webbed fingers.

Chloe. A student at Chancler Prep. Died three days ago after her designated driver had too many beers. At least that's what she heard when she visited her house. She didn't remember the accident, didn't remember getting into the car. The last she remembered was getting into a fight with a friend. She said such awful things to Jess, she wanted to forget the whole night, just wake up the next morning in bed, a hangover acting as her penance.

Instead she woke up with gills and double vision. Sunday didn't actually have two sets of eyes, right? They blink at the same time like an alien in a scifi movie. With her silvery fish eyes, the world had turned blue, Sunday's skin was tinted and freckled and the flowers out the window had tips dipped in white. What happened to her?

"You died," Sunday said.

She closed the door behind her and sat in the armchair.

Do all people die like this?

Sunday shrugged. "I'm not exactly an expert. Other spirits visit me; they're not completely human just like you."

The teen spirit dropped her face in her hands. Her gills gasped between sobs. Sunday ran her fingers over her own cheeks. They were wet just like Chloe's, but she hadn't cried. She drew a shaky breath in. What was happening to her?

Chloe didn't get to apologize. She tried. She saw how sad her family was. Her mother fell to her knees when she heard the news. Her cries came out in choking gasps that reverberated through her whole body. She wanted death, begged for it. She didn't want to live in a world where Chloe died.

"I can't apologize for you." Sunday dragged her hands over her face to mop up the tears. "I don't do that anymore."

The spirit's gills flared red. Chloe wiped snot from her nose and stared large tear-filled eyes at Sunday. It was the barista spirit all over again. What was Sunday supposed to do? Run from spirit to spirit to do their bidding? While each visit made her ache for her father. The hole in her heart throbbed like a wound. She could follow in his footsteps, wear her heart on her sleeve and help, follow his faith and respect the Other World, the spirits. Stephen had worshipped them.

But she'd seen how Matty and the Ghost Gurus worked. Money exchanged, a job done. The spirits and creatures of the Other World were invaders, and the Seers could banish them. Was she supposed to banish this teenage girl?

What did she believe? What was she supposed to do?

Chloe showed Sunday her final moments of memory.

The teenager's face contorted with anger. She screamed at her friend, and Jess screamed back. Chloe stormed from the room, biting her tongue to hold off her tears. She met a few other friends from school and tossed her head back with a shot. And then another. And another.

Then black.

Sunday squeezed her eyes shut and pressed her hands over her ears. She didn't want to see the visions or the spirits. Chloe moaned in her head, hating herself.

She was a nasty friend, a horrible daughter. And now she was dead with nothing to show for her life except for broken hearts and hurt feelings. What was wrong with her? She had loving parents, a younger brother she only fought with on occasion. And how did she show them she cared about them? By getting drunk and dying in a car wreck. Stupid. Stupid. Stupid. Stupid! STUPID!

"Okay!"

Sunday held out her hands. She needed Chloe to stop. Needed the screams in her head to go silent.

"I'll write your family a letter, okay?"

Chloe sat up taller. Her bottom lip still trembled, but she dropped her hands away from her face and into her lap.

In her small office, Sunday dug out a pad of paper and a pen. She got an envelope from the bottom drawer of her desk, then went to retrieve a stamp from the box beside it but her fingers felt only the inside of the box. No stamps. She cursed under her breath.

She remembered her father dropping off a large book of stamps, said he got a deal on them. Had she stored them in the closet?

Sunday stood on her tiptoes to reach the top shelf of the closet. Her knee hit the handle of a file cabinet and she cursed again. At the back sat a small slender cardboard box, the top covered in a layer of dust. She snatched it, stumbling on her toes and flinging her arm off the shelf. Her elbow hit the other boxes stored on the shelf beside her which sent them crashing to the floor.

"Shit!"

Sunday rubbed her elbow. She dropped the stamps on her desk on top of the other letter-writing supplies she'd pulled out and knelt down to pick up the mess. One plastic box held spare sheets. The other cardboard box had broken in the fall. The lid was still intact, though. She picked it up and gasped.

When had she stored her father's things in the closet? The weeks after his accident had been a blur. Now, she collected the items off the floor, dropping mail and pictures into the upturned lid. She gathered a pile of old magazines, and a cell phone fell from the middle of the stack. It landed on the rug, black screen pointed toward her. Her father's cell phone.

What was on there? Sunday thought of the encrypted emails Detective Bell had mentioned. Could she access them on the phone? She knew his passcode: 0817. Her birthday.

The magazines slipped from her rigid fingers. She left them scattered at her knees, seized the phone, and pressed the power button, then sighed. Dead. It would be after six months. She found the power cable in the mess on the floor and plugged it in under her desk. Once the charger was plugged into the phone, the screen lit up, an outline of a battery filling itself continually.

Sunday stared at it, watching the animated battery green fill to the top increment by increment before disappearing and starting again. She'd have to wait hours for it to charge. Then a chill sent goosebumps down her body.

Chloe stood in the office doorway. Her shorts exposed her legs, the skin scaled like a fish.

"I'm almost ready," Sunday muttered. She gathered the pad, envelope, and stamp book. Her eyes kept falling on the charging phone. "Let's do this in the living room."

She led the way out, feeling for the first time since her father's death like she had control. The teenage spirit trusted her, relied on her to move on to the Other World. Sunday settled back into her armchair and positioned the pad on her lap, ready to help Chloe. For the first time since the accident, Sunday felt that she could do it on her own.

The pen glided across the paper, recording the words Chloe put in Sunday's head. Her redemption and her family's closure.

Afterward, with the letter in the mail and the spirit gone, Sunday didn't feel alone like before. She returned to the office. The phone had to be charged enough to turn on.

A photo of Sunday smiling next to her father at her high school graduation filled the screen, the same one hanging in her hallway. The photo was almost ten years old. Did neither of them have any other pictures together?

In the top right corner, the service bars had a cross through them. Sunday didn't remember canceling his phone plan, but she must have. Beside the crossed-out bars, the radar symbol blinked as the phone connected to her wifi. Sunday's stomach quivered, anticipating what she might find. She almost called Matty to invite him over so they could search the phone together, but she decided this was something she wanted to do on her own. It connected to the wifi and began buzzing in her hand as the notifications came in.

Email, text, and voicemail icons spread across the top of the screen. She scrolled through the emails, most of them spam. There were a couple names she didn't recognize: Hazel O'Neill, Hasan Carver. Other

Seers perhaps, but when she clicked on the message, the phone asked for a password. She tried her birthday again. Didn't work.

Most of the voicemails had come in after Stephen's accident. She listened to a couple condolence messages before scrolling past the rest and stopped at a message from Hasan Carver, the same man with encrypted emails. She hit play.

"Stephen. Don't give up just yet. I've been looking into my ancestry. There has to be some way to use Shu's powers. The Sight can't be the only way his blood manifests in me. I was wondering what you know about your blood line with Isis. Get back to me as soon as you can."

Sunday frowned. Her father had mentioned Isis in his letters to Janet. Was she the goddess her family descended from, like Reap had explained? Sunday moved on to the text messages, hoping to find more answers. Half a dozen of them had been sent after his accident. Meant for whom? For her father in the Other World? Sunday? Or just for them, a way to say goodbye? She scanned through them. Luke McCann, a man her father regularly worked with in the antique furniture business. Raphael Tran, an old friend from college. Jillian Hewitt she didn't know. Sunday hit the message exchange and scrolled up several messages, all sent weeks before Stephen's accident.

Stephen: *Makes me uneasy*

Jillian: *Uneasy? The Warvils attacked me. No instigating, nothing, just attacked. I have the bite marks to prove it.*

Stephen: *I believe you. You're not the only one in trouble. Other World beings are acting strange, others feel like they're being followed by people of our world.*

Jillian: *I'll look into it some more. Let you know what I find*

The exchange ended.

Did she know what had happened to Stephen? Was Jillian even alive, or was she on Reap's list? Sunday scanned the other text messages and stopped at another name she recognized: Janice Woodbridge. She opened the conversation. Instead of texts, they'd sent voice messages back and forth.

Sunday clicked one from her father. The voice made her heart skip a beat, and the phone fell from her hand. She couldn't believe her ears. Her breath caught in her throat as she picked it back up and listened.

"I looked him up, but the best I could do was a Google search. Can you ask Jeremy? He's still working for the police department there, right?"

Tears filled Sunday's eyes, real, not Chloe's ghost tears. She let them run down her cheeks.

She hit the next message from Janice.

"Can you send me the spelling again?"

Sure, Stephen texted back. *Jax Fraser.* Followed by another voice message, "Get back to me when you can. I don't want to go to Texas half-cocked. If it's anything sensitive send it through email. That's faster than your letters and I've got that locked up. And Janice, be careful."

Sunday cradled the phone in both hands. She could've hugged it. She would never let it go, would listen to his voice every day. Through his voice she tried to imagine the scratch of his stubble against her cheek and the smell of his aftershave, then lowered the phone back to the desk. She couldn't remember how his aftershave smelled, couldn't remember how her father smelled. Her heart pattered in her chest. What aftershave did he use? What else was she going to forget?

She sniffed and wiped away the tears. Focus. Sunday listened to the voice messages again. He had mentioned a name, Jax Fraser, and he was asking a cop to look up information on him. Maybe another Seer.

Her father knew something was threatening people with Sight. Could he have been trying to reach out to Seers and warn them?

The phone screen fell dark, the only light in the dark room. A chill ran down Sunday's spine. She hadn't noticed the darkness until then. The messages on her father's phone whispered half-secrets to her, words she didn't understand. She had to look into Jax Fraser. He could be the next piece of the puzzle.

She left the phone to finish charging in her office. Her eyes were tired from staring at the bright screen and her shoulders ached with tension. The clock in her bedroom read after midnight. She'd sleep and call the others in the morning. They had a lead.

CHAPTER 17

Dr. Morris,

I'm sure you've figured this out already. I don't know when I'll be coming to another session again. Possibly never. I just need to stay alive. If I make it through this, I'll reach out. These letters alone have helped me keep my head on straight. You're helping and you don't even know it.

There's been so much death. The last time I went to a funeral before all of this was when I was seven years old. It was my grandmother's funeral. That was right before I saw you. Another time of loss in my life. Is that what I'm destined for, continual loss? Grandma, then Dad. Mom might as well be dead. She may be. I have no idea. Now Jaime. Are my other new friends next? It could also be me. The final loss. All I want to do is cry. I'm going to picture you telling me that is all right. Then you'll leave me to it.

•••

"It's open!" Matty shouted from inside the house when Sunday knocked on the door a few days later.

Her stomach had tied into knots as she'd gotten ready. She'd sent a message to Matty the morning after Jaime's attack and murder; he'd agreed that they all needed a couple days off. Sunday had forced herself to go back to work just to keep her mind from mulling over their impending doom all day. On her next day off, she had suggested they get together at Matty's house again to figure out what needed to be done to save their lives. She didn't ask any questions: about the Other World, or Jaime, or Gail. Those could wait to be asked in person.

The curtains were still drawn, so Sunday stepped into the dark living room. Matty walked down the hallway pulling a T-shirt over his head.

"Did I wake you?" She reached for her phone to check that her "on my way" message had sent.

"Nah."

He winked. She wrinkled her nose.

"Everyone has their own way of dealing with tragedy, right?"

He dropped into the armchair, the same one he had sat in just days ago, before.

Sunday forced her eyes away from the view of the back yard. It drew her in through the windows and sliding glass door. Instead, she took a seat across from him on the worn couch.

"You seem to be feeling better." Sunday thought about the last time she had seen him, with his clenched jaw and balled-up fists. Now he sat back, melting into the chair.

Matty shrugged and rubbed his hands down his thighs. "I'm managing. How are you doing?"

"Same." Her eyes wandered around the room, finally settling on the view outside. The sight left a weight on Sunday's chest. She needed to look away from the damaged fence and upturned lawn. The view alone brought back sounds; screaming and crying filled her head until she felt dizzy.

She closed her eyes and took a deep breath before changing the subject. "Where's everybody else?"

"They're not coming."

Sunday frowned. It hadn't even occurred to her that she could bail. Part of her wished she had thought of that before everyone else did.

"They're cowards." Matty sat back in his chair. "Said that they liked Stephen's idea and they're going to hide. Lot of good that did him."

How long would it take the mention of her father's death to not break her heart?

Matty's hand flung to his mouth. He jolted up, like he'd been shocked. "I'm an ass. I'm sorry."

Sunday shrugged. "So they really aren't coming?"

"No. I guess we just have to wait for their names to appear on Reap's list, or we catch this guy before he gets to them."

"No pressure, right?"

They chuckled.

"Hey, baby, do you have anything to eat?" A voice sounded from down the hall.

Sunday recognized it, but it took her a moment to place it outside of work.

Shelly bounced down the hall in an oversized sweatshirt. Sunday had a strong suspicion it didn't belong to her. She raised an eyebrow.

"Hey, Sun!" Shelly smiled. "Matty mentioned you were coming over. Your day off too?"

She didn't reply but looked at Matty. His cheeks were pink and his hands resumed their journey up and down his legs. When he finally met Sunday's gaze, he smirked. She rolled her eyes.

"My fridge is kinda empty," he said over his shoulder. "I haven't gone grocery shopping in awhile."

Shelly shrugged. "That's okay. I should get going anyway."

They didn't talk much as Shelly got dressed and gathered her things. Sunday wished Matty had just followed her back into the bedroom. Instead, Sunday entwined her fingers in her lap, shifting her gaze around the room. Anywhere but Matty.

He lived in the definition of a bachelor pad. The couches were in good shape, but they were worn from age. The walls were painted white and empty. A whiskey bottle transformed into a lamp rested on a side table by the couch, the only light in the room.

Shelly's heels clicked as she exited the bedroom a second time. This time she was accompanied by the Toko. It sneered at Sunday.

She gave a wave to Sunday, saying she would see her at work. Matty walked her to the door. She pecked his cheek. While walking out, the Toko flipped Sunday off and cackled.

Sunday resisted the urge to return the gesture. She waited for the front door to close before turning to Matty. "Was that thing watching you the whole time?"

He chuckled nervously. "It was tough."

Sunday scoffed.

"You're upset?" His lips turned down. He plopped down on the chair again and waited for her answer.

Was she angry? Jealous? She had admitted to herself a long time ago that she found Shelly attractive. That was how she got Sunday to do anything outside of work, but she had no interest in actually dating her coworker. And Matty? She studied the lanky man in a white T-shirt and dark basketball shorts. She sighed.

In the end, though, none of it mattered. Between grieving for her father and the now very real threat on her life, she couldn't wrap her head around dating anyone. Thinking about it now tightened her chest. She forced a deep breath in and brushed the thought away. There wasn't enough time, Sunday didn't have the energy. Shelly and Matty would be good together and Sunday would worry about taking care of herself.

"A little disgusted, I guess."

"I can live with that." Matty stood up.

"It's your life. Do what you like." She followed him into the kitchen as she spoke. He pulled out two cans of Coors and handed her one. "I lock myself away, you slum it with the easiest waitress in town." She bit her tongue. Maybe she was a little jealous, though she had no idea who she was jealous of.

The cans hissed open. Matty chuckled and held his beer out.

"Cheers." Sunday tapped the top of her can with his before taking a sip.

He grinned. Sunday rolled her eyes.

"Let's go save our skins, shall we?" He brought the can to his lips and tipped his head back as he led the way back into the living room.

The cool, crisp beer tingled down Sunday's throat. The shift in topic softened her breathing, and the drink loosened the hand squeezing her chest. In the living room, they leaned over Matty's laptop. Sunday gave him the name her father mentioned in his text exchange with Janice. She ran a hand over her front pocket where she'd tucked his phone away, a piece of her father kept close. He typed Fraser's name into the search engine.

"Jax Fraser is a priest." Matty scrolled through the website glowing on their faces. On the surface, it appeared to be a bulletin board for a church. The posts announced events, and people could comment and ask questions. As he continued to scroll down, though, the posts became more aggressive and unusual. The most recent one read:

THE DEVIL IS AMONG US

The time of reckoning is here, my children. It is our turn to sacrifice for God. To show God our loyalty at any cost. God will forgive. He is all powerful. I will lead you to your salvation. We cannot make it when the Devil is among us, though. Be warned, my children. The Devil is tricky. The Devil must be found and must be obliterated!

"He's enthusiastic," Sunday said.

Matty laughed. "That's a polite way of putting it. He's bat shit crazy, and his church is like some weird cult. The followers who comment on the posts are hanging on his every word."

"Where's he from?"

Sunday skimmed the post and comments as they talked.

"Utah."

Something caught Sunday's eye:

I have seen the face of God. He came to me in a waking dream. He gave me my mission: to destroy those who are servants of the Devil. Only then, when all servants are destroyed, will the gateway to Heaven be opened.

"He sees things." She pointed at the screen. "Like we do?"

Matty looked over the post. "It's possible."

"He's not seeing God, though," Sunday said.

Matty nodded. "Something he's convinced is God, but not the actual big guy in the clouds."

Underneath the post, a comment by HarlowKinsey3 read:

If you saw God, can we see Him?

The comment had hundreds of replies. Matty clicked the "read more" option to expand the thread.

JakelFitz: What makes you worthy of seeing God?

AnnaLogg: He chooses when and where to reveal himself

Rudy_17: Sinners just want. They take and take and take until we have nothing left to give. They deserve to burn in Hell

JakelFitz: Well said. We don't need those people around us. They're toxic.

Rudy_17: We won't let them drag us from Heaven's light

lcnielson: The devil may already be inside her

Hayden1967: "Though you have not seen him, you love him. Though you do not now see him, you believe in him and rejoice with joy that is inexpressible and filled with glory, obtaining the outcome of your faith, the salvation of your souls." 1 Peter 1:8-9

JakelFitz: "Trust in the Lord with all your heart and lean not on your own understanding; in all your ways submit to him, and he will make your paths straight" Proverbs 3:5-6

The comments continued. HarlowKinsey3 was chastised for posing the question to their leader and considered a non-believer. She didn't reply. Matty scrolled through the rest of the site. They couldn't find her anywhere else.

"Seems like an innocent enough question. I want to see the big guy too." Matty closed the thread.

"You're right. It does seem like a cult. I'm thinking this 'HarlowKinsey3' isn't a member anymore."

Reaching over Matty's arms to type, she created a new tab and typed the username into the search engine.

"Maybe 'HarlowKinsey3' is her name. At least, I hope so. It's unique," she said.

The name was indeed unique. Only one person popped up with the name Harlow Kinsey. The rest were websites for Kinsey Designs and news articles about Angela Kinsey. Sunday recognized the star from *The Office*. She scrolled past Angela and clicked on a news article.

CLERK SPEAKS ABOUT ROBBERY

OREM, Utah - Laurence Pilkinson speaks to reporters about the horrors of Friday night. He was working his shift at the Stop and Go gas station when his worst nightmares became a reality.

"They came in all bundled up, hoods up and coats zipped up. I didn't think much of it with it being winter and all. But after doing a walk around the place, they came up to the counter. The woman pulled a gun out of her pocket."

The Caucasian woman, identified by police as Harlow Kinsey, had shoulder-length-blond hair and was described as 5'6" and about 115 pounds. She had entered the gas station with a Caucasian man with a shaved head and septum piercing. He was 6 feet tall and around 140 pounds.

They approached Pilkinson with a box of soda and a gun. After confronting Pilkinson with the gun, they covered his eyes and mouth with tape and tied his wrists and ankles. They were emptying the cash register when a regular, Laura James, entered the station.

"I knew something was wrong. The two people behind the counter didn't work there," James told the reporter.

The woman pulled James over the counter and tied her up beside Pilkinson. They threatened to soak them in gasoline and light them on fire if they tried to call police. Pilkinson heard one of them clicking a lighter.

The pair got away with two hundred dollars in cash. Police still don't know the identity of Kinsey's accomplice. If you have any information about this crime, contact the Utah County Sheriff's Department.

"I wonder if they were just thirsty but couldn't pay for the sodas." Matty chuckled at his own joke. Sunday raised an eyebrow.

The article showed a screenshot of a surveillance video. Harlow was a slim woman, too skinny to be healthy, with matted sandy blond hair. The quality of the camera footage made it difficult to make out any details of her face, but she held the gun to the cashier's face. Another sickly skinny man stood behind her. His arms were out and his mouth opened like he was shouting.

"This happened years ago," Sunday noted. She scrolled back up after finishing the article. "Are we going to find her in jail?"

"You want to find her?"

"I want to ask her questions about this priest." Sunday gestured to the screen. "If she was kicked out of the cult, she might be willing to tell us all about it."

She ran her hand over her father's phone again, which reminded her of the emails. "Hey, Bell mentioned you had locked emails between you and my dad, right?"

He nodded. "It's nothing useful. Just didn't want anyone reading about our Sight. Thought it was best to keep that quiet."

"Sure, but," Sunday pulled the phone out, "he had emails from other people, also locked." She opened the phone and held it out to him. "You think you can get in?"

"I don't know." He tapped the phone's screen and frowned. "This is his encryption, different." With a shake of his head, he returned the phone. "Sorry."

The sound of yelling pulled their attention to the front door. Sunday looked back at Matty, eyes wide.

"Are you expecting someone?"

Matty shook his head. "I told you, everyone else bailed."

It was garbled noise; they couldn't understand the shouting. Matty rose to his feet and Sunday followed close behind him. As they approached the door, the yells transformed into words.

"I'm here! I'm here! I'm here!"

London barreled through the door as soon as Matty unlatched the lock. Her windblown hair stood on end and her cheeks glowed pink. She gasped in the entryway with her hands cupping the back of her head and her chest heaving up and down.

"Did you run the whole way here?" Sunday frowned.

She shook her head. "Just a few blocks. Parking is a bitch!"

London stripped off her backpack and dragged it to the couch. Sunday sat beside her. London pulled her bag onto her lap, unzipped it, and produced a book. Its gold cover was stamped with three symbols, hieroglyphics. No other words were printed on the hardback front.

Sunday's eyes jumped between the book and London. Her gaze narrowed as she watched the woman sit on the couch beside her flipping wildly through the pages. She glanced at Matty, who shrugged his shoulders and shook his head, clearly ignorant. Sunday waited for an explanation; after none was given, she prompted her.

"I thought you were going into hiding?"

London exhaled loudly. She sat up from her hunched position over the book, giving an exaggerated eye roll. "I had a disagreement with my girlfriend. She was the one who wanted me to go into hiding. Worried about my safety and shit."

"How callous of her," Matty said sarcastically.

London snapped the book shut and dropped it on the coffee table.

"I know. I know. Her heart was in the right place, but she just doesn't get it."

Again, Sunday and Matty waited for more explanation. However, London seemed to believe she had explained enough. She reached for the book again.

"Doesn't get what?" Sunday prompted.

"Well, first, that hiding doesn't seem to be working. Didn't work for Janice, or your dad. Second, that I would be abandoning you guys. Like a soldier leaving his platoon. I couldn't do that."

"So you convinced her?" Matty said.

She scoffed. "No. She's too stubborn for that."

"But you are here," he said.

"We're both stubborn asses. I packed a duffel bag and left while she was taking a piss. I don't think she'll be there when I get back." She grinned at each of them, with a glint in her eye that left Sunday feeling uneasy. "I guess I should say *if* I get back."

London ran her fingers over the embossed book cover. "I've had it since I was a kid. All the mummies and mythology fascinated me." She picked at the frayed corners. "Glad I held onto it."

She flipped to an earmarked page. On the left side a colorful illustration of a woman stretched over the top half of the picture, her feet resting on one end and her hands resting on the other, like an exaggerated bridge pose. Her skin was colored in shades of blue with dots of white scattered all over her body, giving her the appearance of the night sky. Underneath the sky woman a green man lay between her feet and hands. He peered skyward with his own arms reaching for her. The man lay beside the Nile River, surrounded by colorful bushes and shaded by a tree. Standing over the green man, a final figure made of wispy lines had his hair blowing in the wind. The figure, a man, stood like a pillar, holding the sky woman up. Opposite the illustration, the chapter began, the title reading: *Mythology*. London read the text underneath out loud:

"The Egyptians were polytheistic, meaning they believed in many gods and goddesses. There are countless gods and goddesses in the ancient Egyptian cultures, each with their own tale, but a few stories are repeated in ancient writings:

1

"The first is the story of creation. The ancient Egyptians believed that Ra, the sun god, created their world with his grandchildren, Geb and Nut. Ra discovered a prophecy: Geb and Nut would be the end of his reign over the world. When Geb and Nut fell in love, Ra forced them apart. Geb became the god of earth, and Nut the goddess of the sky. Shu, Ra's son, was given the task of keeping the two away from each other. He was the god of wind. Like all prophecies in the ancient stories, though, Ra and Shu were unsuccessful in keeping the two apart. Geb and Nut had a son, Osiris, whose sister (and wife) tricked Ra out of his reign, making Osiris the new king."

"Skip ahead," Matty interrupted. "We don't have time for a full history lesson." He pulled the book from London's lap, slipping through the pages. "I just want to know what happened to the gods." His eyes scanned the page, an index finger tapping another passage before he read out loud:

" ...no god should sit on the throne. Instead, man will have a piece of soul from a god, and he would be the rightful king of Egypt. Through that piece, the gods would have one final connection to Earth. So the gods became stories and tales, all powerful and just out of human reach. They judged the dead and protected the living. The ancient Egyptian gods lived on through the people in Egypt and beyond."

"So I have a theory." London scooted to the edge of the couch, leaning closer to Matty. "I think all of us with the Sight have a piece of an ancient god's soul in our blood line." She grinned. "We are the descendants of kings and queens!"

Sunday took the book from Matty's lap and flipped through it. She admired the illustrations, stopping to read the text if the picture interested her.

"Very cool." Matty leaned back and rested his feet on the coffee table. "Who are my subjects?"

"I'm serious." London rolled her eyes.

Matty nodded and sat back up. "I know. I see what you're saying. It sounds good, but how does that help us not get killed?"

She shook her head. "That's where my theory ends."

"Hey, I've seen her."

Sunday pointed to a painted profile of a woman with a cow head. In the typical ancient Egyptian painting, the woman was pictured in profile and wore white robes. Sunday couldn't mistake the cow head and headdress, though. It was the same spirit visiting her at home. Even in the picture, Sunday felt the spirit's tranquil presence. She ran her fingers down the image, warm to the touch like she was touching the actual goddess. Who was she?

CHAPTER 18

"That's Isis," London said.

Sunday raised her eyebrows. Isis. The same name from Janet's letters and mentioned in Hasan Carver's text messages to her dad. She must have the same connection her father had. Was Shu an Egyptian god too?

"Where have you seen her?" Matty asked.

Sunday shrugged.

"Around. Outside of my apartment. In my dreams. I also heard a man mention it to my father." She pulled the cell phone out of her pocket again and explained what she'd discovered going through his phone.

"Could that mean that Isis is in Sunday's blood line?" Matty looked to London.

She shrugged. "If my theory is correct, maybe. Is she threatening, like the Hounds?"

Sunday shook her head. "I think she wanted to help. She doesn't speak, though. Just stands there. Naked."

"Weird," Matty said.

"Hot," London said.

They hunted Harlow Kinsey online and found an address listed in Nevada.

"You think she's still there?" Matty scanned the online white pages.

"It's a place to start." Sunday gathered her small purse off the couch.

She was leaving the state again with London and Matty, and it surprised her that she didn't hesitate. She watched the others get ready to leave. Matty closed the laptop. London closed her book and held it at her side. Her trip to California had been riddled with panic and anxiety. She'd gotten into the car with strangers to break into a dead woman's apartment. How could she trust that they'd have her back, trust that they wouldn't hurt her? But now, she realized, the thought of Matty in the driver's seat and London behind her felt safe. When had they stopped being strangers and become her friends? With the Girdwick? The ambush? Did it even matter?

London met Sunday's gaze and smiled. She returned it. The trust she put into the two of them felt like a harness while rock climbing or a seatbelt in a car.

"You ready?" London asked.

"Completely." Sunday hitched her purse higher on her shoulder and led the way to the front door.

"London has an overnight bag," Matty continued, his voice carrying from his bedroom down the hall. "I'll grab mine, we stop at Sunday's for hers, then we're off to Nevada."

London grabbed Sunday's arm as they walked through the front door, pulling her to a stop. She stared ahead with narrowed eyes. Sunday followed her gaze and saw a black sedan parked a few houses down the street. A man sat in the driver's seat, but Sunday could only see the back of his head.

"I saw that same car at my house," she whispered.

"What car?" Matty joined them in the doorway.

"The black one." London nodded in the direction of the vehicle. "I swear, it's the same car. I noticed the license plate because the letters were b-u-t. It just caught my eye."

Matty chuckled. "Butts."

"Are you five?" Sunday scowled. He shrugged.

"Guys! Focus. Some car is following me." London tightened her grip on Sunday's arm. Sunday patted her hand.

"Let's just go," Matty said. "We'll see if the car leaves too."

They piled into Matty's beat-up Honda. As he reversed out of the driveway, the women kept their eyes on the sedan. It remained parked at the curb. The man in the driver's seat didn't move. At the end of the block, as they turned right to get out of the neighborhood, the sedan rolled forward.

London slapped at Matty's shoulder.

"It is!" she yelled. "It's following me!"

"Cut it out!" Matty pushed her thrashing hand away. "I'll make random turns. We'll see if the car is still behind us."

They turned onto a busy road.

Without signaling, Matty turned right.

The sedan followed.

They pulled into a shopping center and rolled past the shops.

The sedan parked at the end of the shopping center.

Matty continued back in the direction they had come from.

The sedan pulled out of the parking spot and continued tailing them.

"Slow down," Sunday said. "I want to try to get a good look at the guy. We can go to the cops."

Matty decelerated. The sedan stopped a lane beside them at a stop light. Sunday recognized the driver as he stared back through the driver's side window. The distinguished Officer Bell wore cliché aviators, hiding the exact location of his gaze. He raised an eyebrow over the sunglasses and his nostrils flared. The light turned green and Bell's car inched forward.

"What the—" Matty leaned over London in the passenger seat.

"The cop is following us?" London flung both arms in Bell's direction.

The car in front of Matty rolled and Matty lurched his own car into motion again. They sped past Bell.

"He saw us, right?" Sunday studied Bell's black sedan as they drove by him.

Her stomach twisted. Wasn't Bell the good guy? Why was he following them?

Matty turned the car toward the interstate. Bell didn't follow.

"Do you think he has been tailing me since Jaime and Gail?" London pondered after the stop to pick up clothes and a toothbrush at Sunday's apartment.

"Maybe." Sunday balled her hands in her lap. "He definitely knows where we live."

"He's just trying to figure out what's going on." Matty glanced over his shoulder before moving to the middle lane on the highway.

"Why's he following us, though? We haven't done anything illegal, right?" Sunday turned to London.

"Unless you count breaking into the crime scene in Monterey." London shrugged.

That was illegal. Sunday no longer thought of snooping in Janice's apartment as a break-in, but just as another clue. She couldn't believe how much of a mess her life had become.

"What did he say when he interviewed you about Jaime's death?" Matty asked.

"Oh." London scratched her cheek. "That was interesting."

"Mm-hm," Matty urged her to continue.

"Bell called my shooting an act of self-defense. He went over what happened with me like a half a dozen times. I think he believed me in the end. I asked him what was going to happen with the men who attacked us. They had the guy I shot, but the others had gotten away. If they could get that guy to talk, they could work out a deal where he'd plead guilty to everything. Then we wouldn't have to testify. I didn't get the impression the guy was talking much, though. Bell was on edge."

"Isn't he always?" Sunday asked.

"Well, yeah, but even more so. I saw the shooter on my way out. They had him in a holding cell. It was strange. He looked like such a regular guy, like he would be an accountant or engineer, and he wouldn't even know how to shoot a gun."

"Did he say anything?" Matty asked.

"He was praying."

"Praying?" Sunday frowned.

"On his knees, elbows on a bench, palms together, praying. Spoke to the Lord, asked for forgiveness. It creeped me out. I was expecting some large man, tough military type, maybe scars, at least a scowl, something that makes him the bad guy, but he was just…" London paused with a shrug, "normal."

Matty and Sunday nodded in agreement. When no one responded, Matty flipped on the radio.

Sunday looked over her shoulder. She didn't see Bell's car, but she couldn't shake the feeling that she was being watched.

The drive dragged on in its monotony. By the time Sunday took her turn at the wheel, not even the view could provide entertainment. The expanse of the desert went on as far as she could see in every direction, all cracked earth, dry spiny plants, and cloudless skies. London kept herself busy on her phone. Matty dozed in the back seat, his head laid against the rest behind him, mouth slack, breathing deep. She glanced at London from the corner of her eye, unwilling to ask her new friend what she could possibly be doing for hours with the screen lighting her face, but at the same time desperate for a distraction from the horror of her life.

They pulled into a motel. It had taken time to locate Harlow Kinsey. Her address in the white pages was incorrect, as well as her forwarding address. At that address, a small house in desperate need of a new porch roof, a woman suggested they go to an apartment Harlow frequented.

"You're not looking to hurt her, are you?" The middle-aged woman who had answered the door raised her painted-on eyebrows. She brought the cigarette resting between her fingers to her lips while waiting for their answer.

"Of course not!" London frowned.

"We just need to ask her some questions. We need her help," Matty added.

The woman took another drag from the cigarette and shrugged her shoulders. "She's been staying at that motel there since Benny kicked her out." She pointed to the two-story building across the street. Without bothering to wait for the trio to answer, she shut the front door, lock clicking.

"So what are you guys thinking?" London asked. "Are we going to knock on every door asking for Ms. Kinsey?"

Sunday shrugged. They sat in a parking spot with a view of the front of the motel. The rectangular building had two levels with rooms lined up and down the long side. Second-floor visitors could step out onto a balcony and walk to either end to get downstairs. Under the balcony, an office glowed in the evening light, a room surrounded by windows.

"Seems to be the best plan we got," Matty said.

"Wait." Sunday pointed at a woman in a tight black pencil skirt and gold-sequinned top walking slowly on six-inch heels across the parking lot. "Is that her?"

The tall woman limped to the stairs at the end of the building. The chain strap of her purse swung close to the ground, the bag itself clutched in her hand. Her hair used to be tied in a bun, but now it hung limp, pieces of hair coming loose from the bun and gathering around her neck.

London scoffed.

"God, I hope so," Matty said.

Sunday reached for the car door.

"Wait," London interrupted. "Just Sunday and me, okay Matty?"

"What?" Matty's hand mirrored Sunday's on the door handle. "No way, I'm not letting you guys go in there alone."

"And you don't think she wouldn't be wary of three strangers approaching her? She'd blow us off. I'd do the same."

"I don't know…" Matty's hand remained on the door.

"She's right," Sunday said. "And we won't be alone. We'll have each other."

"Exactly." London winked at Sunday. Sunday felt good having the young woman beside her, a friend.

"I guess." His hand slipped into his lap.

"You wait here." London opened her own door. "Be ready, like a getaway driver."

"Okay," Matty called after them as they climbed out of the car, "but be careful!"

They caught her just as she approached the stairway. The humming light above them glowed orange.

"Harlow Kinsey?" Sunday asked.

The woman turned around. The bags under her eyes and wrinkled leathery skin screamed hard life. She could have been thirty-five or sixty. She stared at the pair through half-closed eyes, her shoulders drooping.

"Yes?"

"We just have some questions for you," London said.

"We really need your help," Sunday added.

Harlow stood up straighter. She raised her eyebrows and looked down at them over her nose. Eyes now free from the heavy eyelids, Sunday saw their striking blue color.

"What do I get out of it?" she sniffed.

Sunday shouldn't have been surprised by her answer. Of course she wanted something.

London didn't miss a beat. She pulled a couple twenties out of her back pocket. Harlow snatched the money from her hand. She fanned the two bills out quickly, and then shoved them into her purse.

"Okay," she said as she turned back to the stairs. "You mind if we go inside to talk, though. I want to get out of these shoes."

The setting sun left Harlow's room in shadow. As Sunday followed in behind London, a musty disinfected smell enveloped her, like no clear air had actually entered the room in a decade. A small table sat beside the door, with a chair positioned on either side. Harlow flipped on the lamp on the nightstand and bounced onto the bed to remove her shoes. The thin bedspread sported reds and pinks with a tropical flower pattern.

"Have a seat." Harlow gestured to the chairs and tossed her shoes on the floor. "I'd offer you water or a drink or something, but I don't have anything."

"That's fine," London said.

"So what do you want to know?" The gaunt woman flexed her feet and wiggled her toes. She squinted at a brown stain on her blouse, then scratched at it.

"We were hoping you could tell us anything you know about Jax Fraser," London said.

Harlow's fingers froze over the stain, but she didn't look up. The dim room hid her expression.

"Jax?" Her voice squeaked. She cleared her throat. "How do you know him?"

Sunday's stomach twisted into knots. They filled her up to her throat, making her breathing shallow. The smell of stale cigarette smoke wormed its way through the disinfectant in the room. Harlow adjusted her seat on the bed, jostling her purse. It popped open, revealing cash overstuffing the bag for a moment before she hurried it closed again. Was she a prostitute? A tremor shook Sunday's body. She sensed the danger in the room and scanned the shadows for any otherworldly beings. Anything that could hurt or help, but they were alone with Harlow.

"We don't know him," Sunday whispered.

Harlow stood up and crossed her arms.

"We read about him," London said. "And saw your username in the comments."

"So you also saw that I was kicked out of the church."

"I'm sorry to hear that," London said.

Harlow put her hands on her hips and cocked her left hip to the side. "You here for the damn details or somethin'? Why you bringing up such a shitty part of my life?"

That was a shitty part of her life? Sunday frowned at her, then scanned the room again and pitied the woman. She had a feeling Harlow hadn't been given much of a chance to escape the hard road she took. She took a deep breath to push the knots back into her stomach.

"We wanted to know more about Fraser's teachings," Sunday said, more confidently this time, though the knots were still twisting up her chest. "What he preaches about."

"He talks of the end of the world." Harlow let her arms fall to her sides. Her shoulders hunched over again, transforming her back into a small, broken woman. "The unworthy and ungrateful will drag human-kind down, but He will rise again." Her gaze rose to the ceiling, blue eyes glossed, trance-like.

"God?" London's voice brought her back.

"Not God," she spat. "*Him.* The All Powerful."

"Does He have a name?" London sounded like a teenager inpa-tient with her mother. Sunday half expected her to roll her eyes.

Harlow's narrowed eyes gazed sharply at them. "We are not wor-thy to hear His name." She spit the words at them like venom.

The knots continued to twist in Sunday's stomach. It wasn't the shady motel room. Something else was wrong. London sensed it too. She flicked her gaze in Sunday's direction. Her lips pressed together, but her eyes were calm. She raised her fingers up, gesturing to Sunday to wait. Sunday trusted her. If London felt she could get more out of this woman, Sunday would help her. She nodded and London looked back to Harlow.

"We aren't worthy," London agreed. "But is there a way to become worthy?"

Harlow seemed to forgive them for questioning her. She dropped her eyes and shrugged.

"How did Fraser know about Him?" London continued.

The corners of Harlow's mouth turned up, her childlike grin half hidden behind the stringy hair that had fallen over her face.

"The All Powerful would talk to Jax. He showed Jax His world, another world. And His power. The All Powerful was searching for worthy humans to help spread His power to our world. Jax was the chosen one and he guided us to join the All Powerful too."

Another world? The Other World? Who from the Other World talked to him, though? Something powerful. Something that wanted to get into their world. Sunday couldn't imagine it being a benevolent power, and it had a direct connection into their world through Jax.

"He saw creatures?" Sunday asked.

Harlow frowned. "How do you know he saw creatures?"

"Well, you said Jax heard Him," London said.

The woman pondered this. She drummed her fingers against her hips, frowning as she thought. Nerves continued to quiver in Sunday's stomach. London reached across the table to lay her hand on top of Sunday's. Sunday took a shaky breath. London's soft warm palm soothed her trembling fingers. She wanted to wipe her own sweaty palms against her jeans, but she didn't want to leave London's grasp.

"I guess." Harlow bit her lower lip. Her eyes jumped to them, each movement rigid, robotic. "Jax wasn't like the infidels, though. He saw the creatures because He needed him to."

"Infidels?"

"The heretics. Traitors to humankind. Like Judas and Hitler." She shook her head and her loose bun slid further down her head. "They didn't want Him to return, to save us. They'd rather the world stay as it is, where children starve, women are beaten, and men are sent to jail. They sit pretty in their two-story houses with a yard and kids while others suffer. They're selfish, ya know. What the hell do they have that I don't? Why do they get to decide whether He can return to make Earth better for everyone? They don't. That's why they have to be eliminated."

The word hit Sunday in the gut. She gasped. Eliminated? "You mean killed?" she whispered.

"Good riddance." Harlow stepped closer to them and leaned over the table, forcing the window open, then dug through her purse. "Either of you have a lighter?"

London pulled one out of her back pocket and held it out. The woman leaned forward, cigarette between her first two fingers and her lips. London released the flame and Harlow lit her cigarette.

"That was my job, ya know." She spoke between puffs. Smoke spilled out her mouth and nose. "We were called the cleanup crew. Jax would give us a name of an infidel and we'd eliminate them."

"How?" London asked.

Harlow shrugged and blew smoke at the ceiling. "Jax created a community. We all worked together. I'd never been around so many people who cared. I arrived with nothing, ya know, and these people gave me clothes and food." She shook her head. "Then I had to open my mouth. It's always gotten me in trouble, ya know, my mouth. That's why my ma kicked me out, why Taryn left me, and why the church asked me to leave. They asked me." She scoffed and took another drag. "Fuckers were so kind, even when I screwed up, they asked me to the door and gave me money to help me outside."

A car alarm sounded outside. Harlow looked past them, out the window. She pressed the lit side of the cigarette against an ashtray by the bed, left the butt in the tray and then sat back down on the bed. Her eyebrows furrowed.

"I never mentioned creatures, right?" she asked. "I only told you about the All Powerful."

"Sorry?" London asked.

Harlow stood up slowly.

"The creatures you asked about. How did you know about them?"

"I—" London started.

"Do you see them?" Her gaze bounced between them.

London squeezed Sunday's hand. Sunday pressed herself against the back of the chair. In the small room, Harlow approached them with only a few steps. The door soon became blocked by the woman, with Sunday and London cornered in their seats.

"Ya know." Her smile spread across her face. She giggled like a schoolgirl. "If I kill a couple infidels, they might let me come back." Tears filled her eyes. "I could go home."

They were infidels. The others who saw the creatures but didn't want the All Powerful to leave the Other World. She was like the men who killed Jaime and the stranger with the ax. Seer killers.

"We can't see them." Sunday's voice shook.

"Liar!"

Her wide eyes bulged out and her face reddened with her scream. The veins on either side of her forehead protruded and she leapt at them with her teeth bared. London's hand was yanked from Sunday's. Harlow knocked her from the chair and landed on top of her. She howled and clawed at London's face. With each blow, she grunted like an insane animal.

CHAPTER 19

"Infidel!" Harlow Kinsey screeched.

Sunday acted without thinking. For once, her chest didn't have a chance to tighten in panic. Her breath flowed into her lungs unhindered, and oxygen pumped to her brain keeping her thoughts clear. She wrapped her arm around the mad-woman's waist to throw her off London.

Harlow clawed at London while Sunday yanked her away. She dropped to her knees with the manic woman flinging her arms and legs latched against her chest. With London no longer in her grasp, Harlow turned at her waist and raked her nails down Sunday's arms and face.

"You're one of them!" She screamed over Sunday's cries for help. "You'll burn in Hell with the devil!"

Sunday unlatched her grip on Harlow's waist and scrambled out from under her. Harlow fell to her stomach. She pushed herself to her knees and stretched her arms out for Sunday's boots. She had become a rabid dog. White spittle gathered at the corners of her mouth and dripped down. Her eyes glazed over and burned. She tracked London and Sunday. Sunday pressed her body against the wall opposite the door. The woman crawled closer. Sunday kicked her wiggling fingers away from her. Harlow crawled closer. The motel room shook. A crash pulled Sunday's eyes away from Harlow.

London stood behind her, crouched over with her hands wrapped around the motel lamp. She tugged at the chain keeping the lamp latched to the wall.

Sunday bounced her eyes back to Harlow. The woman jumped to her feet. Sunday thrust her arms in front of her, landing them on Harlow's face. Her fingers pressed against Harlow's nose and forehead, into her eyes, but Harlow continued pulling at her clothes. She shrieked and moaned. Sunday swung a leg. Harlow jumped back, grinning an evil grin. Sunday held her hands out, bracing herself for the next attack. She'd aim better this time, land a kick in the woman's stomach.

Harlow crouched, then launched herself at Sunday. Her arms and legs spread wide to latch onto her like a spider monkey. Sunday envisioned the woman stuck to her face like in the *Alien* movie. Harlow would scratch and suffocate until Sunday couldn't fight her off. She smelled sour sweat, unsure if it belonged to her or the woman landing on her. Just as Harlow's scream blasted her ears, just as her legs clamped onto either side of Sunday's hips, a *thud* silenced the room.

Instead of attacking, Harlow fell against Sunday. Her shriek became a whimper. She pressed her hands against Sunday's shoulders to push herself up.

Another thud.

The grip on Sunday's hips loosened. Harlow fell to the floor. Sunday stumbled against the wall.

"Come on." London held out one hand. Her other squeezed the freed lamp.

Sunday stepped over Harlow. She stared at her back, searching for a sign of breath. London tugged on her hand. Harlow groaned. London raised the lamp and Sunday lurched for the door, yanking it open with her eyes still glued to the woman pushing herself up on her hands. London and Sunday jumped through the door.

"Shut it!" London waved the lamp in front of her.

Sunday slammed it shut. Her toes stepped in the shadows of London's heels as both women raced to the stairs. Sunday peeked over her shoulder to see the door yanked open again.

"Go! Go! Go!" She shoved London in front of her.

Their feet slammed on the concrete steps and they thundered down.

Matty waited at the bottom of the stairs with the car. Had he heard the yells? How could he, they were upstairs behind a closed door. She didn't bother asking questions. She climbed into the front seat and whipped her head behind her when she heard Harlow's scream.

"Burn in Hell, cunts!" She clambered down the stairs.

Sunday smacked the lifted door lock down. Matty put the car in drive and hit the gas before Sunday could reach for her seatbelt.

"Holy shit!" London gasped.

Sunday turned around. London was twisted in her seat, peering out the back window. A dozen Hounds growled and barked behind them. Their red eyes glared at Sunday through the car window. The ratty fur on their backs stood on end. Their bony tails whipped, sending cracking sounds through the quiet evening air. A dozen Hounds. Sunday had never seen so many, and now they all raced behind the car, chasing them. How did they know they had the Sight? What threat were they to the bad omens?

"Where did those come from?" Sunday wheezed. She forced a full breath into her chest.

"They hunted, looking for us." Matty glanced between the rearview mirror and the road. "You two hadn't been gone five minutes before I saw the first one cross the street and stop in front of the car. The others quickly followed. I was surrounded."

London frowned. "I think they hunted me on my way home after Jaime died." She glanced over her shoulder. "I didn't think much of it, just thought I was careless in watching it, you know, distracted and tired from the day and didn't play it off well enough that I couldn't see the Hound. It lunged at me. I made it to my car pretty quick and drove off, but could it have been actually targeting me?"

"Sounds possible," Matty said.

Sunday noticed a tuft of hair fluttering in the wind at the base of the car's antenna. She could only imagine the condition of the front bumper. She looked through the rear window again. The forms of the Hounds grew smaller. The car engine roared as Matty drove them away faster.

"Why were you guys running?" Matty asked.

"That nut job attacked us," London explained from the back. "Didn't you hear her screeching after us?"

Sunday had only just noticed the gash running from underneath London's left eye to her jaw line. It could have been a tear streak, except instead of tears it dripped blood.

"Are you okay?" Sunday gestured to the wound.

London waved her off and continued sharing what happened in the apartment. "She was crazy. Talked like Fraser was a god."

"He's working with something from the Other World," Sunday said.

They couldn't get the information out fast enough. Sunday's heart pounded in her ears. Adrenaline pumped through her body. She vibrated in the seat.

"So we are dealing with someone human?" Matty asked.

"Yes," Sunday said.

"No," London said at the same time.

"Well, which is it?"

"Both," Sunday said. "Fraser is working with something from the Other World. Harlow called it the All Powerful."

Matty let his foot soften on the gas and the car slowed closer to the speed limit. The flat Nevada scenery flew by them in an orange haze. She looked at the clock. After seven. Her body grew heavier. Her limbs stopped vibrating and became heavy blocks attached to her body. Her head pounded behind her eyes. The panic missing in the motel room now landed in her chest again as if Harlow were still sitting on her.

She closed her eyes and focused on breathing.

"This feels impossible," London said from the back seat.

"I know," Matty replied. "We'll figure something out."

"Will we, though?"

Sunday opened her eyes. London's gaze jumped between the two of them, eyes wide and brimming with tears.

"We can't win, can we?" She shook her head, dropping her eyes to her lap. "What choice do we have? What is plan b or c or whatever? We might as well join Fraser's cult."

Matty scoffed. "What do you mean? 'If you can't beat 'em, join 'em'?"

London wiped her eyes with the back of her hand. "I mean, I kind of see where Harlow was coming from. She's been royally screwed over by life and if this All Powerful can help, why not let it?"

"London, it's helping kill people," Sunday said.

"How do you know? Maybe it's just Fraser sending his followers out. The All Powerful may just be desperate for help."

Matty raised an eyebrow and found London's eyes in the rearview mirror. "What do you think? Want to join a cult?"

London shoved Matty's shoulder. "Cut it out. I'm serious, kind of."

He scoffed again. "I get it. There's a lot we don't understand. It looks bleak, but we're not joining the side that kills people."

London licked her thumb and rubbed it over the blood on the back of her hand.

"It's a shame, though," Matty said. "I hear cults throw amazing parties."

London smiled and the mood lightened. She sniffed back the remnants of her tears, used the rearview mirror to wipe the last of the blood from her face, and then pulled her phone out of her pocket. The car now cruising closer to the speed limit, Matty flipped on the radio. The joke seemed to break the tension, lessen their panic. Matty had a way of bringing just enough humor into a situation to relieve the stress. Sunday's own breathing slowed. Her limbs grew heavier as the adrenaline seeped from her body. She pondered a nap before she had to run for her life again.

•••

"How are you doing over there?" Matty said.

Sunday jerked awake. She rubbed her eyes and sat up straighter. "I'm good."

They turned onto the freeway, heading south.

"Where are we going?" London asked

"I've got a real idea of what to do next. I know someone who can help us out," Matty said. "He might be able to tell us what was going on with the Hounds, might know more about this Fraser."

"Who?" Sunday asked.

"My dad." Matty sighed.

"Are you sure?" London's phone screen still shone up at her face, but she no longer watched it. She understood something that Sunday did not.

"Do you have a better idea?" Matty said.

London didn't answer.

"I'll be okay," he continued. "We see each other over the holidays without killing each other. I think I can manage one visit."

"Where's your dad now?"

"California. He's living with his new girlfriend, I think."

Sunday wanted to buy an actual map and track their route. They'd started in Arizona, driven to Monterey, back to Arizona, Nevada, and then California again. The map would be a spider web with all the back-and-forth.

LA traffic lived up to the hype. The air conditioning stopped working halfway to California. When London took over driving, she rolled down all the windows. Sunday leaned against the passenger door. Heat radiated off the asphalt, mixing with the smell of diesel, no relief from the warm evening. Despite the hot air, the open window relieved the suffocation from sitting in the car for hours on end.

"Are we there yet?" Matty groaned from the back seat. Sunday agreed.

"No," London snapped. "Four more exits."

Matty moaned and dropped his head against the headrest. The car inched forward another foot.

Sunday watched the traffic beside them, an assortment of trucks, vans, and sedans. They hadn't talked much since they'd agreed to go to Matty's father for information. Matty had grown unusually quiet. Even after he'd been relieved of his driving duties, he had stared unblinking at the road ahead of him, his clenched jaw visible as he ground his teeth to nubs.

London had moved to the back seat again when Sunday had taken her turn driving. She had watched the top of London's blond head. Her face never rose from her phone screen. Her fingers never stopped scrolling and tapping. How could she start to question them? London knew some of the story, as much as Sunday could make out from their cryptic conversation.

As their destination loomed closer, the idea of going blind into the situation made Sunday's palms sweaty. Did she need to brace herself for a man shriveled by heroin, or maybe some freaky half-human, half-creature from both worlds? Scenarios raced through her head. Traffic only freed her mind up more for her imagination to run wild.

Besides, they'd been through so much together over the short time they'd known each other. Sunday thought of them as good enough friends to ask. A small smile turned up her lips. Friends.

"So what's up with your dad?" Sunday broke the silence.

London raised her eyebrows. Matty sat up.

He sighed. "That's a fair question."

Matty described a partnership between him and his father. Lars Merhi, the Other World expert. A family business.

"I was his pride and joy," Matty explained. "As soon as he found out I was going to be a boy, he dreamed of taking me under his wing, teaching me all he knew. He used to be my hero. Growing up, I adored my monster-fighting dad."

The story felt familiar. Sunday pushed herself off the car door and rested her other elbow on the center console.

"I was a teenager when I began to understand the scope of his business. He taught me the theory of the Other World to prepare me for when I got my Sight. First, there were Tokos. God's gift to Earth, Dad called them. Using ancient magic, he latched Tokos onto potential clients, driving them to the brink. Desperate, they'd do anything to break the curse, pay any price. Merhi, Inc., was ready to help.

"Hounds were a window into the future. The future could also be bought. Dad straddled the border between our world and the Other World, not literally, but still. He's a con artist.

"I left for college and I didn't go back," Matty said. "Dad didn't stop me. He decided my heart was big and it made me too soft."

London took the next exit off the highway. The single lane road rounded up a hill, enveloping them in the shade of surrounding trees. The air cooled and freshened. Outside of Los Angeles, traffic slowed and houses grew larger. Sunday watched the houses through her open window as they continued on the incline. No home looked like another, each one customized for the resident. White plastered homes stood next to stone walls. The sleek shining cars in the driveway boasted the owners' wealth, barely visible behind viny fences and walls. Sunday peered through the small openings, allowing her quick glances into the yards, half expecting a celebrity to walk down the driveway to fetch their mail.

They stopped in the driveway of a two-story house. The large windows shone in the evening sunlight, obscuring any view inside. The second story sat farther back, the empty space in front fenced off into a large balcony. Sunday squinted past the reflecting light of the windows. Through the dark splotches dancing across her vision she got her first look at Lars Merhi.

The dark tone of the man's skin carried the orange tint of an artificial tan. He rested his elbows on the fencing around the balcony. His half-buttoned top fell open, revealing a chest covered in gray curly hair. Large sunglasses protected his eyes from the sunset, and the large gold bracelet around his wrist sent dancing beams of light through the windshield. The only thing shinier than the bracelet was the crystal tumbler in his hand.

"Son?" he shouted from the second floor as the trio climbed out of the car. He lowered his sunglasses to the tip of his nose and squinted down at them. His mouth turned up in a smile. "What are you doing here?"

"Can we come in?" Matty waved his arms.

"Of course. Of course."

His flip-flops slapped on the balcony floor, the noise echoing in the open space around them. Matty led the way to the front door. He held his hand out for a handshake when Lars opened it.

"Dad, this is London and Sunday." He introduced the women standing behind him.

"Nice to meet you." London accepted Lars's hand with a smile. Sunday grinned when he directed his contagious smile to her. His skin was wrinkled by decades in the sun, a stark contrast to his white smile which lifted his cheeks and squinted his eyes in a look of pure joy.

"Come in. Come in." Lars ushered them through the front door and into an elaborate sitting room.

They took a seat and Lars slapped his sandals to a bar cart. A fountain as tall as Sunday lapped in the corner beside a pop art print of Lars's face which stretched from ceiling to floor. The actual Lars poured them each a drink in the same twinkling crystal tumblers he'd held on the balcony.

"Really, Mr. Merhi, we are okay." London waved her hand when Lars offered her the glass. "I can't speak for them, but I've been on the road for days. A drink will put me straight to sleep."

"Then you really need one."

Lars forced the tumbler into London's hand. She accepted it, but left it resting on her knee.

He winked as he handed the tumbler to Sunday. She smiled back before snapping her gaze to Matty. She bit her lip, searching his face for some sort of guidance on how to react to his father. Matty rolled his eyes.

"Dad, we're not here on a social call." He accepted the tumbler only to set it down on the glass coffee table in front of him.

"I know." Lars nodded and sat down on an ottoman opposite Sunday. "I might have a heart attack if you actually showed up just to say hi." He shook the glass in his hand, listening and watching the stone ice cubes bounce around the glass. Then he took a slow sip. "What do you need? Money?"

Matty scoffed. "No!"

Lars shrugged.

Sunday met London's eyes, not the only one uncomfortable in the room. Sunday noted London's stiff posture. She sat perched on the edge of the white chaise lounge chair, the tumbler still on her knee and her eyes bouncing between Sunday and the smiling face of Lars on the wall. Sunday brought the glass to her lips. Might as well. The smooth liquor slid down her throat, calming her jittering stomach.

"We need information about the Other World," Matty said.

Lars leaned back on one of his hands. The gleam disappeared from his eyes, drooping to reveal his age.

"You noticed the killings too?"

All three of them nodded.

"I wondered if you would show up. Glad to see you still have a good head on your shoulders. This isn't a time to be stubborn about a disagreement."

"What do you know, Dad?" Matty sighed.

"I know plenty. But not much of it will help. He's coming back and there is nothing we can do about it."

"Who?" London said.

Lars took a large drink from his glass. "That, I don't know. I know he's old, a being or creature that has been around almost as long as man. I don't know which one he is, though."

"You said that he's coming back," Sunday said. "So he's been here before."

"Of course!" He waved his arms around the room. "They've all been around before. Who do you think the ancient gods and goddesses were? Who started the Trojan War, brought down Atlantis? The beings from the Other World used to roam freely in our world."

"What changed?" Sunday asked.

"It is hard to tell. Ancient writings weren't saved on the Cloud. Most of it wasn't even written down!"

He took another drink. They waited quietly for him to continue.

"Let me start at the beginning." He pulled a napkin off the bar cart and a pen from a drawer in the coffee table and leaned over the table to sketch on the napkin. "So there are layers to the Other World, right?" He drew three horizontal lines across the napkin. "First, you have the WayStation. This is where your soul is judged, a literal way station between our world and the Other World. The Egyptians got this right with the scale and the feather. The spirit is judged on their lives. The Egyptians called Anubis a god, but they're really just ancient human spirits, old and powerful. They all are, the mermaids, centaurs, satyrs, they're all dead humans twisted by the Other World until they become something else, but I'm getting ahead of myself."

He wrote WayStation at the top of the napkin.

"Anubis judges your soul by weighing your heart and that determines where you'll go next. There is the divine level of Arcadia, then the AfterWorld, and finally the LowerLevel. You don't want to go there."

He added the final three levels as he listed them.

London frowned. "So Fraser could be working with a mermaid?"

Lars finished his drink. He held it out to Matty, who took it and poured him a refill. "No. Mermaids aren't nearly powerful enough to contact our world from the Other World. It has to be an ancient spirit, one that ruled our world in ancient Egypt."

"Why Egypt?" Matty handed Lars his glass.

"The veil between our world and the Other World was thin during early human civilizations. The beings of the Other World moved between the two, bringing their power to early humans. There was Dagan and Nergal in Mesopotamia, and the eight immortals in ancient China. They ruled over our world until ancient Egypt. The power led to their destruction, constant fights amongst the spirits, like children."

He clinked the ice against the crystal tumbler and then took a sip.

"It was Set who started the beginning of the end. He warred with Osiris, ruler of Egypt. Killed him, took the throne. Of course, you can't kill something that is already dead. Osiris was trapped in the Other World. From Arcadia, he banished Set from our world and decreed an end to spirit rule. His son Horus was the last spirit king in our world. Osiris strengthened the veil between our worlds and Horus's successor would become the first Seer, his son. All the spirits left a piece of themselves in a human blood line. Their last connection to our world."

He gestured to all of them and then raised his glass for a toast.

"And so we exist. To us."

"So who is Fraser working with?" Sunday asked.

"One of them." He waved his hand in the air. "Whoever's blood runs in his veins. One of them has decided it's time to bring the spirits back to our world."

"Set?" Matty asked.

Lars turned his lips down and bobbed his head side to side as he considered the suggestion. "It's possible. He'd been banished, but he's had thousands of years to get the power he'd need to contact his blood line. If Fraser can combine his blood with Set's, Set would be free to cross into our world, no doubt with plans to rule it again."

"Why would he have a blood line in the first place?" London leaned her elbows on her knees.

"Shit if I know!" Lars scoffed. He took another gulp of his drink. "Maybe it was an all-or-nothing thing. This wasn't exactly recorded for the history books." He tipped the remainder of the liquid into his mouth. "What I do know is Fraser is bringing them back. He's knocking off Seers, cutting off the blood lines of the other spirits so they can't stop him."

"Wait." Matty frowned. "If Osiris strengthened the veil, how do the Hounds and Tokos get in?"

"Those slimy little creatures can slip through any seam. There are ways to cross. You should all understand that, but the ancient spirits stay in the Other World." He grinned. "Until now."

The bird songs outside carried through the open windows as the room fell silent. Sunday studied the napkin sitting on the coffee table. The same theory her father had had. Could it all be true?

"Mr. Merhi?" she asked.

Lars raised an eyebrow.

"What's going on with the other creatures? A pack of Hounds attacked us. A Kappa harassed me too. They're not acting like they should."

He nodded. "I noticed the changes too. The darker creatures, like the Kappas and the Warvils, have turned wild toward me. They're aggressive!"

Just like the Warvils mentioned on her father's phone. Sunday kept the connection to herself, not wanting to interrupt.

"Maybe the creatures are working with Fraser and the ancient spirit," said Lars, "or maybe they're just sensing the change in the air and are losing it, but they're attacking humans with Sight. Well, not just humans. I knew a dog who would frequent the coffee shop at the bottom of the hill with his owner. The German shepherd had Sight! I've seen it in animals before, not very often, but this dog had it! I watched him at that coffee shop. The owner thought the dog barked at nothing, but I saw the Toko or Nymph pulling on the dog's tail. I was ready to offer the old man whatever he wanted so I could buy the dog. That would be good for business, a dog sidekick.

"Before I could make an offer, though, Warvils ate the dog alive. They didn't even wait until he was out of view of people. There was one, then two, then thousands! The dog became a bloody pulp on the sidewalk. I ran away to get away from the screams more than anything."

He shuddered, his hand shaking as he brought the tumbler to his lips again.

Sunday no longer cared what Warvils were. She never wanted to meet one.

"Death has a list," she said. "He can see how many of us with Sight are dying."

Lars nodded. "Makes sense."

"So what are you doing about it, Dad?" Matty sounded exasperated.

Lars chuckled. The rest of them frowned. What was so funny? The man lived in his own reality, one that only he understood.

"You actually caught me just in time, son. I'm heading to Laos in a couple hours."

"Laos?" Matty asked.

"I've definitely not kept a low profile here in LA. All of the United States, actually. I've done work in just about every corner of the country." He chuckled again at a joke that only he understood. "It's only a matter of time until the Hounds, or the Warvils, or maybe even the big guy himself finds me and gets me. It might take the big guy to actually take me down."

He winked at Sunday. She leaned farther away.

"But why Laos?" Matty's words ran together with impatience.

"It's a small, quiet country. Secluded. Almost untouched by the twenty-first century. I figure if I could hide anywhere, Laos should be it." He shrugged. "In all honesty, I don't think hiding is actually possible. Earth is a rat's maze and we're just running around to these creatures. They can see everything. Take anything they like. Remove any rat they want."

He stood up.

"So why hide? Why not fight back?" Matty asked.

Lars laughed, a large belly laugh. Over-exaggerated and difficult to sit through, like bad acting. Sunday leaned further away from the man. London wiggled closer to Matty. Lars watched them, but his eyes glossed over.

"How would you suggest I do that?" He quieted to a chuckle and wiped his eyes dry.

"That's why we came to you," London said. "We were hoping you had an idea of how to fight back."

He threw his head back to finish the drink in his hand. His lips smacked and his flip-flops clanked loudly against the tile as he ventured past them for a third refill.

"There isn't a way to fight back. You don't understand. This is just one spirit from the Other World. Powerful, yes, but he'll open the floodgates from the Other World. Creatures from the bowels of the LowerLevels will climb into our world. There are creatures that can live inside of you, see your inner thoughts, and use that to control you. Before you know it, you'll be taking a steak knife to your wrists, removing yourself from this world for them. There are monsters who are just waiting to feast on your flesh, and then others waiting for your flesh to be gone so they can feast on your soul. Don't you get it?" He looked at each of them, eyes wide and mouth hanging open. "Those with Sight are a threat to the Other World. We can see them for who they really are. And so we will be annihilated."

Sunday shivered. The tiny hairs on her body stood on end and she couldn't shake the feeling that an invisible monster sat behind her. It desired her flesh. She strained to glance back without moving her head. All she saw was the back of the white leather couch.

"Why don't you come with me?" Lars said. He gestured to Matty. "You can bring the girls. They seem like good company. We can live out our days as kings in Asia, beautiful scenery, beautiful women, all the food we can eat. What do you say?"

Without responding, Matty stood up. London and Sunday joined him. Lars stopped him before he could turn toward the front door and rested a hand on Matty's shoulder.

"What are you doing, son?" he pleaded. "Come. This is a time to be with family."

Matty shook his head.

Lars nodded, his lips pressed together in a thin line.

"You're a better person than me. Better than I could be, even if I tried." He followed behind them as the trio made their way to the front door. His shoes continued to slap against the tile. The sound echoed and bounced unpleasantly off the tall empty walls of the entryway. "I don't know how you turned out this way. Your mother and I are both terrible people." He chuckled and shook his head. "Good for you."

London and Sunday stepped out first. Matty turned around to face his dad one last time. Lars put his hand on Matty's shoulder again. The crazed look in his eyes was dulled by tears.

"Good luck," he said.

"Thanks, Dad." Matty turned and left. Lars shut the front door and slid the deadbolt into place.

THE APOSTLES OF THE LORD BLOG
"NO REST FOR THE WEARY"

With Reckoning Day upon us, it is time for the final push. Every day we're surrounded by liars, cheats, and sinners, but don't be discouraged. Remember the plan. Small maggots are not your Goliath. We must cut off the heads of the dragons to destroy the horde.

God has whispered in my ear. I see his shining light. I hear him through the music of my radio. Elvis Presley played after Van Halen, both warning us of the Devil. The street signs glow, guiding me to the doorway. I look past the fire of the non-believers and see the way, and so must you. I have Faith, dear apostles. Follow our Lord and together we will save the world. Reckoning Day is upon us. Don't be weary.

CHAPTER 20

They were silent in the car as they drove back down the winding road to normal civilization. This time around, Sunday didn't crane to see inside the yards of the rich and famous. She watched her hands balled in her lap, taking deep breaths to push down the twisted knot in her chest. Were they really crazy not to run? It didn't seem to do any good either way. She'd rather go down fighting than chased and cornered in Lars's rat maze. She took another deep breath. Better than chased down like a rat. She may be anxious now, but if she hid, she wouldn't get any rest or reprieve. She'd be a sitting duck wallowing in her fear.

"Were we too quick to turn down Lars's offer to go to Laos?" London interrupted Sunday's thoughts.

"What?" Matty frowned. He slowed the car along a sharp curve.

"I'm serious! We have no idea what we are doing right now. We're going to get ourselves killed."

"We'd get killed in Laos, too," Matty scoffed.

"So you admit this is a suicide mission."

Sunday bit her bottom lip. They couldn't hide. They had to try to stop Fraser. She was sure of that, right?

"At least we would be putting up a fight, not hiding like cowards," Matty said.

"At least you would be with your family, not driving around the country going god knows where."

Did London talk to her family? Sunday found herself wondering as the other two argued. London had mentioned her witch mom, Seer dad, and two brothers, but not where they were or whether she talked to them. Maybe that was where London should be. Matty with his dad. London with her family.

But where would that leave Sunday?

Her grandmother came to mind, how Sunday had last seen her not long after she developed her Sight. She had asked her mother if Grandma had always had pig feet. Was that why Grandma wore long skirts all the time, even to the beach? And then her mother had slapped her across the face. Sunday had cupped her hot cheek and her mother's fingers had flung to her mouth. Sorrowful tears had filled her eyes as she backed away from Sunday. And then she had left.

Sunday had no other family, no one to run to.

"Maybe I should just go, then." London's sharp voice pulled Sunday away from her memory.

They'd left the wealthy neighborhood and made it to the bottom of the hill. As the car slowed, Sunday's heart leapt to her throat. Matty couldn't stop the car. London couldn't get out, she couldn't leave, Sunday didn't want her to. She needed these two to stay with her, her friends, the only people she could rely on.

A dark sedan blocked the road in front of them. The driver's door stood open and a man leaned against the frame of the car with his arms crossed. He wore a grey suit, hair trimmed short, with the same grim look on his face as the last time Sunday had crossed paths with him.

Detective Bell remained in the middle of the road as Matty

approached and rolled his car to a stop. The car idled as they watched him from their seats.

"Where the fuck did he come from?" London rested her hands on the dashboard when she leaned forward. "Had he been following us the whole time?"

"Apparently we didn't lose him." Sunday slid herself between the passenger and driver's seat.

"No shit." London unbuckled her seatbelt.

"Where are you going?" Matty said.

"To talk to him!" She gestured toward Bell. "He obviously isn't going anywhere. Do you guys have another idea?"

When Sunday and Matty didn't respond, London climbed out of the car, slammed the door, and made her way to Bell. He uncrossed his arms while London drew near. She stopped in front of him, jutting a hip. Her head rocked side to side while she talked. Bell's mouth appeared unmoving from the distance, but London threw her arms in the air in response to his words.

Sunday took a deep breath.

"I'm going to join her." She turned to Matty. "Are you coming?"

Matty shrugged. "I guess. What else are we going to do?"

London turned her head. She smiled over her shoulder at them as they joined her.

"So we didn't actually lose him on our way to see that lunatic in Nevada," London explained. "He's been following us the whole time."

"You guys have been on quite an adventure." Bell raised an eyebrow and smirked, voice reeking of sarcasm. He didn't seem to believe anything that London had told him.

"I explained why we went to talk to Harlow," London said. "And your dad." She waved a hand at Matty.

"So you guys really have no idea why armed men attacked your home and killed your friend." Bell might as well have been laughing at them, but instead he looked at them like they smelled rancid.

Matty shoved his hands in his front pockets. "We'll still be killed whether you believe us or not. We have to do something."

Bell sighed. He looked to the ground and Sunday followed his gaze. The detective was obviously uncomfortable with the conversation. He avoided their eyes, probably trying to figure out how he should handle the situation. Should he arrest them? Call in a 5150? His eyes were drawn down, but not to the large bug crawling at his feet. He couldn't see it without the Sight.

"I'm not here officially," he said. "Something hasn't felt right since I interviewed the shooters."

"Who were they?" Sunday asked.

"I tracked down Kenny Everett and Nial McClure. One didn't make it out of intensive care. His name was Che Smart."

Sunday flicked a glance to London. She'd killed one of the men. None of them had had any other choice, but London had been the one who pulled the trigger. Was she okay?

"But who were they?" Matty asked.

"Losers as far as I can tell. Nial McClure used to be a lawyer until he showed up drunk at a hearing, a couple of them actually until he was finally disbarred. Che Smart had been picked up several times for possession of heroin. Kenny Everett lived with his mom, worked at a gas station. He had a restraining order put on him for harassing a young woman at a local college. I couldn't find any connection between them. McClure was from New York. Smart from Seattle. Everett lived in Montana."

"Did you talk to them? Did they say anything?" Matty asked.

Sunday squinted to get a closer look at the bug. It crawled onto his brown shoe. Feelers protruded from its head, touching every surface it could reach.

"A whole lot the moment I mentioned a death sentence, but none of it made sense. They seemed to be working off a hit list, called the people on the list infidels."

The same word Harlow had used.

The black body of the bug stood out against the leather shoe, segmented into three round pieces like an ant. Shaped like an ant, but ten times larger, the exoskeleton shone in the evening light.

"They wouldn't name any other names, though. Nobody else on the list or who produced the list. Just kept going on about a new age, a healed Earth, and something called the All Powerful. I thought they could be involved in some sort of cult, but I couldn't find anything in our databases. It must be a new group."

"We know who's leading it," Matty said.

"Actually, I was hoping you did. And hoping that you would be more honest with me, no matter how unbelievable you think your story is. Something weird is going on here, nothing good. I want to help."

As if on cue, the bug turned to Sunday. Large red eyes narrowed, daring her to do something. Sunday scratched at her arm, her whole body twitching and itching at the thought of the bug crawling on her. It opened its mouth, revealing several rows of razor teeth. Its mother of pearl wings fluttered in the sunlight. It bit down on Bell's foot.

The detective shook his foot, not quite aware of why. The thing's insect-sized teeth didn't break all the way through his shoe, but Bell still felt enough of the creature's presence to try to shake it off.

The monster insect lifted its face with a piece of shoe in its mouth. It chewed on the leather, spit it out, and bit again. Sunday frowned. Time moved slowly while she tried to wrap her head around what was happening. Why was it biting Bell? He didn't have the Sight. The next bite made contact with his foot.

Bell yelped and gave his foot a violent shake. His wide eyes snapped to the ground, searching in vain for what had bitten him.

"What was that?" he screeched.

"Warvils!" Matty hopped higher in the air than Sunday had thought humanly possible. He landed several feet back and pointed past Bell, toward the ground behind the detective's leather shoes.

The oversized monster ants writhed down the hill. Their bodies melded together to create a wave of shining mother of pearl. The setting sun left a warm hue on the glimmering Warvil wings. Thousands of red-eyed black insects chomped on foliage and dirt as they inched closer to them. Their razor teeth snapped twigs and scraped against rocks. They crawled over the front of Matty's car, teeth now screeching against the metal hood. When the creatures found the vehicle empty, they moved in tandem, one large motion in their direction.

"Get it off! Get it off!"

Bell hopped around, shaking the foot with the Warvil latched on. It nibbled on his foot, undisturbed by the jolting shakes. Blood coated his shoe. The surface grew more slippery. The thin insect legs of the Warvil struggled to hold on. It lost its grip and flew from his foot. Bell sent the large insect flying in the air. He continued to wave his foot around, not seeing that he'd freed himself from the creature. Finally he realized the biting had stopped and let his foot rest on the ground. His eyes darted, searching the road around him. The invisible menace escaped his view.

London screamed and stomped on the creeping Warvil. She stopped one, but a half a dozen more followed behind it, climbing over the corpse of their fellow Warvil to get to her. Sunday eyed a small group closing in on her. All she could picture was Lars's Sighted dog, the one eaten by Warvils. These creatures intended to eat her. When they were done, all that would be left would be tufts of hair and bone.

"What is it?" Bell pulled his gun from his holster. His eyes never stopped searching the ground. Holding the gun in both hands, aimed down at the ground, he leaned most of his weight on his right foot, the one that hadn't been recently gnawed on by a Warvil. "What was on me!?"

"Warvils!" Matty repeated. "You can't see them."

Bell looked behind him. To the right. To the left. His finger remained off the trigger, but the gun followed his gaze. Something had bit him. He'd kicked it off.

"Give me that!" London held her hand out.

Bell hesitated. His eyebrows came together in a frown. He looked at London, scanned the road, and then looked back at her.

"I can see them. Give me the gun!" She waved her hand impatiently. She leapt backward when a Warvil took a biting dive at her. It missed and landed on the front end of Bell's car.

He growled in frustration but handed the gun to her. London snatched it, clearly comfortable with the weapon. She aimed for the Warvil chomping at the bottom of her jeans. She squeezed the trigger over and over again, easily hitting the one chewing on her and the layer of Warvils underneath. It was like shooting at grass and aiming for a blade. If you missed the one you were aiming for, you would still hit something.

There was too much grass, though. The gun quieted. London pulled the trigger several more times. It clicked. London groaned and threw the empty gun down in a swarm of Warvils. One burst into a gooey lime green mess under the firearm. The rest scaled the obstacle, unhindered.

"Fuck!" She jumped back.

While London shot, Sunday and Matty ran to Bell's open car door. Bell scrambled into the driver's seat and cranked the engine. London toppled in behind Bell, climbing over him to get to a seat. The moment her legs lifted off his lap, Bell slammed the door shut. London fell onto the passenger seat face first. Sunday kicked at a couple of Warvils that had climbed in after them. Her shoes left the same lime green stain on the car floor.

"Where do I drive?" Bell looked at the two in the back seat through his rearview mirror.

Sunday watched the Warvils swarming from the hill. The black wave continued crawling from the shadows, never ending. Where should they go? Did it matter? Away. They should drive away.

"Down!" Sunday pointed toward the freeway.

The monster insects surrounded the car. Dozens of them managed to climb up the back of the car and over the rear window. Their teeth scraped against the glass. Bell placed a heavy foot on the gas pedal and reversed away from the swarm. They left a trail of green goo behind them; the Warvils trapped under the rolling tires didn't stand a chance. The few that had managed to climb on had nothing to hold onto and slid off the metal frame as the car picked up speed. Bell spun the car around, slammed on the brakes. Sunday was flung forward as he put the car back in drive and roared forward. Sunday slumped back in her seat, too exhausted to reach for the seatbelt.

Bell flew down the freeway, driving well over the speed limit. He continued without any direction from the others. Didn't ask for it, and they didn't offer. London's eyes watched the speedometer. Sunday's flashed between Bell and London's face, searching for some hint of their speed. How worried should she be for their safety on top of the attacks of Other World creatures? She suspected they were easily going over a hundred.

"How's your foot?" London nodded toward the pedals where Bell's bitten foot sat heavy on the gas.

Bell grunted, almost a gruff chuckle, like he wanted to laugh at the craziness, the unbelievability, but he couldn't quite bring himself to it.

"What's a Warvil?" he asked instead.

London and Sunday looked to Matty, the only one who knew the name.

"Other World insect," Matty said. "Carnivores. Nasty."

Bell grunted again.

"Why'd the Warvil attack Detective Bell?" London asked. "He isn't a Seer."

She looked to Matty, but he didn't have an answer.

"It bit him when…" Sunday frowned. That couldn't be the reason.

"What what?" London asked.

"When he said he was going to believe us, to work with us."

"Like it knew what we were saying?" Matty narrowed an eye, unsure.

"That would be one smart bug," Bell said.

"I don't know." Sunday tugged on the hem of her T-shirt. "Could've just been a coincidence."

London's face crumpled. She covered her eyes with her hand and faced the window.

Matty leaned forward to rub her shoulder.

"If you need to cry, then cry," Bell grunted. "This is fucked up. Cry for me too."

London sniffed and shrugged Matty off. He sat back and her shoulders shook with silent sobs.

Sunday turned to the window and watched the road soar by her. Well after rush hour, there weren't as many cars on the road. The sun had disappeared behind the hills, giving off enough light to tint the sky, but not enough to light the road in front of them. Other Los Angeles drivers flicked their headlights on. The red taillights or brake lights illuminated Bell and London's faces. Bell avoided cars by staying in the far right lane and swerving to the shoulder when cars didn't move over for him. He weaved through traffic with ease, as if his responses were automatic. Although his eyes were narrowed, he glared at the road, and his lips were pressed together so tightly they appeared flush with his skin, Sunday doubted he focused on the road. He pondered the Warvils, their story, attempting to wrap his head around it.

"So is this the same world where the gunmen's All Powerful lives?" Bell asked.

"Yes," Matty said from the back seat.

Bell shook his head. "Who are you people?"

London stared at her lap. She answered with a shrug. "No one."

Sunday nodded in agreement. "We're just people who happened to have the genes that see these creatures. Kind of like if we happened to be born with eyes of two different colors."

"I can give you the short version," Matty said. "You'll have to suspend some disbelief, though."

Bell nodded. They took turns, adding what they knew about the All Powerful being plotting to take over their world. Sunday explained the vision of Isis, and her friendship with Reap and the information he had provided. Matty added his knowledge of the creatures and the Other World, explaining how they had just left his father's house before they were attacked by the Warvils. London described Harlow's attack and the information she provided. Bell listened. He asked a few clarifying questions, but mostly just listened without comment.

"Sorry about your foot," Matty said after they had made it back to the present in their story.

Bell shrugged. Sunday saw him shift in his seat as if he were flexing his foot below the steering wheel.

He shook his head. "That's an incredible story. You all sound nuts."

His frowning eyebrows shadowed his eyes, still narrowed and glued to the road. He gripped the steering wheel tightly. Sunday let out a slow breath. He wasn't going to believe them. He was going to take them off to jail for god knows what. There they would be sitting ducks for Fraser and all the Other World creatures trying to kill them.

"What if I don't believe you?" he asked. "What happens then?"

"You let us out of the car," Matty said. "We'll find another way to get to Fraser."

"What are you going to do when you find the guy?"

"Stop him."

Bell grunted. Sunday wiped her sweaty palms against her jeans, afraid to do anything that might turn Bell against them, like making a sudden movement would scare away a wild animal.

"So you say this Fraser guy is in Utah?" He raised one eyebrow.

Matty snatched Sunday's hand and squeezed it. Sunday looked at him. He smiled, eyes bright. Sunday lowered her shoulders and relaxed her clenched jaw.

"Don't get any crazy ideas back there." He looked at them through his rearview mirror. "I'm not saying I believe all this crap about different worlds or dimensions or whatever the hell this is. But you do have something here with Fraser. He's up to something and there are people dying. I'll help you look into this, but if this gets hairy, we're backing down and calling in local authorities. Understand?"

"Yes, sir," Matty said.

Sunday widened her eyes. Could the police help? What if Fraser succeeded in bringing the All Powerful to their world? How could the police fight what they couldn't see? How would they fight as Seers? And Matty had agreed so readily. He squeezed her hand and she looked at him again. He shook his head, curt, almost imperceptible, but Sunday couldn't have imagined it. He agreed. Bell would help. And when things got hairy, they were not backing down.

Bell pulled off the freeway and slowed at a stoplight. The sun had disappeared completely and the sky had darkened. Sunday had never thought Los Angeles would be empty, but the roads off the freeway were deserted.

"I just need to stop and look this Fraser guy up." He gestured to the large screen on the car's dash; it took the place of a CD player and radio that would be in any other car.

They pulled over and the three of them watched Bell search Jax Fraser. The screen worked like a tablet. Bell typed Fraser's name into a police search engine. A short list of names glowed on the screen. Bell clicked through the first few, the ages of the men not matching their description. The fourth on the list slowed Bell's scrolling. Jax Fraser, resident of Spring, Texas, used to be a youth leader for a local Catholic church. According to church records, he was no longer employed.

"Does it say why he doesn't work there anymore?" Matty asked.

Bell shook his head. "That would have to be something we ask the church. I have his most recent address. I say we head to Texas, go to the church, and then decide our next steps." He twisted to look at all three of them at once. "I'm not acting as an official detective. You hear me? My bosses wouldn't exactly be on board for this wild goose chase, invisible monsters or not."

Sunday nodded. Matty and London followed suit.

"Good," Bell muttered. He turned back around and started up the car again. His fingers tapped the large screen again, switching off Jax Fraser's information and opening the navigation system. He typed Spring, Texas, into the search bar and put the car in drive.

CHAPTER 21

Dr. Morris,

Wow. When was the last time I wrote you? Feels like a lifetime ago, but it's been less than a week. Just taking a moment to process this. I feel like I'm being pulled in every direction. To fear and terror, then to anger, then to determination, and then exhaustion. I don't have the energy to even write to you. The thoughts are buzzing in my head, but my hand moves heavy across the paper. I promise to reach out if I survive this. I'm sure I'll need more therapy.

• • •

The church could have been pulled out of a picture book. The red brick façade was shaded by white paneling. Light shone through a small circular stained glass window, and a bell tower gleamed over the tip of the roof. Sunday imagined it ringing while their parishioners filed inside wearing their Sunday best.

They walked across the parking lot. London dragged her feet

beside Sunday, her gaze on the pavement. Sunday wondered if London still wanted to leave. She hadn't mentioned it since they'd been interrupted by Bell and the Warvils.

"Listen," London began, like she had read Sunday's mind.

Matty looked at them over his shoulder with an eyebrow raised. He pressed his lips together. London scratched her arm without meeting either of their gazes.

"I'm sorry about earlier," she said. "I just freaked out a little back there."

Matty scoffed. Sunday frowned at him and patted London's shoulder.

"It's okay," she said. "A freakout is understandable."

She said the second part for Matty's benefit. He shrugged and turned back around. London lifted her eyes off the ground and gave Sunday a smile. "Thanks."

It was Wednesday afternoon, only a small group climbed the church steps in front of Bell. Three women listened intently to a curly-haired blond woman between them. She waved her arms, describing a small fender bender that had occurred earlier in the week.

"My seatbelt locked, so when I flung forward, it nearly cracked a rib!" The blond woman wrapped a hand around her waist. The small woman beside her gasped. She continued, "I didn't know what to do. I just rolled to the curb and sat there with my hands shaking against the steering wheel. I could see the car that hit me pull over too, and do you know who climbed out?"

"Who?" The same small woman hung onto the blonde's every word.

"You'll never guess!"

They turned down a hallway once they entered the church, taking the answer with them. As Bell led the way into the pew-filled hall, the surprised exclamations of the women carried back to them. Sunday watched them as they disappeared around another corner. Inside the meeting room a woman dusted the ornate stage at the end. She didn't respond to the four of them entering, instead continuing her work and quietly singing along to the music playing in her earbuds. London found the directory, pointed them toward a Father Antonio's office, and they left the woman undisturbed.

Father Antonio was in his office, his back to the door. His knees were pressed to his chest as he crouched down, running a finger along books. The bookshelf covered half the wall opposite the door. The priest, dressed in navy slacks and a pressed white shirt, stood up with two hardbound books in his arm and turned around.

"Hello." He smiled and set the books on the desk. "Did I forget a meeting?"

His smile spread to his eyes where crow's feet had formed in the corners. Sunday assumed he didn't actually believe he forgot a meeting. She, Matty, and London all looked like they hadn't showered in days. She could feel the grease in her hair when she touched it. Her clothes had been stretched out and were stiff from days of wear. All three of them trailed a smelly cloud behind them wherever they went. Bell would have been the only one presentable except for the bottom of his pants leg splattered with blood. Despite their appearance, the man smiled politely at them.

They sat down in the chairs around his desk. He sat across from them and set aside a pile of thick folders before giving them his full attention.

"We have questions about a former priest at your church." Bell's thick eyebrows furrowed and his mouth was set tight. He stared at the man of the cloth in front of him with narrowed eyes. "Jax Fraser? Do you remember him?"

Sunday watched the priest for a reaction. His face darkened. Father Antonio's eyes no longer smiled, though he maintained a small grin on his lips. "I'm sorry, who are you?"

Bell pulled out his badge.

"You're from Arizona?" Antonio handed Bell back his ID. He leaned his elbows on his desk and entwined his fingers together in front of him.

"I'm investigating Jax Fraser. He's a person of interest in a case I'm working on." Bell followed Antonio's eyes toward the other three in the room. "They're with me."

"Please." She spoke without thinking, taking the lead because she knew what she could do. She'd relate to the man, believer to believer. Father Antonio believed in God and Sunday believed in the Other World, but they both understood worship and conviction. With her friends behind her and her father's faith in her heart, Sunday laid her hand on the father's desk. She begged him with her eyes and he looked back, genuinely trying to understand her request. "We need your help. It's important, or we never would've bothered you."

Father Antonio sighed. His face sagged, revealing the wrinkles of age and stress on his face. He leaned back in his chair. "Of course I remember Jax Fraser. He used to be a favorite at the church, always brought smiles to people's faces."

"What happened?" London asked.

"The change was subtle. Fraser began constantly reading his Bible. When I asked him what he was doing, I thought he'd tell me that he was catching up on next week's sermon, or he felt God's desire for his devotion. Instead, he watched me with dodgy eyes. He looked around the room, his room, like he was searching for someone. I swear he looked like he was searching for approval, permission to answer my question. Then he leaned in close to me and whispered. He said that he was missing something. I couldn't get him to explain what he thought he was missing or what he thought he was looking for. The whole encounter made me uncomfortable, but I admit, things got busy around the church and I forgot about it."

Antonio looked at each of them slowly with his eyebrows raised, then went on.

"We had to let him go when his sermons began scaring the parishioners."

"What about his sermons scared them?" Bell asked.

"He called for—" Antonio paused, sighed, and shook his head. "He wanted the parishioners' help in punishing non-believers. They were a threat to God. And when I invited him into my office to talk about my concerns, he continued his ramblings. He demanded a witch hunt, calling for the death of infidels. He wasn't even talking about the Catholic God."

"Who was he talking about?" London sat up straight with her hands on her knees to lean closer to the father.

"He called his god Set." He looked down and shook his head.

Sunday frowned. She wasn't concerned or even surprised that Fraser had gone off the deep end and began frightening people. It was just as Lars had said. Thousands of years of biding his time, obtaining power, and now Set wanted back into their world.

London solved the problem for her. "Set? As in the ancient Egyptian god?"

Father Antonio nodded. "I didn't know what to make of it at first. One moment he was talking about God's plan to punish the sinners. Then suddenly instead of God's plan it was Set's plan. Instead of God showing us the light, Set showed us the light. He was inconsolable. I was afraid I'd have to call the police if he didn't calm his screaming."

The phone rang. At first they all stared at it. The machine pulled them out of their trance. Antonio finally reached across his desk to answer it.

He greeted the person on the other line. Sunday waited impatiently as he discussed an upcoming summer event for teens. He turned his chair away from them to talk, so he couldn't see her eyes boring into his head, willing him to get off the phone.

"Sorry about that." He spun back and hung up the receiver. The small smile was back on his face, this one reaching his eyes. "We have an event this weekend, a lot to coordinate."

He took a moment to reposition himself in his seat. The smile faded again.

"I'm willing to guess that Fraser didn't stop his unusual behavior since you did remove him from the church," Bell said.

Antonio nodded. All evidence of the animation he'd had while talking about the upcoming teen event was gone.

"At first, I just reassigned his sermons. I was happy to allow him to stay at the church, completing his other clergy duties, those that did not involve talking to parishioners. I caught him about a month later. I came back to pick up my phone charger. Apparently Jax had been holding his own talks after church hours. He had about a dozen people in the room listening to him spew his nonsense about another world filled with powerful beings and how they will rise and take over our world. It was crazy talk, and people were listening to him." He messed with a stapler on his desk, tapping the top against the bottom gently. "I had to call for help, hoping to get him into a hospital, to get the help he needed. The last time I saw Jax, though, he was pacing in front of the church." His shoulders slumped forward as he shook his head

"And how long ago was that?" Bell asked.

He thought about it for a moment. "About three months ago."

"What happened to Fraser?" Matty asked.

Father Antonio shrugged. "He moved, didn't stay long after the church let him go. By that point, all the Catholics in town either feared him or hated him. Still had a couple dozen people following him, though."

Now more like hundreds, Sunday thought.

She scanned the rest of the room. Father Antonio's desk sat in front of the large bookcase he'd been searching through when they entered. The sun beamed through a window with a view of a grassy courtyard. The walls were covered with framed pictures of youth groups surrounded by hand-drawn pictures of Father Antonio and church saints, each labeled with a name and date written in childish scrawl. No Warvils or Hounds. The church had rid itself of Jax and his darkness, wiping their hands of it after releasing him to the rest of the world.

"Do you know where Frazer is now, Father?" Bell asked.

Father Antonio shook his head. "I wish I could help you more."

Bell thanked the priest for his time, standing up to leave. Sunday and the others followed him.

"Wait a second, I just remembered something."

Antonio pushed himself off his desk, stood up and walked back to the bookshelf. The wooden crate on the bottom shelf scraped against the Formica surface when Father Antonio tugged on the handle. He dug past a spare shirt and socks to retrieve a Bible.

"I found this among his things when he left. He left a few things behind, mostly useless junk, but I couldn't let this go." He held the Bible out for Bell. "It gave me the creeps, but I thought that if anything were to happen with Jax Fraser, this would help clear things up."

Bell opened the book. Sunday could make out the scrawled-on pages. Text had been crossed out, words written in the margins. At the end of a section, the blank space on the page had been filled with sketches of Other World creatures, the red eyes of Hounds, the mischievous grin of a Toko. Bell leafed through the pages, his face unreadable.

"Thank you." Bell fished out an evidence bag from his blazer and dropped the book inside. Sunday puzzled over a man carrying evidence bags in his pockets while off duty. Bell continued, "You've been a big help."

Father Antonio nodded. "I'm glad."

Bell explained where the priest could reach him if Father Antonio thought of any new information. Father Antonio accepted Bell's business card and Bell offered him his hand.

"We appreciate your time." London stepped around the chair toward the door.

Bell trekked forward with his hand continually rising to pat the Bible-filled pocket of his jacket. The rest of them followed him back to the car. Once inside, he pulled the Bible out again. All of their eyes fixed on it.

"Are we going to read it?" London asked.

"We have to, don't we?" Matty replied. "It's the only way to find Fraser."

Bell smoothed the plastic bag over the book.

"We don't have another choice," Matty urged from the passenger seat.

The detective grunted and opened the Ziploc seal of the bag. Matty accepted the freed book and opened it across the center console. All four of their heads bent over the book to read:

Who is to say what God is. God was the creator of this world. He was here before man and since man was not around at the creation of the world, then man is left to piece together how our world was created and who God is.

What if we got it wrong. God is not all powerful. God is not above human sin. Despite his shortcomings, however, He deserves to be worshipped and praised. Still, God is not benevolent.

He deserves to be a part of the world He created. Trapped on another plane for thousands of years, He needs a savior. He needs his creations to get him back from the other plane. Long ago, humans had unjustly banished

Him from His world. We have come to believe we are the engineers of the world. We are the decision and creators, the leaders of our destiny.

We are wrong. He's our leader. Our savior. He is our king. Our ruler. To guide us to the world he intended to create. He'll return. It's our duty as His creations to open the door and allow him to return to our world.

The words were scrawled sloppily across the pages in thick black ink over the original text from the Bible. The ramblings of a mad-man swam in her head. Sunday glanced up when Matty turned the page. The sun set in front of the parked car. Bell squinted at the text and his white knuckles held one end of the open book. London checked her phone and then tucked it back into her pocket. Matty muttered under his breath as he started the next page:

He came to me again. In all his glory. I have been blessed by the Heavens. I have been chosen to bring back our Savior from his solitude. I can see the door. He places visions in my head. A graveyard, weakened by superstition. A doorway cracked when the sun crosses the celestial equator. Only then will the window between our world and his purgatory open. Only then can I save him. He needs me. I'll bring Him back to His throne. I'll show him my devotion.

A graveyard had been sketched beneath the text. Rectangular grave markers jutted up across flat land. A large barren tree loomed over them. The bare branches had been sketched with a quick flick of Fraser's pen. Sunday reached forward and ran her fingers over the tree. He'd pressed hard while drawing, leaving divots on the paper. A few strokes had ripped jagged holes in the thin paper. Underneath he traced over the name of the graveyard several times. A couple of the letters cut off at the ripped paper, but it was still readable: *Stull Cemetery.*

"What does he mean by 'celestial equator'?" Sunday reread Fraser's words. That was when the veil would be lifted, when Set could break free from the Other World.

"It's the fall equinox," London said.

"When's that?" Bell asked.

"I'll look it up." London pulled her phone out again.

Matty turned the page in the Bible. Fraser's notes grew more disorganized and frantic. He scribbled "Stull" across the page, writing the word small, large, forward and backward. The letters were sharp and dark. Some he wrote quickly and others he took his time with, writing the name in block letters, shading each. Bell turned the next page. The repetition of "Stull" continued. He released the book to Matty and dragged his finger over the small screen on his dashboard, typing in "Stull."

"Looks like we're going to Kansas." He zoomed in on the map to reveal a small farm town.

"When's the equinox, London?" Matty studied the pages of the book.

"In two days."

Sunday shivered. London's answer echoed in her mind. *Two days.*

London leaned forward to study the screen with Bell. "Who's to say that Fraser is even there? The last time he wrote in this was three months ago. He could be anywhere by now."

"Stull, Kansas, has a cemetery." Bell pointed to the satellite image on the screen. "It's the best lead we've got."

Sunday peered over Matty's shoulder. His fingers traced the scratched-over Bible. Sunday's chest tightened at the sight. She sat back, forcing herself to take slow deep breaths as Bell pulled out of the church parking lot, enroute to the rural town.

CHAPTER 22

The infamous Stull, Kansas, had long ago been deemed evil. Legends of demons and the Devil blended into the town's history. Buildings disappeared. Poor luck plagued the residents with strange and unexplained deaths. Kansas residents called the town the gateway to Hell. Most avoided the evil region. They drove an extra twenty minutes just to circumvent a drive through town. Teenagers visited late at night for a thrill. They clenched their fists and squealed as they rolled past the church and a few shops that lined the only street of Stull. No one ever had the guts to stay through the night, though. Many claimed one glance at the cemetery planted ice in their bones. Their teeth chattered for miles as they fled the town. Braver thrill seekers trespassed onto the cemetery grounds. Enough jumped the small fence surrounding Stull's dead that the town was forced to put up a large gate and lock.

As Bell drove down the road, once named Devil's Road, the town looked abandoned. If Sunday hadn't known any better, she'd have assumed it was a ghost town. The cemetery expanded across one side. The ancient headstones had been hidden by moss, half sunken into the earth. The large black gate shone, a contrast to the decrepit backdrop.

In the distance, a single tree stood watch over the graves. The remnants of a building sat beside it.

Across the street was a modern church and large market. Half a dozen homes were sprinkled around the main road, but no people. At least nobody alive.

One woman stood watch at the end of the cemetery. Her grey skin clung to her bones and her hair whipped around her face in a wind not felt by the living. Instead of human lips and nose, a long black crow beak pointed in their direction. Protruding from her billowing hair were two long ears of a brown rabbit. She stood on long spiny legs that ended in hooves. She turned to them as they approached. Her black, beady eyes saw through Bell's tinted windows. Her gaze washed over Sunday like an ice bath.

Prudence.

The spirit spoke her name proudly. It reverberated in Sunday's head. A grin spread across the spirit's beak, an unnatural sight that stretched what should have been a hard bird beak like it was the flexible skin of what used to be the spirit's face. Sunday shivered.

Prudence Chaderton. Her family was from England, Puritans forced from their home by persecution.

Prudence never felt God like her family did. She never felt His protection. Instead, He bothered her. He spied on her, taking note when she pulled tight-faced Susie's hair in school or kicked the cat and giggled at the thump of the animal hitting the wall.

As she developed into a woman, Prudence fell in love with the Devil. She'd seen visions of his creatures, his children. His power over Hell lit a fire in her loins. She ached for his touch, for his surrender to her.

Some called her a witch. Fine. She was a witch. She fit the description. She was devoted to the Lord of Hell. She sacrificed the family cat to him to demonstrate her faithfulness. It wasn't the sacrifice she wanted to give, though. She didn't care for the family pet. It was a nuisance, a waste of space. Prudence wanted to sacrifice something that mattered.

She'd give her body and soul to the Devil. He'd be hers and she'd be his.

The Devil loved her body. Loved to use it, took pleasure in touching it. She was his playground. His fingers. His tongue. She groaned at night. She ached in the day.

He planted his seed in her. She bore the Devil's child. Prudence cupped her swollen stomach and smiled. She loved the child moving inside her more than the Devil. She hadn't known that was possible.

Her sister ratted her out. Prudence knew it. The cunt couldn't keep her nose out of anyone's business.

"Your bodice seems to be too tight, sister." She raised her eyebrows and judged Prudence's growing abdomen.

Prudence should have bashed her head into the wall right there. That would shut her up.

She would tell the town that her sister was whoring around with Goody Cranwell's husband.

Eye for an eye, sister.

The rope was rough. The bristles scraped against Prudence's delicate neck, a prequel to what would come next. Men and women spat at her feet. They cursed her and her baby. The Devil's child wiggled in her stomach. The fetus knew she was in danger, but there was no way out.

The town cursed them to Hell, Prudence and her unborn child, like it was a punishment for her sins. She laughed, throwing her head back to see the thick branch her rope had been tied to. They were just sending her to her love. The Devil would hold her in his arms for eternity.

She wouldn't let them see that she mourned for her child. She couldn't forgive them for the cold-blooded murder. She was only a fetus. She'd never seen the world. Never harmed a living creature. She'd be slaughtered by the pious breadsplitters of the town. Prudence would reside in Hell with the

Devil, but not with her child. She placed one hand on her abdomen. If she could, she'd keep her baby in her womb forever. Keep her safe from purgatory. That's what the Bible thumpers taught. Unchristened children go to purgatory after death, a fate worse than Hell.

Sitting on an agitated horse with a rope around her neck, Prudence glared at the angry faces around. They screamed their righteous words, but did Prudence ever keep a mother from her child? Did she ever banish an infant to purgatory?

Her heart broke before her neck. A hand slapped the horse's behind. The whack bounced off the gravestones around them. The horse grunted. It leapt forward. Prudence's thighs caught on the horse's hip bones for a moment, but the rope held her in place. She swung back. The rope tightened around her neck. And her heart shattered. She couldn't go to her Love. Not while her child's death went unpunished. Her breath caught in her throat. The rope pulled tight. She cursed them. Until they suffered like her child, she'd stay. They'd regret the day they thought of harming Prudence Chaderton's child.

The rope hung taut. Prudence's head fell forward, her neck broken. The town shuffled their feet. The body of the witch swung. The tree branch creaked. A cool breeze rustled the grass around them, unusually cool for the August evening.

Sunday tore her eyes off of the angry witch spirit.

"That's the ancient church." London pointed to four stone walls sitting on top of a hill beside the large tree. The same tree they had used to hang Prudence. "It was torn down a long time ago. It's said to be a church for witches and Satan worshippers. It's the gateway to Hell."

"Was that in Fraser's book?" Matty pointed to the defaced Bible in her lap.

"Huh?" London tore her gaze off the church. Her fingers brushed against the Bible's spine and she looked down at it, frowning like she had forgotten it was there. "Yeah." She shook her head. "I read it in here somewhere."

"You must've gone through it a dozen times by now," Bell said.

London set the Bible in the empty space between her and Sunday. "Just trying to figure this guy out. He gives me the creeps."

Bell rolled the car down the road between the cemetery and the town.

"The place gives me the creeps." Sunday's stomach shivered.

"Where is everybody?" Bell leaned forward, craning his neck to get another look at the town. Nobody. "It's three in the afternoon, shouldn't somebody be out and about?"

"Maybe they all went through the gateway," London suggested.

"Seems like an appropriate place for a guy worshipping an ancient god," Matty said.

Bell turned off the road. After a long day and a half on the road, he looked for a hotel. No rooms for rent in Stull. An old Victorian house had been converted into a hotel outside of Stull in a town called Lawrence. The moon had shone above them for hours by the time Bell pulled into the parking lot.

The hotel stood several stories high. In the dark, the intricate architectural detail cast the whole façade in shadow. They followed Bell onto the wrap-around porch and into the large lobby. The entry-way opened on either side, both darkened rooms at the late hour. The front desk sat at the other end of the hall. A man at the counter looked up from a worn paperback book when they entered. He smiled and greeted them.

"You're in luck," he informed them as he ran Bell's credit card, "we're almost completely booked. Some convention in town, I guess. We don't usually have so few empty rooms."

They split into two rooms. The man handed them keys. Upstairs, London shuffled into their room in front of Sunday. As soon as she crossed the threshold, she dropped her bag at her feet. A few more steps into the room and she dropped herself face down on one of the two queen-sized beds.

"I miss beds." Her voice was muffled by the paisley printed bed cover. "I don't even care if the obnoxious wallpaper looks like it would give me hay fever. I get to sleep in a bed!"

She rolled over and wiggled her body all the way onto the bed. Her head rested on a couple pillows, propping her up. She grinned at Sunday.

"You okay?"

Sunday dropped her purse onto the other bed. She sat on the end to untie her boots.

"I'm managing," she said.

London nodded. "You'll have my back, though, right? I'm just scared shitless this whole mission is going to get me killed." She scratched her cheek. "I just don't know."

Sunday nodded. What could she say? That she understood. That they didn't have a choice. That their lives were in danger either way. She could go through the myriad of thoughts that had buzzed in her head the entire drive to Stull, but they didn't make her feel any better. Would they be any help for London? She sighed.

"Of course, I'll have your back," she said. "We're in this together, right?"

London nibbled on her bottom lip. "Right."

Sunday kicked her boots off and her bunkmate rolled onto her side and pulled her phone out of her pocket.

"Don't judge me," London said, "but I'm so beat, I'm not bothering to brush my teeth. I'll be asleep in ten minutes, I'm sure."

The glow from her phone illuminated her face. What could she possibly be doing on her phone so often? Texting? Scrolling through social media? Sunday pulled her own phone out of her pocket and switched the screen on. She couldn't remember the last time she'd looked at it. An email notification informed her she'd received spam mail. Facebook advertised events near them. Her lip twitched into a grimace when she saw a half a dozen missed calls from the restaurant. She assumed she'd be job hunting if she survived this. She clicked her phone off and tossed it onto the bed.

Having London in the room with her felt safe. She could almost convince herself this was a childhood sleepover, staying up late, her friend playing on her phone. No tightness in her chest, no worrisome thoughts. Despite the danger, Sunday pondered turning on the TV and watching reruns of some show with London even later into the night.

Sunday ran her tongue across her teeth. What was the last time she'd brushed them? The gritty feeling told her it'd been too long. She pulled her toothbrush out of her bag and quietly locked herself in the bathroom.

The mint toothpaste was refreshing as the toothbrush bristles massaged Sunday's gums. She stared at the corroded faucet as she pushed the toothbrush around her mouth, enjoying the feeling of control. It relaxed the vise grip on her chest and freshened her sour breath. She rested her free hand on the edge of the sink and relaxed a hip to the side. Her mouth filled with toothpaste foam and spit, but she prolonged the process. Her eyes grew heavy and she allowed them to close. Just as her breathing began to slow, something brushed against Sunday's calf.

Her skin attempted to jump off her bones. Her eyes shot open, and her arms sprang out in front of her. The toothbrush hung from her mouth. She spun around. No one stood behind her. Her gaze traveled to the ground. Two baby blue eyes stared up at her. Lavender opened her mouth to meow, but no noise came out.

"You 'cared the 'hit out of 'ee!" Sunday hissed at the ghost cat, toothbrush still in her mouth.

She turned back around and the toothbrush fell from her mouth and bounced in the sink. She shrieked as her hands flew to her tooth-paste-covered lips. Lavender no longer peered up from her from the floor. In the mirror reflection Reap stood next to the toilet with the cat in his arms.

Her heart pounded in her ears. She wiped her mouth with the back of her hand and turned to face her friend.

"Are you trying to give me a heart attack?"

"No," Reap whispered, "but I had to talk to you, in private."

The cat jumped from his arms and brushed its cool body through Sunday's legs.

She put her hands on her hips and cocked an eyebrow. He had to know he was being difficult. "Why?"

"Same reason you're driving across the country. I have had the hardest time trying to find you." Reap gestured in Sunday's direction. A small piece of flesh dropped off his left index finger. Sunday frowned. Reap always had some flesh still clinging to his skeletal form, but it never fell off. It remained there, permanent, like a tattoo.

"What's wrong with you?"

Reap followed her eyes to the spot on the ground where his flesh landed and sighed. "I'm dying."

Sunday frowned. "You can't be dying. You're Death."

Reap chuckled. "Almost poetic. We should really come up with a better word to explain a Grim Reaper's death. Dying makes it a para-dox, don't you think?"

She shook her head. Even if she did understand paradoxes, she couldn't care less about Reap's choice of words.

"How can you be dying?"

He shrugged. The movement sent a few more pieces of flesh float-ing to the ground. A larger piece of his cheek landed with a plop.

"It was bound to happen eventually. Just as every empire must fall, every being must become extinct."

Sunday looked around for a place to sit. She couldn't handle the conversation standing up. Reap stood in front of the toilet. The walls of the bathroom seemed to shift closer around her. She crouched down, keeping her feet on the ground and her head between her knees, hoping to get a full breath in. Extinct. Dinosaurs were extinct. Saber-tooth tigers and mammoths. Not Death. Not Reap. It didn't make sense. As she inhaled, the lemon scent of industrial cleaner burned her throat. She stood back up.

Reap watched her. His lower lip jutted out. When he bit it, a chunk sloughed off.

"You're going to have to explain this better." Sunday pressed her fingers against her temples. "Did you just say you were going extinct?"

"That's the short version, yes." Reap picked at his trench coat, found some sort of fuzz, and flicked it away.

"How?" Sunday shook her head. "Aren't you an immortal being?"

"There have been plenty of immortal beings that have gone extinct. Have you heard of the Julapee? Seen a Cthulhu? You haven't because they've gone extinct. Poof!" Reap made a small explosion motion with his hands. "Gone from existence."

The sink dripped behind her. Sunday looked over her shoulder and then whipped her gaze back to Reap. Her breath caught in her throat. Would he be gone? When would he leave? He couldn't leave. She couldn't breathe.

"But why?"

Her voice cracked. Her eyes were dry, but the sob in her chest suffocated her. Her thoughts moved a mile per second, words formed in her head, and she struggled to get them out. Should she say goodbye? Should she demand an explanation? How could she help? Could she stop this? She had to stop it. He couldn't die. She couldn't allow it.

Reap shrugged. His gaze fell to the ground as he kicked at the confetti of flesh that had gathered around him. "The way the world is moving is making Grim Reapers obsolete."

Sunday frowned. "The world is moving toward no deaths?"

"Of course not!" Reap leaned against the toilet. "But death won't include a Grim Reaper."

She placed her hands on her knees and leaned over.

"I suspect some big guy in the Other World has decided to speed this process along." Reap leaned his weight on one leg and brought his fingers to his chin. "They're not too happy that I've been helping you guys."

Sunday's head continued to spin. She felt sick. She didn't know if she would pass out or throw up. Her best friend was dying. Was he even upset? Her own life was in danger. The weight of Sunday's world closed in around her, pressing on her. She wheezed as her vision darkened. It was happening again. The same attack as before when she saw the Hound at the bar. She was ready to accept it, let the panic overtake her.

That was easier than fighting it.

She was so tired of fighting.

"Oh no, you don't!" Reap grabbed her shoulders roughly.

Sunday pried her eyes off the ground to look at him. He guided her into an upright position.

"Don't let this take over you." Reap squeezed her shoulder with one hand and shook a finger at her with the other. "You *are* strong enough to be by yourself." He smiled. "The monsters don't have anything on you. *You* made you and your dad strong, not him."

Sunday frowned, still struggling to get a full breath in her body. "How do you know?"

Reap's grin grew larger. "The way that man talked about you, how you took the world in stride." He shrugged. "You were his hero. Didn't you see that?"

Tears brimmed in Sunday's eyes. She shook her head slowly. Reap leaned closer, forcing eye contact. His dark eyes blazed with passion, his last fight against his rotting flesh.

"He did you an injustice by keeping you busy with his antique business. I suspect it was fear. Fear that you would leave for a bigger horizon and forget all about him. Nietzsche said, 'The higher we soar, the smaller we appear to those who cannot fly.' You were meant to fly. Your father chose not to."

The hot tears ran down her cheeks. She bit back a sob.

Lavender hissed at the closed bathroom door. They both watched the small ghost cat as a growl erupted from her throat.

"What's wrong with her?" Sunday's throat ached from holding back the tears.

Reap pulled her close. His bony fingers dug into her arm.

"Something is out there," he hissed.

Lavender growled again. She lifted herself on her toes with her fur standing on end.

London was out there. Sunday imagined the Warvils or Kappas finding their way into the room, or one of Fraser's followers. Had they found them? Was London hurt? Sunday had just promised to protect her. She had to get out there.

Reap's fingers pulled her back.

"This is what I came for," he said quickly. "Be careful who you trust. Especially the detective with you. His aura is black."

Sunday's eyes widened. Black. A death sentence at its best. Evil at its worst. "Who is he?"

"I don't know," Reap moaned. "He's not of the Other World.

Maybe he works with Fraser, but he's dark, darker than any human I've seen. I don't want him to hurt you."

Lavender snarled at their feet.

"I have to get out there." Sunday pulled her arm from Reap's grasp. "London needs me."

"Of course." Reap nodded.

Sunday leapt for the door. Lavender howled on the floor in front of her. She couldn't look back. Couldn't say goodbye. Would she see Reap again? But she didn't have time to worry about that. She had to get to London.

CHAPTER 23

A figure stood between the two hotel room beds. Her breath caught in her throat. It was a man, tall and wide. Was it Fraser? One of his followers? Had he hurt London? He stood so Sunday could only see his side. His face was turned toward London's bed. Her view of London was hidden behind the bathroom door. Sunday squinted. The dark room filled with shadows.

She pulled the door shut quietly, closing herself back in the bathroom. Reap and Lavender had disappeared. Sunday scoured the tiny room for a weapon. She settled for the porcelain lid of the toilet tank. It was cold and heavy in her hand. Heavy felt good. Sunday switched the lid between both hands in order to wipe the sweat off of them onto her jeans. The last thing she needed when storming out there to face a crazed killer was to have her weapon slip from her fingers.

Silent and leaning against the door, Sunday didn't know what she expected to hear. The quiet on the other side unsettled her. With the toilet lid in her left hand, she grabbed the doorknob with her right. She squeezed and threw the door open.

The scream erupted from her. She hadn't planned to scream. She couldn't feel her throat vibrate with it, but it rang in her ears, stopped abruptly and, with a grunt, she swung the toilet lid at the dark figure.

Sunday fell forward and landed on the nightstand between the two beds. The porcelain lid banged against the wall and London leapt from her bed. The commotion probably woke the guests next door as well.

It all happened quickly, but Sunday saw each moment like a film had been slowed, revealing each shot. London's eyes leapt open. Sunday crashed down beside her. The man disappeared. London leaned over the edge of the bed. Sunday lay sprawled on the floor.

"Are you okay?" London propped herself up on her elbow. Sunday met her frowning face; London's mouth was stuck open as she took in the disturbed nightstand and toilet lid. "What the hell are you doing?"

Sunday didn't know how to answer because she didn't know what happened. Lavender had growled a warning; a strange man had threatened London. Sunday had stormed out of the bathroom. Her eyes had adjusted to the dark room until she made out a young man. He had one hand raised above the sleeping London with his middle finger thrusted toward her. The sound of the bathroom door opening caught the figure's attention. He had looked at Sunday with the eyes of a snake. She had gasped. A spirit, but the snake eyes hadn't prevented Sunday from recognizing him.

Jaime's thick eyebrows had shaded his golden eyes, burrowed together in a frown. His lips were pursed so tight they formed a thin line over his chin. Sunday had fully understood the phrase: if looks could kill.

She was already running toward Jaime at that point. There was nothing stopping her momentum, so she had continued awkwardly, not sure if she was still protecting London or if she was attacking the unfortunate ghost of a friend. Admittedly, Jaime was a new friend who Sunday had not known very well. Maybe he wasn't the goofy guy she'd thought he was. There was so much hate on his face. Why would a good person carry so much hate?

He had disappeared. Sunday had passed right through his vanish-ing form and fallen into the wall and furniture on the other side of him. The toilet lid hit the wall and she hit the side table. Both she and the lid had bounced loudly to the floor, and Sunday was left to assess her body. Had she broken anything?

She pushed herself up onto her elbows and turned toward London.

"Honestly?" she said. "I have no fucking clue."

After returning the toilet lid to its home and examining a cou-ple new bruises on her arm, Sunday fell onto the bed beside London's. London flipped through channels until Sunday returned.

"I saw Jaime," Sunday said. She left out Reap's visit, his warning fresh in her head. She'd just started to trust her new friends, but Bell's aura was black. Was her judgment that off? She trusted London and Matty. Still did. Was she wrong?

London's eyes widened. The remote control fell softly on the bed beside her and her hands rose to her lips.

"Was he okay?" Her voice cracked. In the dark room, Sunday couldn't make out whether there were tears in London's eyes.

She shrugged. "I mean, he's dead, so probably not doing great. He looked so angry."

"Angry?" London frowned. "Did he say anything? I mean, the communication you have with spirits. Did you receive anything?"

"Nothing much." Sunday ran through the scene in her head. Jaime's angry face, flipping off London. She recounted it for London.

"He looked so upset. I don't know if I have ever seen so much hate in someone."

London didn't make eye contact, but instead studied the thick curtains over Sunday's shoulder. Her hands rested in her lap, her fingers tangling and untangling themselves. Sunday waited for her to explain. London knew something. She had to.

"I had my suspicions," she whispered. Her fingers untangled themselves one last time and she ran her hands down her thighs. "We didn't know what was going on." She finally looked at Sunday. Her eyes were wet as she leaned closer. Words tumbled from her mouth. "You weren't there. No one had a clue. But Gail and I saw it. Jaime would have an unexplainable answer to our questions, and we would look at each other. How did he know?"

Sunday frowned, thinking back to her time with Jaime. "What do you mean?"

"They were just bad feelings. I mean, he seemed all smiles and jokes, but it could've been an act to get close to us. To get information on us, I mean."

"Are you saying that he was working with Fraser?" London was confirming her worst fear. She'd trusted this group of Seers, trusted them with her life, and she'd judged wrong. It didn't make sense. Jaime had the Sight. He was one of them. Why would he be trying to get them killed?

"I hardly believe it myself." London shook her head. "But what other explanation is there?"

"How? Why?" Sunday shook her head.

London shrugged. "The internet. Fear?"

She sighed, thought of her father running away, Lars hiding in Laos. Fear, fight, or flight. Could Jaime have fought for the other side to protect himself? The heavy weight of her anxiety sat on her chest. She couldn't trust anyone. She'd surrounded herself with people she barely knew. Reap had warned her about Bell, and now Jaime?

Her limbs hung heavy at her side. She wanted to get up, leave. She wanted to stay and cocoon herself under the bedsheets. She needed sleep. She needed a break from the terrifying roller coaster she found herself on.

PRAYERS OF JAX FRASER

My Lord, Set, I have found the gate. It was exactly where You had shown me. I will bring You back to rule Your world, to make it great again. I'll stand by You as Your servant, all powerful Set.

CHAPTER 24

Sunday woke to a small light blinking in the top corner of her phone, informing her of a message. She wiped the sleep from her eyes, clicked the phone screen on, and opened the message. It was forwarded from Matty:

Young Mother of Two Victim of Drive By Shooting

Her heart leapt to her throat. The article title glowed on her screen. Her thumb hovered over the link, but she couldn't bring herself to click to the full article.

"Did he send it to you too?" London pulled her eyes from her phone. She mirrored Sunday, her elbow propping herself up, her face lit by her phone screen. "Did you read it?"

Sunday's shaking finger still lingered over the link. She shook her head, eyes flicking back to her phone. A deep breath pushed the panic from her throat. She tapped it.

GILBERT, AZ - Tragedy struck downtown yesterday evening when an unknown culprit targeted a sandwich shop. Witnesses reported a tan sedan stopping in the middle of the road and open-ing fire on the storefront before speeding away. Three patrons were injured and, unfortunately, one was killed.

Authorities are searching for the assailants....

Sunday's eyes scanned words. She couldn't focus on the prose; there wasn't enough oxygen getting to her brain. The words blurred together and jumped lines. Instead, she searched for a name. Did the article name the victim? Any description? Mother of two? Maybe she had blond hair instead of brown. Maybe she had two boys or girls instead of one of each. She reached the end. No name given. Where was Gilbert, Arizona? Still, Sunday's chest squeezed. Matty had sent the message for a reason.

Citizens are left in shock over the random act of violence. "We're a small town. Nothing special," a patron shared. "I just don't understand."

Matty added a note beneath the attachment: *Gin sent me the news. He says him and the kids are fine, with police and searching for a place to hide.*

Gin. Sunday pictured Gail's husband at the hospital, Rose on his lap and a sleeping Jacob at his feet.

"Poor Gail," London whispered. She held a dark phone in her palm.

Sunday blinked to fight off the tears. Her screen went black too. She pushed herself up and leaned against the headboard. The phone was discarded in the tangle of blankets beside her. She stared at the open bathroom door across the room. Images of Reap and Lavender visiting the night before flashed in her mind. Lucho. Her father. Even Jaime. Now Gail. She didn't understand either. Didn't know if she should be scared or grieve. Run and hide or continue on.

She pressed her lips tight. No. She wouldn't hide. Even if she managed to outrun Fraser and his death toll, she couldn't run. Then Gail's death would be in vain. They all would be. She'd find them justice.

Kicking her feet over the edge of the bed, she spoke to London over her shoulder. "I'm sure Matty and Bell are waiting for us." She pulled her boots to her and shoved her feet into them. For the first time since her father's death, since this whole mess, Sunday was taking the lead. She knew what she had to do and felt ready to take it on. She strode to the door. "Come on," she said. "We need to get Fraser."

Downstairs, Bell greeted them in the lobby. "I'd say good morning, but that doesn't seem appropriate. We're going to get this guy." He gestured over his shoulder to the large dining room. "Matty's eating in there."

Sunday slid into the seat beside Matty with a plain bagel. He gave her a curt nod before scooping another bite of scrambled eggs into his mouth. Anger and frustration radiated off of him. He glared at the sugar packets in front of him. How long had he known Gail? She hadn't known her long, unlike the rest of Matty's Ghost Guru crew. Only two of them remained: Matty stewing in the seat beside her and London tapping on her phone screen across from them.

The room buzzed with conversation as other guests at the hotel enjoyed their complimentary breakfasts. Gail's death lingered in the space around them, looming in the mix of silverware scraping against plates and chatter.

"The guy last night did mention they were pretty booked." Sunday nibbled on her bagel.

"Looks like it." Bell took a sip from a steaming mug.

"Why are there so many people, though? Is there a local event or something?" Sunday looked around. Nothing remarkable about the crowd. A couple dozen people sat at tables in groups of two or three.

They varied in age, gender, and ethnicity, an excellent example of the American melting pot, but not helpful when figuring out why so many people were visiting the middle of Kansas. The couple next to them caught Sunday's eye as she scanned the room. The woman with ruffled red hair gave her a small smile. The man beside her wore dark sunglasses indoors. He stared at Sunday with pursed lips. She looked away quickly, but still felt the man's eyes on her.

"They're kind of creepy," Matty muttered. His hunched shoulders straightened and he glared around the room.

Bell nodded in agreement.

"Must be some sort of convention this weekend." London shrugged and took a bite of her bagel.

"I doubt there'd be a convention here. We're in the middle of nowhere." Matty narrowed his eyes. Sunday gazed around the room, unease tugging at her gut.

"I'll take a walk around." Bell stood up with the small white mug the hotel provided for coffee. "Get a refill. See if I overhear anything."

Sunday followed him to the buffet to pick out breakfast. There was a decent spread of fruit and toast and oatmeal. At least she'd have a good breakfast to start the day. She left Bell who had taken his refilled mug and leaned against the door jamb. As he brought the coffee to his lips, he watched the room. He almost looked casual, but his unreadable expression still screamed cop. Reap's warning passed through her mind. Was it all an act? Did he make himself appear official to throw her off, lessen her suspicions? Or was Reap wrong? Did Bell's black aura mean something else? Sunday's shoulders raised to her ears as she navigated back to their table. She pushed them down after sitting. She had to relax.

Bell returned a bit later with his lips pressed tightly together. Sunday chewed on another bagel. He laid both hands on the table and leaned forward.

"You guys done?"

Her eyes followed his to the couple next to them. The man in the sunglasses stared at the whole table now while the woman across from him chattered about the perfect hard-boiled egg.

"—can't keep them in too long because then the yolk gets all dried out." She took a bite of her own egg and examined the inside. "It's really a science."

The man barely nodded. The woman continued.

"I have some eggs left." London pushed her food around her plate.

Bell's eyes moved across the room. He stood up abruptly. His knee hit the edge of the table, jostling the glasses. Matty lifted his glass of orange juice, leaving a ring of spilled liquid behind.

"I'm done." Bell took a step back. "Go up to your rooms and get your stuff. Meet me in the lobby in ten minutes. We need to get moving."

He walked away without another word. Sunday frowned and looked at Matty for some explanation. He just shrugged.

"That was weird, right?" London took another bite off her plate.

"For sure," Matty agreed.

They finished up and found Bell sitting on a loveseat beside the check-in desk. No one was manning it, just a bell left on the counter with a sign reading: Ring if you need assistance!

"Took you long enough." Bell stood up. "I grabbed my bags already. Why don't you get yours? I'll be in the car, meet me there in ten minutes?"

"We're checking out?" Sunday looked from Matty to London to make sure she wasn't the only one taken off guard by Bell's urgent need to leave.

"I know." The only part of his face moving were his lips. His even tone matched his expressionless face. "I'll explain everything in the car. Just trust me, okay?"

The words left a sour feeling in Sunday's stomach. Should she trust him? She couldn't trust Jaime. London met her wide-eyed gaze. She took Sunday's hand and led her to the elevator. At least she had London and Matty. She could trust them. The three of them had been working together from the beginning of this whole mess. Their lives were at stake too. They'd save each other. Matty followed them into the elevator and hit the third-floor button. As the elevator car climbed, Sunday forced a deep breath past the weight sitting on her chest and squeezed London's hand.

In the room, London packed quicker than Sunday, announcing she would meet her at the car. She walked out the door before Sunday could even look up from her own bag. The room grew quiet. She had thought that London had closed the door behind her, but the ding from the elevator and loud voices in the hall told her otherwise. It disrupted the quiet, unsettling Sunday's nerves. With another deep breath, she tucked her toothbrush into her bag, already scanning the room for any items she might have forgotten. A name snapped her attention back to the conversation in the hall.

"—Fraser asked for another meeting tonight. That'll be three extra meetings this week." A young man spoke.

"The fall equinox is tomorrow night. What do you expect?" An older man replied.

Sunday stepped to the door on her toes, moving silently over the carpeted floor. Her heart pounded in her throat. She touched the door with shaking fingertips, wanting it closed off from the two talking on the other side, but at the same time not wanting to draw attention to herself.

Was that why Bell was acting so strange? The other guests were with Fraser? They were his followers. She thought back to Harlow Kinsey. London and Sunday had been barely able to get away from her once she found out they had the Sight. She didn't want to let a hotel full of Harlows know about them.

Frozen at the door, she didn't know what to do. She could stay there, but someone would come looking for her. She should leave. Would anyone notice her panic? How wide were her eyes? How sweaty was her forehead? How pale were her lips? She shoved her trembling hands into her pants pockets.

The pair's voices faded as they continued walking. A hotel room door beeped, unlocking, and the speakers stepped into a room. When the door shut behind them, Sunday was left in the quiet once again.

She strained to hear through the silence. It rang in her ears. The more she listened, the louder it grew; it was dizzying. She couldn't stay at the door forever. Someone would come around at one point, probably London or Matty looking for her because she hadn't met them at the car. And there they would find her, frozen in fear at the door.

And what if they were working with the crazy cult people? Sunday still hadn't figured out who she could trust. Jaime was threatening London in his own spirit way, so Sunday thought she would probably be all right trusting her. Knots still tied up her stomach and twisted her chest. Probably didn't relieve her panic. Probably didn't allow her to trust any of them waiting for her in the car.

She forced the knots lower with a slow long breath in through her nose. She had to get moving.

Her heart still pounded as she tossed her bag over her shoulder and squeezed the doorknob. The hallway remained quiet, but it didn't put her at ease. She pulled the door open. Bright cream-colored walls surrounded her. No talking. No war cries. No one around to see her leave. No one to notice that she had the Sight.

Sunday's blood pumped loudly in her ears as she stepped across the threshold of her room and made her way to the elevator. She might as well have been trying to cross a busy highway; it felt just as impossible. Her neck swiveled. A glance over her shoulder, then eyes forward. Someone was behind her. Another glance at the empty hallway, then eyes on the elevator again. At any second a hand could wrap around her arm. It could pull her back. She stomped to the elevator, stealing glances over her shoulder. No one there. But she still had to check.

Her feet wouldn't move fast enough. She wanted to be in the elevator, the lobby, and in the parking lot. She wanted to be driving away from the cult-infested hotel. But she was still walking in the hallway.

She didn't see it, never would have. Everyone in the dining hall had appeared so normal. They laughed, chatted, and drank coffee. Which one of them killed? Which of them murdered innocent people? Who had hit her father's car?

And what were they doing here?

The couple in the hallway had mentioned the fall equinox, just like Fraser's Bible. Were they all lining up to accept Set as their new god, their leader and father? They wouldn't even be able to see the ancient god from the Other World, would they? And what would happen to Sunday if Set came through the gate of Hell? Or the gate to the Other World? Or whatever it was?

The elevator doors opened. A short man in a white cowboy hat stepped out and gave Sunday a smile. She couldn't bring herself to return it. This man could be the one who had killed her father. She brushed against him as she scrambled into the elevator. Immediately her fingers pressed the door close button. She held it down, holding her breath as the doors slid closed.

She almost let out a breath of relief. No person could fit through the crevice left between the sliding doors. She would be alone in the elevator, safe for the minute or two it took to make its way down to the lobby.

The crevice couldn't fit a person, but it fit a hand. The hand slid in at the last moment. Sunday released the close door button. She fell against the back of the elevator. Her skin kept beat with her thumping heart.

"You got it!" A woman's voice sounded from behind the doors.

They slid open much faster than they had closed. The man and woman who had sat at the table next to them at breakfast now stood in the entryway of the elevator. Just as at breakfast, the woman immediately gave Sunday a large, warm smile before stepping in. Sunday tried to return it, but she didn't trust that her face was doing what she told it to do.

The man stared at her. He no longer wore sunglasses. Pale blue eyes gazed at her, making her want to shrink into nothing and hide behind the woman. He saw through her and inside of her. He knew. She had the Sight. He hunted people like her. She needed to be killed.

"I haven't seen you around," the woman said, making small talk as the elevator doors attempted to close again. "You with the group?"

It could have been a group of knitters traveling cross country, or groupies following a band on their tour. Instead, the group the woman was referring to was a lethal cult that believed the villain of ancient Egyptian gods was meant to be king of our modern world. She smiled at Sunday as if this were the most normal, even mundane, question she could ask.

Sunday shook her head. She needed to speak. She told her mouth to form words. She couldn't look suspicious. But her lips didn't part. No words were spoken. They remained stubbornly pressed together.

The doors finally closed. The woman pressed the button labeled L. The man's eyes never left Sunday. They bored into her profile, watching every move she made. Sunday forced a large breath past her tight chest and tried to speak again.

"No," she squeaked and then cleared her throat to hide her nerves. "We just got in yesterday. Just a pit stop."

The woman nodded. "It's a cute place. I'll have to remember it the next time I'm around."

Sunday didn't attempt to continue the conversation now. The elevator shook when it stopped. She gave the woman a quick nod before scuffling out of the half-open doors. She forced her feet to slow. She itched to sprint out of the hotel, but she didn't want to bring more attention to herself. She wasn't sure how well she was blending in. Her lips must be blue from lack of oxygen, her face pale and sweaty with panic. But no one looked her way as she shuffled toward the exit.

Except for the man in the elevator. His gaze bored into her back. She didn't dare turn around to meet it.

They had all been waiting anxiously at the car. Matty saw her first. Sharp eyes glared at her as she all but sprinted across the parking lot. He threw his hands in the air as an unspoken question. *Where were you?* Sunday felt compelled to justify her tardiness, to temper Matty's frustration. She explained what she had overheard outside her room and how she had worked her way to the car.

"So it's just like Fraser said in his book?" Bell said. "The fall equinox, here in Stull."

Sunday nodded. Her purse felt heavy on her shoulder. She wanted to crawl into the car and sleep.

"Okay. Then we need a plan." He climbed into the driver's seat and started the car, signaling that it was time to leave. As they pulled out of the parking lot, Sunday was relieved to have the hotel full of cult members behind her. "We'll find another place to stay tonight. Be ready for tomorrow."

•••

Sunday couldn't sleep. She tossed in the creaky bed, eventually flipping over to face the motel room door. London snored beside her. Behind London, the clock mocked Sunday. The glowing red numbers inched toward morning. Sunday played the plan over in her head again.

They had stopped at the store and created the same Ghost Guru bag they'd used with the Girdwick: salt, rope, markers, water, flashlights. The next evening, they'd sneak into the cemetery, to the ancient church in the back. They assumed that was where the gate would be open, hidden behind the crumbling walls. All Bell needed was some concrete evidence of illegal activity. They'd hide on the other side of the walls, watch through the windows. At the first sign of wrongdoing, Bell would call the local police.

The plan made her nauseous. They had no idea what to expect. How would Fraser open the gateway to the Other World? How could they stop it? What if they didn't stop it? What then?

Sunday resisted the urge to check the clock again. Knowing and hating what it read felt better than not knowing. She couldn't tell if a minute or hours had passed. Maybe she'd finally fallen asleep and the sun was rising behind the closed curtains. She threw the blankets off her body and kicked her legs off the bed. She couldn't convince herself otherwise. Sleep eluded her; she gave up trying.

Outside, the dark sky hung over her. The thick air hovered around her. Without the sun beating down, the moist air wasn't unpleasant. As Sunday walked across the parking lot, a cool breeze brushed against her skin. The quiet only heard in the middle of the night was peaceful. The trees waved in the small breezes, showering her in the sound of leaves brushing against each other.

Sunday stopped at Bell's dark sedan. She rested her back against the driver door and dropped her head against the window to watch the night sky.

She couldn't do this. How was anyone supposed to stop Fraser from opening a gate to the Other World? Her chest constantly felt tight, and her breathing had been shallow for the last two days. She wasn't sleeping. The anxiety left her exhausted. No rush of adrenaline when facing the enemy. Just a cold sweat and bags under her eyes.

"Reap!" Her words cut through the quiet warm night. Nothing followed. She tried again. "Reap!"

He didn't come. She hadn't really believed him when he said he was dying. He couldn't die. He'd always been in her life, around when she needed him and when she didn't. The only one left she could trust.

Crushing loneliness took whatever shallow breath she had right out of Sunday's lungs. Her legs buckled beneath her and she slid down the car, collapsing on the ground. She tried to take a breath, but nothing could push past the weight sitting on her chest. Without disrupting the quiet night, tears overflowed and ran down her face.

She had no one. No father. No Reap. She traveled with a group of people she'd just met and didn't trust. And none of it mattered. The Other World wanted her dead and they'd probably be getting their way tomorrow.

She inhaled. It wailed out as a sob. Ragged breaths filled her lungs. Sobs heaved out. She gulped, but never felt the relief of a deep breath.

She was alone. She would die alone. No one would miss her when Fraser or one of his followers finally killed her. Her apartment would remain empty. Her landlord would miss her checks. Work would miss her role keeping the restaurant running. Not her.

Dark blotches sprinkled across her vision. Lack of oxygen. She needed to breathe or she would pass out. Air still struggled to get past the crushing in her chest. She dropped her head between her knees.

A hand touched her back. She gasped and flung her head up.

"I heard you leave your room." Matty sat down against the car beside her. He didn't say anything else, just opened his arms to allow her to fall into his chest.

Her sobs were muffled by the stale-smelling T-shirt, the same one he had been wearing for the past few days. But the warmth of his body relieved the panic. The feel of his chest lifting up and down gave her an example to follow. She tracked his breathing, matching it with hers. A shaky breath pushed past her chest and filled her lungs. Then another. She sniffled. Another. Her mind cleared. Her eyes grew heavy.

"It's going to be okay," Matty said once Sunday's sobs quieted. She continued following his breathing with her trembling breaths. "We'll protect each other. You trust me, right?"

Sunday thought over that question. She wanted to have a friend to rely on, someone to have faith in. Why not Matty? He had helped her at the bar, introduced her to his friends, worked side by side with her. Wasn't that a friend? Sunday honestly didn't know, her only friend being an Other World creature, but it felt right. She sniffed and nodded.

"I trust you," she said. The words comforted her, slowed her panicking breaths. No more questioning. She would put her trust in Matty and give him and London reason to trust her in return.

Matty squeezed his arms tighter around her.

"We'll kick ass tomorrow," he said. "I'm sure of it."

CHAPTER 25

How Sunday was going to kick ass on three hours of sleep was beyond her. Now that everyone was up and making plans for breakfast, Sunday hoped that an adrenaline rush would come late in the game. With that and a breakfast sandwich from McDonald's, she might be able to pull it off.

At least, that's what she kept telling herself.

Bell parked in the church parking lot across the street from the cemetery. The gray headstones stood silent behind the tall black gate. The woods beside the cemetery swayed in the wind.

"It's kind of creepy." London looked down the deserted street. "I haven't seen anyone since we left the hotel."

Sunday silently agreed. Last night's quiet had almost felt peaceful. The silence that hovered over Stull was deafening, wrong. She was tempted to walk the mile or so to the next house and pound on the door just to confirm that other people were in fact around them.

The noon sun was blocked by grey overcast. The weather rose to the occasion. The cemetery stood across the street, dark gravestones daring them to come over.

"Are we ready?" Bell looked between the other three.

Matty shrugged his shoulders, enough of an affirmation for Bell. He pushed the door open first. The others followed. With backpacks stuffed with supplies hanging from their shoulders, the mismatched group ventured across the country road.

Sunday didn't know what she expected. Her heart thumped in her throat as they approached the cemetery entrance.

Was she going to be struck down by lightning the second her foot crossed the threshold?

Or would she be overtaken by Warvils and eaten alive, a trap set by Fraser?

Her feet grew heavy as she forced them to take one step after another. She followed behind London and Bell with Matty behind her. They crossed into the cemetery. Her lungs ached for her to let go of the breath she held.

She trudged through the entryway, ready. Hell could shower down on her and she'd be prepared. No turning back now.

Nothing happened. They stood on the other side of the black gates. The breeze rustled leaves in the distance. The graves remained silent, just like the town.

"Anyone else feel like our entrance was a bit anticlimactic?" London wandered between a couple rows of graves.

Bell smirked and followed her. He leaned over to read a few epitaphs.

"There's the church." Matty pointed to the decrepit building. A strong wind led the leaves in a choir again.

A chill ran through Sunday's body and the tiny hairs on the back of her neck stood on end. Her breath caught in her throat. Something was behind her.

She turned around. Along the cemetery gate, Prudence, the witch spirit she had seen when they first arrived in Stull, hovered inches from the ground. Her eyes glowed red like the barista ghost, but her crow mouth still smiled, like her beak was made of warped rubber.

"Guys," Sunday whispered.

The witch spirit raised an arm.

"London, look out!" Matty said.

London leapt away from an uprooted tombstone. Prudence raised both of her arms and smiled at the sky. Stones rained down around them and landed on the cold dirt with heavy thuds. Prudence's laughter echoed in Sunday's head. Her curse rang louder than the others' cries. Sunday pressed her hands to her ears, but she couldn't escape the witch's voice in her head.

Murderer. No baby slayer shall escape my wrath.

"We didn't kill your baby!" Sunday screamed. A stone fell down onto her cheek and she grunted. Sunday touched her face and pulled her hand back to see the blood.

"Let's go!" London snatched her arm and dragged her toward the spirit.

"What are you doing?" Sunday yanked at her grip, but London held tight. "Let me go."

"It's okay."

London continued to pull Sunday toward the witch spirit.

Sunday searched for help. Stones rained down around them, smaller, but they still stung when they struck her. Why was London pulling her to Prudence? She couldn't make sense of what was going on.

She found Matty standing behind the spirit. He waved them along. How had he gotten past her? Matty met her gaze. The same warm feeling of trust washed over her, and she allowed London to pull her to Matty. She'd trust these two. Whether they made it out of this fight alive, she wouldn't have it any other way.

When crossing the spirit, Sunday avoided her cold gaze. Prudence towered over them, red anger beating through her. Sunday dropped her gaze and gasped. The spirit had been encircled in salt. She looked back to Matty and saw the empty bag of salt in his hand. The stones had shrunk to pebbles and the spirit shrieked in Sunday's head, but Prudence couldn't cross the salt. London and Sunday stomped past the spirit and up the hill. Prudence's screams faded and Sunday could hear her own heavy breathing again.

"Everyone okay?" Bell followed behind them.

Matty and London confirmed they were all right. Sunday rested her hands on her hips, her chest heaving up and down, and could only manage a nod. She narrowed her gaze at the detective beside her. He didn't worry her as he had before. Had Reap misread Bell's black aura? Or did she just want to trust him, like the others?

"Should we turn back?" London asked. "Are you sure the spirit didn't give us away?"

"It might've, if anyone was watching the entrance, but we can't turn around now." Matty squinted at the stone church at the top of the hill.

The decrepit building was now just a shell. There must have been windows and steps leading to double doors once. Now, just four walls remained standing, open to the elements from the sides and above. Matty led the way to the stone church.

A few feet up the hill, Sunday's steps slowed. Chanting carried down to them. Soft, barely audible. She stopped walking, eliminating the sound of her feet crushing twigs and dry leaves. She listened.

"Wait, guys!" Matty held his hand out. He cocked his head to the side. His ear pointed toward the church.

"Voices?" Bell asked.

"Shh!" Matty brought his finger to his lips.

"I hear it, Matty." London resumed walking. "We all do. It must be a sign we are going in the right direction."

The rest of them continued their trek up the small hill. As they got closer to the collapsing church, the chanting grew louder. In a foreign language, many voices spoke in unison. Sunday couldn't make any sense of the words. The rhythm left a beat in her stomach. She felt sick.

A stick broke to Sunday's right. Her gaze snapped to her side. The growling stood the hairs on her arm on end.

Hounds stood guard around the church. The black canines bared their teeth. There was no fooling these creatures that Sunday couldn't see them. They knew she had the Sight. They were ready for the hunt.

Growling softly, one of the Hounds narrowed its eyes. Sunday needed to run. Her legs wouldn't respond. She demanded they move. Run. Run as fast as they could. Get away from the supernatural dog. It would tear her to pieces. Her limbs refused to move.

London's scream shook Sunday out of her frozen panic. She didn't look for London. She turned from the church and ran into the adjacent woods.

The Hound's paws cracked and crunched the ground behind her. Each snap of a twig pumped her legs faster. She glanced over her shoulder. It was right behind her. Its mouth hung open. Its tongue flapped against the side of its muzzle. She spun her gaze back in front of her, willing her feet to move even faster.

Branches and trunks littered the route before her. She dove behind a tree. Her eyes darted up and down the trunk, searching for any branch in her reach. Could the Hound follow her if she escaped up?

The wind rustled her hair. Sunday's chest heaved up and down. Her legs trembled from her mad sprint from the Other World beast. Even over her panting she could hear the quiet. No sound of the beast.

She peeked around the large trunk.

No Hound.

She whipped her head around, eyes scouring the woods.

No sound. No sight of the Hound.

It had vanished.

Sunday bent over, resting her hands on her knees, wheezing. Her body became heavy and weak as the adrenaline seeped through her pores. All she wanted to do was curl up beside the tree and sleep. Only the thought that the Hound would be back kept her on her feet.

Matty.

The thought brought her standing again. What had happened to the others? She hadn't even caught a glimpse of them before her mad dash away from the Hound. Did they run too? Were they caught? Were they...

She didn't allow the thought in her head. She took in her surroundings. It was cool under the shade of the trees. They all looked the same. Sunday had heard stories of hikers and campers being turned around by the woods. Surrounded by bark and foliage, there was nothing unique to mark the direction she'd come from. She understood how those hikers and campers would get lost in the woods for days, weeks. She had no idea which direction the cemetery would be. Had she run in a straight line? Or had she turned while winding around trees? With no way to know for sure, she headed in the direction she thought she had run from.

Her eyes bounced from tree to tree, searching for any hint, any landmark she recognized. Out of all the worst-case scenarios bouncing around her head, she never thought she'd get lost in the woods. A crow's cry shook her. She spun around, hand flying to her chest. Her eyes narrowed. Someone was in the distance.

"Hey!" she shouted more as a reflex. What if it was one of Fraser's followers? What if it was Matty or London? The figure didn't answer.

She walked toward the person. People should mean cemetery. As she got closer, she could see the sun breaking through the shade of the trees. Her feet slowed when she realized that she was approaching something not human.

The figure faced her. Sunday recognized the Cow Woman. The spirit's tan skin contrasted with the green around her. The Cow Woman raised an arm when Sunday stopped walking and stared at her with white glowing eyes.

Peace washed over Sunday. She closed her eyes, euphoria giving new life to her body. When she opened her eyes again, the woman was pointing away.

"I should go that way?" Sunday thrust her thumb in the same direction.

The naked woman nodded slowly. Another wave of calmness enveloped Sunday, like a mother's hug. She actually felt her lips turn up in a smile.

"Thanks." She started in the direction the woman gave her, giving her a small wave as she walked on. A crow cawed above her again. She looked back. The woman was gone.

Her heart now settled into a normal beat. Sunday took a deep breath, inhaling the smell of rotting foliage and dirt, enjoying the sound of the ground crunching beneath her feet. The Cow Woman's visit left her thinking clearer. She reflected on their plan, which really just consisted of showing up at the cemetery and hoping for the best. Sunday rolled her eyes.

What were we thinking?

A voice sounded to her left. Sunday froze.

"I can't believe they got away." The voice was clear and close, the words disheartening. Was someone out looking for her?

Sunday took a slow step back. Just moments ago, the sound of dried leaves under her feet had been pleasing; now it was the crinkle of a candy wrapper, of a forbidden treat. She didn't let her heels touch the carpeted floor of the woods as she made her way to the nearest tree and ducked behind it. The voice was joined by another. Sunday pressed her back against the tree, holding her arms tight at her sides. She forced her breath to soften and strained to view the scene behind her through her peripheral vision.

Two sets of footsteps stomped near her. She crouched low, knowing full well that the skinny tree trunk didn't cover her completely.

"They can't have gone far," a woman continued. "Right, London?"

Sunday gasped. Had she heard her correctly? London?

The pair grew closer. Sunday peeked around the tree. London and another woman split up, moving in opposite directions, obviously searching for Sunday as they craned their necks to peer around trees. Sunday stared, mouth open. What did this mean? It couldn't be true. How could London do this? She'd get them all killed.

Sunday ventured another step back. They'd find her eventually.

Her heart had to have been her strongest muscle at this point. She couldn't remember a single day lately when it wasn't trying to pound its way out of her chest. She kept her eyes on London. Her friend now reapproached the woman.

"They won't go far. They need to stay close to keep the doorway closed," London said.

Sunday took another crouched step back, and her toes landed right on a dry twig. She felt the snap in her stomach. It reverberated out through each limb.

London's head whipped around. The woman peered around her and both of their gazes landed on Sunday.

"Sunday." London's voice was hushed.

Her eyes grew big and round, and her mouth hung open as she

stared at Sunday. Every moment they'd had together ran through Sunday's mind. Her companionship when they confronted the Girdwick in the farmhouse. The camaraderie when the gunmen attacked. Their friendship as they trekked across the country to save their own lives. Sunday had been comforted when London snored in the bed beside her. Her panic had eased with each of London's deadpan, sarcastic remarks. She never reacted. Always remained calm. Now Sunday understood why.

The other woman chuckled, pulling Sunday's eyes away from London. "We actually stumbled on one of them!"

London shrugged. She wrapped her arms around her chest, fingers picking at the shoulder of her T-shirt.

Sunday stood with her hands on her hips.

"Why are you working for Fraser?" It didn't make sense. She had the Sight.

The other woman rested an arm on London's shoulder, cocking her head to the side and giving Sunday a smirk. Her dirty blond hair framed her long face. Her features were narrow and delicate, but her eyes burned with glee. "Sucks, huh?"

London shrugged her off, her gaze set to the ground.

"Nothing to say?" Sunday raised her eyebrows.

The woman turned to London when she still didn't respond. "You okay?" She put her hand on London's arm.

London shook her head, then raised her gaze to meet Sunday's. "I told you guys we should join Fraser. It was a death sentence trying to stop him. But you wouldn't listen."

Sunday thought back to her comments. *If you can't beat 'em, join 'em.* She thought it had been a sick joke.

"I wasn't going to walk in there to be killed," London continued. "I knew you guys wouldn't listen to reason. I did what I had to do." Her eyes fell to the ground again. The woman reached for London's shoulder, but London shrugged her off again. "Let's just get this over with."

She stepped closer to Sunday, hand outstretched to guide her back. Sunday jerked away from her fingers, glaring at her friend. The other woman stepped in front of them and pulled out a gun.

"Is that necessary?" London hissed.

"Yes." The woman narrowed her gaze on Sunday and gestured with the gun for her to start walking, keeping it pointed in Sunday's direction. "Let's go."

As much as Sunday resented being herded back to the rubbled church, she felt satisfaction listening to London's heavy footsteps behind her. She saw the last few weeks in a different light. The constant texting. Had London been talking to this woman? Did she text Fraser's other followers? How'd they meet? Probably online. London was the social media expert. Did London actually believe in Fraser's cause? She couldn't. Sunday understood London's survival instinct, but her body still grew hot at the thought of the betrayal.

She glanced over her shoulder at the woman urging London to speak, fuming as she watched the face of the woman she had thought was her friend. How stupid was London? How did she expect this all to end?

Jaime knew. That was why he had visited their hotel room. That was why he was so angry. He knew the truth, tried to tell Sunday. She went at him with the toilet tank lid instead.

Inside the church, Matty and Bell were seated on a small platform erected in the middle of the building. Two large men stood over them, keeping them at gunpoint. Only a few beams remained of the once vaulted ceiling. A thick breeze flowed through the open windows, not strong enough to relieve the humidity of the day. Sweat dripped down the side of Sunday's face. Her whole body was covered in a layer of sweat just from the walk up the hill to the church.

Fraser stood over Matty and Bell, tall and proud as he addressed the congregation before them. Twenty people stood on the ground in front of the platform. All heads swiveled around to watch the three of them enter the stone building. Fraser and the congregation remained quiet. Their feet crunched on the dirt floor, loud and obnoxious.

Sunday searched for Matty's eyes. He stared at his balled-up hands. A deep frown pressed his eyebrows together and shadowed his eyes. Steam could erupt from his fuming ears at any moment. She didn't want to be in his head. She caught Bell's gaze as she was led to the platform.

Are you okay? he mouthed.

She gave him a curt nod and allowed herself to be sat down beside him.

"Shall we continue?" Fraser spoke above her. She looked up, getting a view of his smile. He beamed at his followers, exposing his yellowing teeth. His eyes bugged out as he addressed the small crowd. He was dressed in all black, wearing a long coat that brushed against Sunday's back. As he moved the coat would catch in the air, sending whiffs of cigarette smoke in their direction.

The crowd watched Fraser with unblinking eyes.

"The day has come. The Equinox is upon us, and it is time to free our Lord."

Sunday looked past the crowd to the open holes that used to hold windows. The sun was setting, giving the world a bluish tint. The air remained warm and heavy. She didn't know if it was the temperature or her fear, but her sweaty skin glued her shirt to her body. She was suddenly exhausted. They'd lost. She was going to die in this ancient church. Her blood would spill onto the dirt at her feet and she would join the legends of Stull, Kansas.

"I know I had many loyal believers ready to start off the ceremony." Fraser continued speaking to the crowd. Two middle-aged men joined him on the platform. There was nothing special about them. If Sunday would have seen them on the street or in a grocery store, she wouldn't have looked twice at them. They had probably been living unexciting lives, running to the store for a last-minute dinner. She never would have guessed they were part of a murderous cult that worshipped ancient Egyptian gods.

"However," Fraser turned to the three of them, "a more worthy sacrifice came knocking on our door."

Sunday's eyes flashed back to him.

Did he just say sacrifice?

CHAPTER 26

Wide round eyes gawked at Sunday and the other two beside her. Their mouths hung open and they stepped closer to her. One of the men stopped at her feet and smiled up at her, raising his hand and wiggling his fingers.

"The heathens are not the blood our Lord requires."

The eyes of his followers snapped back to Fraser. They breathed as one, moving like a soft wave.

The two large men took Fraser's words as a cue. They stepped forward, each taking one of Bell's arms.

"No!" Sunday reached for Bell as he was yanked to his feet. Her fingers snatched his pant leg only to have it pulled from her grasp as he was dragged away.

Bell kicked his legs and grunted in protest. The two men on either of his sides held strong as they guided him to the middle of the platform.

Sunday looked over her shoulder at the gun pointed at her, aimed and ready.

One of the men holding Bell knocked the back of his legs with his shoe so he knelt before the crowd. He grimaced and tried to shake their meaty hands off of him. When that failed, he stared into the crowd, forcing eye contact with each guilty person below.

Tears filled Sunday's eyes. Her breath shortened. Was this what Reap saw in Bell? Had his aura been black because he'd been doomed the moment he met them?

The scene moved in slow motion, but still too fast. She looked from Bell to Matty. Matty stared at his fists. He inhaled through his nose sharply and squeezed his hands together until his knuckles were all white.

The man standing behind Matty held his gun aimed at him, but as his gaze turned more and more to Bell behind him, his taut arm drooped. In that moment, Matty acted. He swung his arm, hitting the man in the gut. The gun went off, ringing in Sunday's ears. Her face contorted with the loud discharge, she twisted to look behind her again. A gun was no longer pointed at her head. Matty had tackled Fraser to the ground, and the two followers leapt to them. Bell remained on his knees, and the man behind him stayed in place.

The voices of the crowd below rumbled. Some in surprise, others in anger.

Sunday pushed herself to her feet. The woman who had searched in the woods with London jumped onto the platform and crouched, her dark hair falling over her face. She gritted her teeth like a wild animal before leaping onto Sunday, who fell backward, swinging her fists at her attacker.

London stood above her. Sunday reached for her with a cry for help. Her friend couldn't walk away from Sunday. She still cared about her.

She had to.

London's response knocked the air from Sunday's lungs.

Guilt. It choked her. Filled her lungs and her gut.

London's whiskers caught the dim light in the church. Behind her a long, thin tail whipped.

So sorry. So sorry. So sorry.

London's face scrunched. Sunday grunted to get the woman off of her, but she'd pinned down her arms and legs.

They'd killed her outside. Sunday felt the cool blade on her throat. All of it had been a lie. They'd promised her safety, her life for theirs, but now they all were going to die. How could she have been so stupid?

Sunday glared at London's spirit. She couldn't agree more.

Another set of hands lifted Sunday from the ground. The woman on one side and a man on the other, each squeezing her arms. She winced as their fingers pressed into her skin.

She had known. London had known what they would be walking into. She had known what would happen once they got to the cemetery and she had walked them all to their deaths. Now they were all doomed.

Matty's shout pulled her eyes to her right. He'd been tossed away from Bell and struggled back to his feet. A dark-haired woman held him back, away from the sacrifice. Another follower pulled a hunting knife out of his belt. He squeezed the handle in one hand and a chalice in another as he straddled Bell's legs. The knife pressed against the detective's throat, the chalice was held in front of his chest.

Sunday stood on the platform but didn't remember getting up. Her body responded again and she dove toward Bell.

She shoved past Fraser, knocking him with her elbow. Bell was right in front of her. She just needed to knock the knife out of the asshole's hand.

The second man held Bell's shoulders, forcing him still. Bell craned his neck to peer down at the knife. He shook his head and pushed against the man holding him down, keeping as much distance between his skin and the blade as possible.

The first man pressed the blade to Bell's neck. A grunt escaped his lips.

The second man looked up from the scene playing out. His mouth fell open.

Again, the world moved slow, but too fast all at once. Sunday pushed her legs, willing them to move faster. She reached her arms out, demanding they stop.

The second man let go of Bell's shoulders and lunged at her. He wrapped an arm around her waist, knocking the air from her lungs and stopping her momentum. She gasped for air. A moan erupted out of her.

The knife slid across Bell's neck effortlessly. One moment, his neck had been sprinkled with stubble, developed from days on the road. The next, a waterfall of red poured from a C-shaped incision.

The man with the knife propped Bell up by his chest so he couldn't fall forward. He held the chalice below the wound to catch the pouring blood.

Bell gurgled. He looked in the direction of Sunday and Matty. His eyes had grown wet and wide with fear. Sunday kicked and scratched the second man. She had to make it to Bell, even if it was too late. The man's grip strengthened around her.

Matty shouted, but she couldn't make out his words.

Behind her, Fraser's voice began as a low thrum. He spoke in another language, repeating the same phrase over and over again.

The ground shook. The deep rumble drowned out Fraser's voice. The shaking traveled up Sunday's legs and shook her guts. The grip around her waist loosened and she was able to spin around to Matty.

Matty heaved for air on his knees, blood dripping from a split lip. As Sunday met his gaze, he wiped away the blood with the back of his hand, only managing to smear it across his chin.

The ground gave another jolt. This one forced a cry from the crowd. The followers standing in front of the platform all held their hands out in front of them. Their feet were planted far apart, keeping their balance as the world shook.

Unbothered by the shaking, Fraser continued chanting. He ogled the chalice held before him by one of his followers. Bell had fallen on his side. His hands were splayed in front of him, and his legs tangled together behind him. His eyes stared ahead, not seeing anything. The wound on his neck now seeped blood onto the platform.

The man held the chalice in both hands. The large gold cup appeared ancient. The stem and wide bowl were intricately engraved around glimmering stones. Bell's blood splashed over the top and ran down the engraved sides, like it ran through a maze. Glimmers of blue and green stones reflected off the setting sun outside, but the blood stained most of the chalice, transforming them into red gemstones.

The man dropped to a knee before Fraser. The blood-filled chalice moved with Fraser's words, stirring the contents without any assistance from Fraser or his lackey. It spun quicker, creating a whirl in the middle. As the spinning increased, the blood grew darker, until the contents were black.

Fraser continued chanting.

The ground trembled. A violent shake made Sunday stumble. She pressed her feet hard to the platform and held out her arms to catch herself. Based on the louder cry from the crowd, they had been shaken to the ground. But she wasn't taking her eyes off the chalice.

Something brushed against her ankles. The sensation forced Sunday's gaze off the ornate cup. She wiggled her toes in her shoes. The solid wood platform had become soft earth. Not the beaten-down ground they had found in the ancient church, but cultivated soil. Reeds grew out of the dirt around her. She was no longer before Fraser and his disciples.

As she raised her eyes, the reeds grew taller. They towered over her like a corn maze. Sunday peered between the stalks. No Fraser. No Matty. She was alone. The church and platform had disappeared. She was no longer surrounded by the horror of the cult, but she could hear the voices of the cult followers and Fraser himself continuing the chant. She couldn't be certain because the language was unfamiliar to her, but it sounded like a few words had changed in his chant.

"Matty!" She spun around and pushed the reed aside. He'd been behind her back in the church.

"I'm here!" Matty's voice sounded to her right. "What the fuck is this?"

She found him still kneeling. His eyes darted back and forth in their sockets. She took his hand and pulled him to his feet.

"Maybe we went to the past, when this area wasn't a cemetery?" She frowned. How could that have happened? But what else could it be? The image of Lars's scribbled-on napkin popped into her head. The layers of the Other World. If Fraser was opening the gateway between their world and the Other World, what part of the Other World would be opened?

"What was the first layer my dad mentioned?" Matty seemed to have the same thought.

"WayStation."

She squinted through the reeds in search of Fraser and his chalice, or the stage and Fraser's followers. Fraser's voice reverberated around her. The ex-priest was doing this, so the field couldn't be good news. The sky above them was dark. She couldn't see anything besides the reeds around her.

"I don't see the others, do you?" Matty asked.

Sunday shook her head.

"Can anyone go through the open gate?" he said.

She shook her head again. "I don't know."

They might not be there. Maybe only Seers could go into the Other World. Her father had never taught her about this. Lars hadn't mentioned anything like this either. People could also be hiding in the reeds. Her heart fluttered and she scoured the windblown reeds for anyone who might hurt them.

"This is definitely not our world," Matty said.

Sunday looked around them. Something felt off. She couldn't quite figure it out, but something about the air they breathed or the way the plants moved didn't seem normal. The air was tinted, like she wore colored sunglasses, but she couldn't identify a single color. She swung her arm in front of her face; it moved like the plants, appearing to move through thick liquid. She parted the air around her with her arm but felt little resistance in her motions. She glanced up and studied the feathery fronds at the top of the stalks. They waved at least a foot above her head. If only she could see over the plant. Maybe Matty could boost her up and they could find a way out.

Time felt off as well. A moment seemed to last for twenty minutes, but then Sunday would check her watch only to discover that the next ten minutes shot past her in seconds. All at once, standing in the same position, time sped up and slowed down. The reed leaves flapped in a wind that she couldn't feel. Shades of greens, yellows, and browns bounced off the tall stalks. Sunday squinted at them, some of them bright like the sun. She smelled the dirt and rotting plants under her feet. It enveloped her, wrapping her in a cocoon of scents.

"That was weird, right?" Matty pushed some reeds aside to look into the field.

She frowned, thinking again of the vivid colors and smells. "Definitely weird."

"Are we high?"

Sunday squinted. "Don't think so."

She craned her neck to look over him through the plants. More reeds. Never ending. She expected to see a pyramid or ancient temple among the reeds, something that matched the creatures of this world.

"It has to be the WayStation, or at least some other layer in the Other World, right?" Matty wondered.

The question made Sunday's stomach flip. They had to be in the Other World. Now that they were there, how the hell were they going to get back?

CHAPTER 27

Fraser ceased his chanting. She looked around, searching for any movement of the reeds, any threat. She searched for Fraser specifically. He had to be somewhere hidden in the field. Her heart thudded in her ears. Just for a moment, the reeds stood still. The moment hung around, like a car teetering on the edge of a cliff. She braced herself, unsure if they would fall over the cliff or save themselves.

The Hounds' snarls interrupted the silence. The reeds parted in front of them. Sunday and Matty stumbled backward.

Fraser stepped out from the tall plants. His eyes twinkled yellow and his face extended into a wolf's snout. He grinned to reveal the row of razor teeth. The frightening grin washed over her. Sunday bit her lip to hold back a scream. Was he dead? Or had the transformation been completed? Just as Lars had predicted, Fraser and Set had combined as one. Set was now free to go through the gateway to their world.

"He has returned!" Fraser laughed. Tears streamed down the sides of his face as he gasped for a breath between the roars of laughter. Matty and Sunday stepped away again. She eyed the Hounds sitting at his feet like master and dog.

"*Tati.*" Fraser snapped his fingers.

The wolves slowed to circle around them. Matty yanked Sunday's arm, flinging them into the reeds before the beasts could enclose them. Sunday leapt to avoid a diving Hound. The hot breath of the creature snaked around her ankle. She stumbled, falling to her knees where she tucked her face in the dirt. Curled into a ball, she accepted her fate. She anticipated the stench of misery coming off the bad omens, prepared for the pain of their teeth against her skin. She heaved, inhaling dust and sweat. She was ready and prayed the relief of death would come quickly.

Matty pulled her to her feet.

"The reeds are thinning up here, come on!" He dragged her.

They broke through into a clearing. The Hounds' growls still followed close behind. Hand in hand, they shambled toward a brown two-story townhouse on display on top of a small hill. A light shone through one of the second-story windows. As they approached the home, the light switched off, only to be replaced by one downstairs.

Matty stopped at the bottom of the hill. Sunday's chest heaved. She glanced over her shoulder, eyeing the reed edge for the Hounds. Why did Matty stop? The beasts were right behind them.

"What is it?" she asked.

Matty stared open-mouthed at the building. "That's the house I grew up in."

When he didn't move, Sunday took the lead. She hurried up the hill and Matty followed behind her. Over her shoulder, she could see the first Hounds spring into the clearing. They sniffed the air. It smelled like smoke from a lit fireplace, billowing from the chimney on the roof. The Hounds growled and sprinted to them.

"Let's go!"

Sunday stomped up the porch steps. They creaked under her feet. She threw the door open and stumbled in. Jumping in after her, Matty snatched the door. Before he closed it, Sunday caught sight of the Hounds approaching the porch. They snapped their jaws and leapt up the steps. Matty slammed the door shut and the beasts rammed into it on the other side.

Breathless, Sunday scrambled to her feet. Upstairs, someone shouted. She looked to the ceiling.

"Where are we?" she asked.

"My house," Matty said.

Sunday dropped her gaze to him and frowned.

"My childhood home," he said.

The shouting continued above their heads. Matty stomped past Sunday. She followed him into the kitchen. Several of the wooden cabinets hung open. An island held a bowl of fruit and a crumb-covered plate.

"What's going on up there?" Sunday gestured upstairs. "And why are the cabinets all open?"

Matty opened the back door and poked his head out.

"It's a bad habit I picked up from my mom." He spoke over his shoulder. "Broke the habit quickly once I was tall enough to whack my head on the open doors."

"And upstairs?"

Matty sighed and shut the door.

"That's me and a girlfriend from college," he said. "I'd lost my temper. I don't even remember what about, but she was done with me. I was an idiot."

He looked up from the plate with sad eyes. Sunday wanted to reach for his hand, comfort him.

Someone rushed down the stairs. Sunday whirled around to see a young woman. Short, at least a half a foot shorter than Sunday. She wiped tears from her cheeks. Her hair was in two French braids that whipped around as she rushed to the front door. Sunday's breath caught in her throat. *Don't open the front door. The Hounds.*

The young woman approached the door, extended a hand to the door knob, then vanished like dust in a breeze.

"She died." Matty's voice brought Sunday's eyes off the door.

"Your girlfriend?" Her heart still thudded in her ears.

Matty nodded. "Car wreck a few weeks after she walked out on me. I never got to apologize."

Sunday peered upstairs. It had grown quiet. Was this Matty's judgment? What would the WayStation dredge up from her life? What were her biggest regrets?

"It looks clear out the back door." Matty's voice was quick and sharp. He opened the door again and leaned out. "I think we should go this way. Try to find our way back to the church."

Sunday agreed and followed Matty out of the house. Outside, a wind stopped her breath in her throat. She grabbed Matty's arm to keep the gale from blowing her away. It whipped her hair around her head. The wind reached into her mouth and snatched the breath before it could reach her lungs. The space around her became an indistinguishable blur of reed leaves, dust, and curly hair.

"What's happening?" She had to shout over the roar of the wind.

"I don't know!" Matty yelled back.

She peered through the windy mess. Where were the Hounds?

Matty took a heavy step forward. His back foot slipped in the dust whipping around their legs. Sunday clung to his arm, fighting against the push of the wind. It forced her left, then right, then back and forward. The reeds made quick nips at her skin. She looked over her shoulder, anticipating the cold eyes of a Hound ready to pounce. The dirt and fallen foliage had been kicked up from the ground, dancing in the open space around them. They wouldn't hear it or see it until it was too late.

"Come on!" Sunday tugged at Matty's arm.

She squinted, searching for any sign of the church. The image of the stone building in Sunday's head guided her forward, but all she could see was dust. She kicked her feet around in front of her, but only kicked air.

Then, just as suddenly as the wind had started up, it stopped. The roar of the wind disappeared. The leaves flying in the air dropped to the ground around them. The absent gusts left a heavy silence that was eerie. The only noise came from Sunday and Matty's heavy breathing. She looked around.

The reeds around them withered and fell to the ground. Sunday stopped. The soft dirt they walked on shifted, some of it falling away as if through cracks in the ground. Then, branches and tendrils snaked through dirt, growing into trees. All sorts of trees erupted around them. Sunday was familiar with some: the lime-green leaves of a blue palo verde and a desert mesquite tree of her home. There were also evergreen trees, willows, and oaks. Dozens of tree species flared up from the ground. Sunday watched, wide-eyed and open-mouthed.

Something brushed against her leg. She cried out.

The gray creature walked on all fours like an ape, holding itself erect and propelling itself farther with its arms. A tendril erupted from its abdomen and latched onto a branch, then it swung itself forward and continued scurrying away.

"What was that?" Sunday gasped.

"I don't know," Matty said. "Never seen anything like it."

Sunday watched the creature. Her eyes settled on a building not far away, and she squinted through the thicket of trees. She recognized it. A two-story home, cream with dark trimming. An old dark blue Chevrolet parked in the driveway. Her childhood home.

"Sunday!" Matty called after her. "Where are you going?"

He chased her through the trees. Other creatures whipped past them. Kappas. Tokos. Warvils. They hurried past.

The lights downstairs shone through the open windows. Sunday could make out the front living room, just as she remembered it. The front steps were just a yard away. Then light exploded in front of her.

She staggered back and fell onto Matty. Around them, more light dropped from above and crashed into the dirt. One landed on a slithering creature, green with a dozen legs on each side of its body. The creature shrieked. The light glowed through its skin as it convulsed. The ground beneath it opened up and the creature fell through. Sunday scrambled closer to Matty. Her eyes darted above her and around her. Where were the lights coming from? They couldn't get hit. With a grip on her wrist, Matty pulled her the rest of the way to her house.

The door shut, blocking out the explosive noises outside. Instead, the noise of cabinet doors being opened and slammed shut came from the kitchen. Sunday followed the sounds and found her father on his knees, halfway in a cupboard. He was muttering to himself, hastily moving things around inside.

"This isn't too far in the past." Sunday spoke to Matty without taking her eyes off her father's hunched-over back. Her hands trembled at her sides and her nerves made her nauseous. First the strange world outside, and now her father before her inside her old home. She continued without thinking. "The remodeling of the kitchen was done just a couple years ago. And I got him that shirt last Christmas."

She had helped make the decisions for the remodel after he decided to sell the house. He didn't need a place so big. Sunday had moved into her apartment and neither of them expected her mother to return. Apart from the living room and bathroom, the rooms were left to the dust.

"Yes!" Stephen Elm knocked his head on the top of a shelf as he pulled himself out of the cupboard.

He rubbed the back of his head and smiled at the old windup radio in his hand. They followed him when he stomped up the stairs and into the master bedroom.

The bedroom was covered in maps and newspaper clippings. Sunday looked over them and recognized a few of the names from Reap's list of the dead. Tim Yeats, who had been poisoned, and Jacqueline Draker's death in the bathtub were two clippings that sat beside an open suitcase on the bed. There was one other duffel bag on the bed and a backpack being filled on a chair.

"Was he going on a trip?" Matty studied the room.

Sunday barely registered his words. Stephen was jumping back and forth across the room. He would go into the closet and reemerge with an armful of clothing. After he dropped the clothes in the suitcase, he practically sprinted into the adjoining bathroom to gather his travel bag. That bag went into the backpack. He emptied Mom's jewelry into the front pocket next. All the while he was muttering under his breath about having to go to the bank to get cash or whether he was packing too light or too heavy.

"He looks like he's going on a big trip." Matty continued talking.

Sunday looked at the calendar on the table beside the bed. She remembered that calendar growing up. It had sections that could be changed to match the date, like a flip book. Sunday noticed the day and her breath caught in her throat.

"This is the night before my dad's accident," she whispered. She couldn't get enough breath into her chest to say the words louder. It wasn't like her father would hear them.

"Where was he going?"

Sunday shook her head. "He left me a message."

"What did it say?"

Matty had turned away from Stephen when Sunday didn't answer.

She still had her eyes locked on her father, filled with tears. One escaped before she began blinking them away. She took a long breath in before finally looking at Matty.

"He left me a message that night." She cleared her throat. "I didn't get to hear the end of it."

Sunday pulled her cell phone out of her pocket. She clicked the screen on and wasn't surprised to see that it didn't have any service. The battery was low too, apparently drained by searching for service in the Other World. Sunday sighed, switched it onto airplane mode to hold onto the last sixteen percent before finding the voicemail icon.

She didn't need service to play an old voicemail message. Sunday scrolled to the last message, the oldest one, because it was one that she would never delete.

She held the phone out between the two of them and hit play.

"Hey sweetie." Her father's voice leapt from the phone. It was like a knife through her heart. She placed her free hand over her heart, which was still stubbornly pounding in her chest. "I was just calling to check in on you. I've been having a bad feeling. I wanted to be sure you were all right." He paused. "I may be hard to reach for a while. I'm fine. I swear! But—"

The recording stopped with a loud screeching sound of tires braking.

The past Stephen continued packing behind them. Sunday watched Matty, allowing her tears to fall down her cheeks now. Matty placed his hand over the phone and guided her outstretched arm back to her side. Then he pulled her in, wrapping his arms around her shoulders. Sunday let him, one of her hands remaining on her chest and the other clutching the cell phone at her side. She didn't sob or cry out like she'd expected. Instead, the tears flowed from her eyes gently. She laid her head on Matty's shoulder, enjoying his closeness for a moment.

There weren't any words. Nothing appropriate and definitely nothing that could fix how she was feeling. She was disappointed by therapy in that sense. Most people grieving hope for that easy fix, a word or sentence that so obviously needed to be said to make it all disappear.

If there was a sentence that could take away all pain, wouldn't the human race have discovered it already? Wouldn't it have taken full advantage of the healing powers instead of paying thousands of dollars to have some yuppie repeat what you were saying back to you in a slightly different way?

She appreciated that Matty didn't attempt any magical fixing words. He held her, gave her that comforting moment, and then let her go. Sunday tucked her phone back in her pocket and then looked to her father again.

"It looks like he's leaving town." Matty spoke for the first time since they'd listened to the message.

Sunday looked over the room again, searching for anything that would point to her dad not running away. She couldn't find anything.

He began zipping up the suitcase and moving the bags outside of the room. Sunday couldn't bring herself to follow.

"What the fuck is that?"

Matty was pointing to the bedroom window. It was dark outside, the trees and lights and creatures gone. It looked like the same view Sunday had seen growing up, but she knew if they were to actually step outside, they would find themselves in the field of reeds. Now, though, something was standing in front of the second-story window, blocking her view.

CHAPTER 28

It stood like a human with the broad shoulders and bare chest of a man, but it had the head of a dark dog. Its nose was long and narrow and its ears stood on end. It stared at them with unblinking red eyes. It was hard to tell in the dark, but it almost appeared to be grinning.

"Do you think it is going to start licking its chops, like the wolf in Little Red Riding Hood?" Matty whispered. Sunday felt his efforts to stay quiet were unnecessary.

The part human, part animal materialized in the bedroom. It stood before them nude, just like the Cow Woman.

Sunday raised her eyebrows and turned to Matty.

"He's well endowed." A smirk twitched at the corner of her lips.

Matty rolled his eyes.

The creature stepped closer, standing a foot taller than them. A scale emerged out of the top of its head, like it was the stand, and two plates balanced on either side. The plates shook slightly as they settled, but the plate with a large feather on it stopped slightly lower than the other.

"Should we be concerned?" Matty leaned closer to Sunday.

They took a step away from the creature as it reached its arm toward them. It seemed to grow longer as they moved farther away. The

fingertips brushed Sunday's chest, radiating heat. Her already thumping heart attempted to leap out of her chest painfully, like it was mag-
netically attracted to the creature's hand. Sunday clutched Matty's arm.
They took a final step back, hitting a wall. Her heart slammed against
her chest. She cried out, hearing a crack of her rib cage. The creature's
fingers pressed against her as it moved closer, shrinking its arm back
to size. Sunday felt the searing limb through her whole body. It made
her ears ring and her mouth hang open. She couldn't hear a scream; her
lungs were burning enough to make sound impossible. Her body radiated pain. Matty grabbed her shoulders. His touch felt strong enough
to break her brittle bones.

And then it disappeared.

Her heart no longer slammed against her sternum. Her ears
became quiet. She inhaled cool air that spread through her whole body.

Her father stood in front of her. He had stepped between Sunday
and the demon dog man, no longer the memory version of himself, but
a spirit looking at her with a small smile and sad eyes. His skin was
developing green scales. They had taken over half his face and continued in splotches down his neck and under his collar. He held out a
tentacle as if to place his hand on Sunday's shoulder. His eyes remained
the same. Tears filled Sunday's own eyes as she looked into her father's
loving eyes, something she thought she would never see again.

It all happened in a moment. In real time, it would have been
over before anyone could register that something had even happened. Stephen stepped between Sunday and the creature. She was
no longer burning from the inside. He now had the creature's hand
in his back.

For Sunday, though, time slowed. She studied his face, enjoyed his
gaze. She heard him without his lips moving.

"You shouldn't be here."

His voice echoed in her head. She could have shrunk down to her knees and sobbed right there. How she'd missed his voice. "Are you—" He couldn't finish the thought.

Sunday shook her head. "We're not dead. Fraser did something, it dragged us here." She spoke out loud. "Are we in the Other World?"

"Yes and no. This is like a train station, a stop on your way to your afterlife."

"The WayStation."

Stephen nodded.

"What are you doing here?" Six months ago he had died. Had he been there the whole time?

"Trying to get back to you. To protect you. But I've been caught in a loop, packing over and over again." Tears filled his eyes. "Pumpkin, I'm so sorry. I never should've left you. I should've told you the truth."

She reached for his hand but she couldn't hold him. Her own hand brushed through him.

"It's okay, Dad."

Stephen grimaced.

"What is that?" Sunday watched the grinning dog man with wide eyes.

"Anubis." His voice came to her softer. "I've been running from him. He's here to judge your heart."

As if on cue, Anubis retracted his arm from Stephen's back. The front of her father's shirt grew darker with blood. In Anubis's hand was Stephen's beating heart.

Sunday knew her time with him was ending. She spoke quickly. "Do you know how to get back?"

He looked down and sighed. "No. I thought if I could find Isis, my connection to her could help me through the veil, back into our world, but I couldn't get out of my loop."

Sunday snuck a glance at Matty. He was still holding onto her shoulders. His expression was unreadable. He stared at Stephen intently, obviously listening. Sunday wanted to know what he thought of her father.

Stephen grunted. Anubis thrust his hand further into his back. Sunday gasped. Her father's last moments flashed in her mind.

Stephen was behind the wheel flying down a two-lane highway. The headlights around him were bright. He adjusted his rearview mirror to keep the reflected lights out of his eyes. By flipping the mirror down, the mirror reflected the back seat.

He let out a cry.

Sitting in the back seat was a smiling Toko. It wasn't the same one that followed Shelly around, but it was the same gray-skinned humanoid. Its smile revealed its yellow, rotten teeth. Its oily hair was gathered in a small bundle at the top of its head and hung down dividing its face in half. It slowly raised a finger to its lips, to urge Stephen to quiet his cry.

The sound of a big rig horn forced Stephen's eyes back to the road, but it was too late. There was no way to tell if Stephen had veered out of his lane into the oncoming traffic or if it was the truck that was off course, but either way the headlights blinded Stephen. He raised his hand uselessly to shield his eyes. He only managed to raise it halfway before his world went black with a sickening crunch of metal against metal.

The impact took Sunday's breath away and forced her back into the bedroom.

Matty was still beside her, still holding her. He looked on the scene with wide eyes.

Stephen no longer faced her. He turned to Anubis, staggering on weak knees with his heart beating in the hand of the creature. He fell forward, reaching for the demon to keep him standing. Anubis allowed him to take hold of his shoulders. He looked down at the ghost of

Sunday's father, holding his dripping heart in his right hand. Without looking away, he placed the still-beating heart on the other plate.

They pulsed up and down, the heart and the feather. Everyone's eyes watched it bounce.

Sunday remembered from elementary history something about a scale and a feather. It was some sort of ancient ceremony.

"He's weighing his soul." Matty's whispered voice filled in the blanks.

"What happens if it doesn't weigh correctly?"

She looked quickly to Matty, but his face was still unreadable. His gaze just continued bouncing up and down.

The scale plates slowed. It was painful watching them. Would they be balanced or unbalanced? It slowed with the heart below the feather.

Matty sucked in a breath.

Slowly the heart raised above the feather.

Sunday's own heart pounded once again in her chest, though it was a feeling she almost embraced after it had nearly been forced out of her.

The heart lowered. It was going to weigh more than the feather. Time stood still as it passed the feather and continued its journey down.

Except it didn't continue down. Time hadn't stopped; the scale did. Matty's loud sigh confirmed it. They were balanced.

Stephen stood up taller. His blood-drenched shirt clung to his chest, but he didn't notice. His eyes closed and the corners of his lips turned up.

"He gets to continue on," Matty said. She was beginning to understand.

There were no bells. No angel choirs to welcome her father to heaven, or the Other World's form of heaven. There was a bright light, but it quietly illuminated the room. Sunday brought her hands over her eyes, but she still couldn't see anything past the brightness. And just as quickly as it appeared, the light faded until it was again just a normally lit bedroom.

Anubis and Stephen had disappeared. Matty and Sunday were left alone in the room.

There wasn't any movement or sound. The silence was actually overwhelming. The absence of sound pounded in Sunday's ears. It took her breath away and pushed her heart up to her throat.

Where did he go?

Is he okay?

Why are we still here?

Are we okay?

How are we going to get home?

Are we stuck here?

Her thoughts were spiraling. She felt it happening, knew the warning signs.

This is bad.

Something is wrong.

We're going to die.

Death.

Die.

Alone.

The attack was coming on. She remembered it from the bar. She remembered the discussions she had with Dr. Morris, her therapist, about the nature of panic attacks and how to handle them. She struggled to dredge up the instructions over the choir of death in her head.

Of course you are freezing up in the Other World. That's how pathetic you are. You'll die here, a failure.

She was ready to curl up in a ball and just attempt to push air in and out of her squeezing chest.

But she wasn't giving in to the urge.

You're okay. She forced her mind to form the thoughts. *Dad is okay. His heart was balanced. You're okay. You can do this. You're okay.*

You're going to die. Matty's going to die. What's the point in—

You're okay.

She gritted her teeth. To push the thoughts away, she pushed her legs to move.

"Sunday!" Matty called after her. She heard his footsteps clomping behind her.

She stormed out of the house and back into the trees. The air outside blew her hair in every direction. The sound roared in her ears. Lights rained down around her, missing some creatures and striking others. Sunday gaped like a fish, unable to get a breath in through the panic attack. Matty shouted behind her, but she was unable to make it out over the sound of the creatures' screams.

Just as Sunday turned around to face him, something drove into her side.

CHAPTER 29

She stumbled sideways. The blow took her breath away. Struggling to stay on her feet, she gasped for air. A Toko scrambled back to its feet. This one was dressed in scraps of clothing made from leaves. It hissed and narrowed its red eyes at Sunday before running off. A light dropped beside it and it leapt away. A beam stretched for the Toko, latching onto its ankle, sending it crashing to the ground. Its chin bounced on impact and it grabbed for anything as the beam of light pulled it closer to the glowing crash site. The Toko disappeared into the light and the dirt absorbed both of them. The fight between the Toko and the light had disappeared, leaving the ground undisturbed.

"Sunday!" Matty pulled her attention off the now-dark dirt. He pointed in front of them. "I see the gateway. The church!"

Surrounded by towering trees was the ancient stone church. The gateway to Hell shimmered around it. Their world was a crystal-clear image surrounded by wavering reeds. It beckoned them. Matty and Sunday raced to the old church, following the other creatures. The Other World beings were rushing to the gate. Sunday realized her father had been wrong. These creatures didn't come to their world by accident, they sought it out, just like Set. Now Fraser and Set had opened the gate and the creatures flocked. Lights continued to pour down around them, striking some creatures before they could make it to the gate. Others climbed through and disappeared into the dim light of Stull, Kansas. Matty dodged in front of her to avoid a light. Sunday stopped on her toes to keep from getting hit. What would happen if they were hit? Would they be dragged under the dirt too?

The view of the church grew clearer as they approached. The wooden stage stood in the middle with Bell's corpse still lying on the platform. The followers lay scattered around the stage. Sunday's mouth hung open as her eyes bounced from the corpses of the followers to the lights dropping around her. All of them faced the sky, their own mouths open as wide as their red eyes.

Almost there.

Matty leapt through the gateway. He spun around and reached a hand back through to grab Sunday. She stretched for his fingers, and then a light struck her back.

Twilight tinted the world blue through the open church windows. Matty and Sunday stood before the gateway, still open and revealing the WayStation on the other side. Creatures crawled through, lights cascaded down.

Sunday frowned. What had happened? How had she gotten through the gateway?

She caught sight of her hands. They glowed, like the light emitted through the twenty-four-legged creature in the Other World. Her breath caught in her throat. The light was inside of her. She jumped her gaze to the ground. When would it open up and take her?

"Are you okay?" Matty shook her shoulder.

A wave of peace washed over her and a smile crept onto her face. "I think so," she said.

She scanned the space around them. Fraser's followers appeared to have met a fate she had feared. Their bodies were strewn on the ground around them dead or dying of lacerations. Dead eyes stared up at her, faces splattered in blood, stomachs ripped open leaving the stench of blood and bowels in the air. She forced herself to look past the dead; Fraser was around here. Sunday could feel it in her bones. The light inside her pulsed like a beacon.

Her arm rose without her doing; the light had taken over her body. She looked to her feet. They were hers, wearing the same combat boots she'd been wearing when she left her apartment a month ago, but not under her control. Sunday sighed with trust. The same trust she'd grown for the man beside her.

"What is it?" Matty took a step away from her. "Sunday, your eyes are yellow like Fraser's."

I am Isis. Sunday spoke, but without her own voice. *I've come from the light. Come for Set.*

Matty narrowed his eyes. "Is Sunday hurt?"

Not at all. Sunday wanted to reassure Matty, tell him to do as the goddess told him, but she couldn't speak. Only wait.

She's safe, Isis answered. *Set is close. I feel him. He made it through the gateway, but he can't leave the cemetery. We need him close to the gateway.*

Sunday had an idea. They needed rope. She thought this and Isis understood. She explained the plan to Matty who nodded in understanding.

He patted his own pockets, searching for anything that could stand in as cordage. Sunday scoured the scene with Isis's eyes. Their backpacks had been discarded on the other side of the platform. There would be some rope in there. Matty rushed to the backpacks and Sunday searched for more. They'd need more. She noticed the ribboned clothing of Fraser's deceased follower; the Hounds had shredded the fabric. Together, Isis and Sunday ripped at the closest tatters of a T-shirt. Bile rose to her throat and Isis calmed her. Isis's blood pulsed through her veins, the same as her own. In tandem, they gathered pieces, like a dance.

Help me gather the longer pieces, Isis instructed Matty, then listened to Sunday for her next words. *Anything long enough to create a hitch knot.*

They yanked at the cool stiff fabric, ripping them away from the bodies. Sunday replayed Jaime's instructions in her mind, focusing on the swift movements of his hands, reminiscing over the allure of his voice as he sang Sinatra to attract the Girdwick. What she wouldn't give to be fighting off a Girdwick right now. Instead she squeezed a handful of fraying fabric in her sweating hands, her breath short and her wide eyes searching for anything else she could scavenge from the dead around her.

"Start wrapping them around the tree trunks." Matty raced down the hill. "I'll see if I can attach any to the grave sites."

Sunday glanced over her shoulder as hers and Isis's fingers fumbled with the fabric. She felt Fraser just beyond the church, the gods inside of each of them working like a radar. Fraser knew she was there too. She understood him, a communication like the spirits. Fraser needed to close the gateway, stop any possibility to send Set back to the Other World.

He's coming back, Isis called to Matty.

They secured another hitch knot around the tree. Sunday watched Fraser. He'd crept closer to the church. She hustled to tie the last of the bloody fabric, the circle completed. They all rejoined at the top of the hill, the gateway still shimmering in the church.

Fraser's eyes narrowed when he found them.

Sunday reached for Matty, but her hand didn't respond. Isis washed another wave of peace over her and moved Sunday's hand to Matty's. Matty squeezed hers back.

Fraser transformed before them. His face morphed into a wolf's, and the same yellow eyes narrowed in their direction. Claws replaced his fingers and he knelt forward on the bowed legs of a canine. A growl rumbled in his chest and Fraser, now Set, snapped his arm forward. Isis leapt Sunday back and Set's claw wrapped around Matty's leg. Sunday cried out inside her head. Isis's calm couldn't quell her panic. She screamed to Isis, begged her.

Do something!

CHAPTER 30

Without a second thought, Isis reached her arm out to squeeze his shoulder. Set turned away from Matty. Isis removed her hand from his shoulder and placed her palm on his forehead. Set shrieked, dropping Matty's leg. He jolted and convulsed in an attempt to throw her off of him. With his leg now free, Matty clambered away toward the edge of the protective hitch knot circle.

Set shook Sunday off, the force sending both of them backward. Sunday landed against a tree. Fraser slid over grave markers. His narrowed eyes followed Matty. He leapt to his feet in pursuit. With his arm stretched out, nails sharp like claws, the creature crashed against an invisible barrier. He pushed himself to his feet again and slammed a fist against the hitch knots, but the barrier remained strong. Matty watched, mouth still hanging open, safe on the other side.

Set. Her voice echoed. It had grown deeper and stronger. *You were banished from this world. This is not your place.*

Dog God, or Set, replied, but not out loud. His voice echoed in her head.

I've been summoned. I am the rightful King.

This is no longer a world of Kings and Queens. This is not your place. The repeated words shook the ground beneath Sunday's feet.

Set cowered under her gaze. He crouched against the hitch knot wall, each movement changing him more, bit by bit. His feet grew long claws. His knees bowed forward. His hands fell back to the ground as paws and a growl erupted from his throat. With a row of fangs and red eyes narrowed, he wasn't half man anymore, but full wolf, larger and more daunting than any Hound.

I banish you, Sunday declared. *Again.*

You have no power over me! Set growled in her head.

He spit the words out with a guttural chuckle. His fangs glimmered in the moonlight as he launched off his back legs. He landed on Sunday, his claws scraping down her chest. His jaw clamped on her shoulder. Another warm wave of peace washed over her, Isis protecting her from the pain.

"Hey!" Matty yelled.

A large rock the size of a bike tire knocked into Set's head, inciting a whine. He released Sunday's shoulder and launched his gaze behind him, glaring down at Matty.

Sunday threw her body forward, flinging the dog off of her. She planted her foot on the dog's sprawled out body, producing another howl from the animal. Set's beady red eyes seared into her.

You will answer to Osiris. She leaned forward and placed her hand on the dog's chest. Set struggled under her weight but couldn't break free. Sunday took a deep breath, a powerful one that accumulated in her stomach. It gathered into a force that released through her hand as she spoke in the same booming, echoing voice.

Now go!

Her voice rumbled the ground. Beneath her hand, Set sizzled and Sunday pushed him to the gateway. He roared inside her head, cursing her and Osiris and Horus. He fought her will inside her head just like he was swinging at her in real life, but she was stronger.

Her touch burned him. Her nostrils filled with the smell of scorched dog hair as he shrunk away. With one last push of power, she shoved him back to the Other World. The foreign power surged through her body. She willed it. He was gone and the gateway closed.

The world stood still. The clouds above them, threatening rain, had slid over the moon and blocked its light.

What time was it? Sunday could only guess. At least evening. How different was time in the Other World? Was it even the same day?

She turned around to find Matty on the ground. He stood straddling a grave marker and watching her with wide eyes.

It was so quiet. It could have been the contrast of the heart-pounding chase and rampaging god, but even the leaves grew silent.

Matty cocked his head to the side as he studied her.

"You still there?" Matty lifted his hand like he wanted to touch her, but halfway up he let it drop.

She wanted to scream: Of course I'm still here!

But he wasn't talking to her. He was talking to Isis. Her body still glowed. She tried to wiggle her fingers. Another ripple of peace ran through her when her fingers didn't respond.

Yes. No longer booming and threatening, the being spoke with Sunday's voice.

Matty frowned. "Isis. The Egyptian goddess."

Yes, she replied.

He nodded, but the frown didn't leave his face. "And Sunday is still with you, right?"

Sunday would have hugged him if she could, his concern for her well-being warmed her heart. She wanted to tell him she was okay, more at peace than she'd been in a long time.

I needed her mortality to banish my brother.

"Sorry?" He wrinkled his nose.

You are our connection to this world. You call it the Sight. We call it our bridge.

He narrowed his eyes. "She's okay, though, right?"

Isis smiled. *Of course. She's at peace.*

The real Sunday felt the goddess's words wash over her. It made her want to close her eyes and sleep.

"She's coming back, though? When you say she's at peace, you don't mean she's peacefully dead or anything, right?"

As soon as we are done.

His eyebrows relaxed, releasing the frown while his head bobbled in an unstopping nod. "While I got you here then, could you explain all of—" He gestured to the cemetery around them. "...this?"

Sunday internally rolled her eyes.

Isis chuckled, a laugh like twinkling bells. "Set wanted to return to Earth. His biggest threats and assets were people like you. You had the power to see him and stop him, but he also needed someone like you to leave the Other World."

She went on to explain her rule of ancient Egypt. It had been an epic tale of dead husbands and jealous brothers. After uprooting Set from the throne several times, Osiris, the king of the gods and humans, decided that gods were not meant to rule over man. Osiris ordered his kind to leave Earth and reside permanently in the Other World.

As she spoke, Sunday's fatigue grew. If she had control of her eyes, she would've had trouble keeping them open.

"Those humans who descended from us gods were left to rule while we retreated to our world. We watched from afar."

"So who am I then?"

Sunday struggled to follow the conversation. She wanted to stay awake, terrified of slipping from consciousness. What if she never woke up? What if she woke up in the Other World with the goddess deciding to keep her body on Earth? Despite Isis's peaceful medicine, Sunday felt panic begin to brew in her chest.

"If you took the time, you could trace your roots back to a god," Isis continued.

"Which god?"

Sunday wanted Matty to shut up so the goddess would go.

Isis smiled. "Horus. You have my son's temperament."

"And Sunday?"

Sunday's own sight was becoming blurred. She was losing her fight against the fatigue.

"She is one of mine. I wouldn't have been able to link with her without the connection." The smile dropped. "She's growing weak. She can't help fighting my presence."

The words were muffled. Sunday strained to hold on. Her own vision was closing in around her. Despite her body still being rooted to the ground, she was falling.

"Sunday?"

Matty's voice was the last thing she heard before she slipped into darkness.

CHAPTER 31

Her cheek was cold. That was the first sensation Sunday noticed as she slowly emerged from the darkness. Her cheek rested on something cold and hard, uncomfortable.

She blinked her eyes open.

She was leaning on a car window. The windshield in front of her revealed the flat open road of a highway. Her mouth was as dry as if it had been stuffed with cotton, and her body ached from her cramped position against the passenger door. She used the hand rest to push herself up, wincing as the kink in her neck shot pain down her arm.

"You're awake!" Matty hollered. She jumped and looked at his grinning face. "I mean, I trusted the goddess. She saved the world and all, but I couldn't help worrying a little."

Sunday rubbed the blurriness from her right eye.

"Where are we?" Her voice came out hoarse. She really needed to wash out the cotton feeling. There was a plastic water bottle in the cup holder between them. She snatched it and took a sip.

"Somewhere in Colorado. We just left Kansas. I can't say I'm disappointed." He rattled on like he hadn't spoken in hours. He probably hadn't. "Are you okay?"

She took inventory of herself.

Apart from the stiffness, she felt fine.

"What do you remember?"

She thought back to their journey in the Other World. Then Set and her possession. Possession. There was no better word for it, but the negative connotation didn't feel right.

"I think I remember everything."

Matty nodded.

Sunday leaned back in the seat and sighed. How long had she been asleep? She was still exhausted.

"When Isis left you, you were out. She told me you'd lost consciousness. Called you a fighter with a smirk on her face. Well, your face, I guess. I liked her."

"Jury is still out for me." Sunday stretched her neck. "It was strange not having control of my body, being forced into relaxing."

"I get it." He shrugged and drummed his hands on the steering wheel.

Sunday lay back on the glass and watched the scenery pass before her. She'd thought she would get tired of the endless flat land, the same bushes and trees, and mesmerizing phone lines, but she didn't. After escaping from the Other World, she actually felt comforted by the unchanging scene. It was beautiful.

"So, I've just been heading home." Matty interrupted her contemplation. "Are you okay with that?"

She thought of returning home. Empty apartment. No family. No Reap.

Tears sprang to her eyes. Just the thought of her Other World friend made the hole in her heart ache.

"What?" Matty glanced at her. "What's wrong?"

"Nothing." She brushed the tears away and sat up straighter.

For the first time since her father had died, Sunday felt whole. She hurt for their loss, her father and Reap, would trade anything to return home to them, live the rest of her life happy and content as a restaurant manager who moonlighted as a Seer now and again. But she couldn't. They were gone. There was nothing waiting for her in Arizona, and for the first time that fact did not scare her. She breathed easily.

"No," she said. "I don't want to go home."

He didn't answer for a moment, but Sunday watched him. He frowned, and then stretched his lips in an upside-down smile and nodded.

"I agree. Home sounds horrible right now."

Sunday smiled and looked out the window again, this time resting her chin in her hand. Signs for Georgetown, Colorado whizzed by them.

"So what is it going to be, descendant of Isis?" Matty smirked.

Someone stood on the side of the road, leaning against the wooden post of a green exit sign.

Argentine Street next exit.

He was a cowboy with his spurred boots and wide-brimmed hat. A face covered in barnacles watched their car approach. He raised a paw to tip his hat at them. Before Sunday could get a closer look at him, they'd driven past him.

Colorado. She pondered.

"The Rockies are supposed to be beautiful. That town back there could be fun." She jutted her thumb back at the cowboy spirit.

Matty raised his eyebrows. "Really? I thought you wanted to avoid the Other World."

She thought of how she had resisted her Sight. Avoided spirits. Avoided people. It had left her alone and scared. Now, as she ached from the journey into the Other World and a battle with an Egyptian god, she felt accomplished, fulfilled. She had someone beside her she could trust and nothing waiting for her back at home. Why was she going there? Why should she go back to her old life, a life that left her so unsatisfied?

Sunday grinned at the friend beside her. "I'm ready to embrace it."

ACKNOWLEDGMENTS

There is so much more that goes into writing a novel than just sitting at the computer and typing. With a feat as large as a novel, comes teamwork. There are so many people I'd like to thank for encouraging and helping *Daughter of Isis* to publication.

I'd like to thank my parents, Michelle and David. They gave me the courage to put myself out there and the support in whatever I want to pursue. I am lucky to have them standing behind me and cheering me on. The same can be said about my brother, Victor, brother-in-law, Seth, and other family, Drew, Kolina, and Chad, as well as my grandparents, Buck and Jackie. There is nothing I can't do without my family at my side.

I'd like to give special thanks to my sister, Kylie. Since childhood, she has been my first reader. No matter how much of a mess the draft is, she is ready to dive into the fantasies I create. She has read work I've written that will never see the light of day, and she helps me chip away the messy pieces of my projects to reveal the shine beneath. I couldn't ask for a better sister or friend. Thank you.

Thank you to my future husband, Aquiles. He is my biggest cheerleader. I've convinced him to read two books since we started dating, and *Daughter of Isis* has become the third. Thank you for talking me down from moments of panic and anxiety and for dreaming with me.

Then there is the support of my friends. Thank you, Maddie, Nicole, Andrea, G, and Hali. Your excitement keeps me going through the slog that can be writing at times.

Thank you Caroyln, Jaime, and David Crow for showing me that you believe in my writing and *Daughter of Isis*. Thank you Angie, Anne, Brie, and Eddie for being some of my first fans. Your words of encouragement made a difference and really helped me believe in my own work.

And finally, I wouldn't have the novel you are holding in your hands if it wasn't for the team that read through my second, third, fifth, sixth, all number of drafts. Thank you, Michelle Meade for working me through my early drafts. Thank you Emily Hitchcock for walking me through the publishing process at Boyle & Dalton! And to project manager Doug Davis for reaching out when I grew stressed about the book launch. Thank you to editors Heather Shaw and Shannon Page for helping me through those final drafts and asking all the right questions to get *Daughter of Isis* really polished and ready for publication. And thank you to Laurence Nozik for your excitement and hard work with the book cover. It's better than I could have imagined!

My writing group on Discord has taught me so much about writing. Special thanks to Grooven for working through an early draft of *Daughter of Isis* and really getting excited about the characters.

There are so many others I could thank for this whole project. I couldn't have done any of this without the care and support of the people around me. So, I say again, thank you.

ABOUT THE AUTHOR

REINA CRUZ was raised in California and currently resides there. Besides writing, Reina enjoys yoga and spending time with her loved ones.

Connect with Reina on her website here:

reinacruzwrites.com

FREE NOVELETTE!

Sign up for Reina's mailing list and receive a free download of *AfterWorld*, a *Daughter of Isis* novelette.

Sign up at the link below!
reinacruzwrites.com

Made in the USA
Monee, IL
24 October 2020